CANYON SACRIFICE

A National Park Mystery
by Scott Graham

TORREY HOUSE PRESS, LLC

SALT LAKE CITY • TORREY

First Torrey House Press Edition, June 2014

Published by Torrey House Press, LLC
Salt Lake City, Utah
www.torreyhouse.com

International Standard Book Number: 978-1-937226-30-5
Library of Congress Control Number: 2014930120

Cover design by Jeff Fuller, Shelfish • Shelfish.weebly.com
Interior design by Rick Whipple, Sky Island Studio
Cover painting "The Chasm of the Colorado" by Thomas Moran, c. 1873, used by permission of the Interior Museum, U.S. Department of the Interior

For Sue, Taylor, and Logan,
without whom...

CANYON SACRIFICE

Wednesday

"To stand upon the edge of this stupendous gorge, as it receives its earliest greeting from the god of day, is to enjoy in a moment compensation for long years of ordinary uneventful life."

— John Stoddard
John L. Stoddard's Lectures, Vol. 10, 1898

One

7 a.m.

A group of middle-aged Japanese tourists gathered in a tight knot twenty feet from the edge of the Grand Canyon, focused on something Chuck Bender could not see. The tourists should have been soaking in the dazzling dawn view from the South Rim of the canyon while spread along the waist-high railing around the Maricopa Point overlook. Instead, they stood huddled together in their matching navy windbreakers, tense and vigilant, cameras forgotten in their hands.

Chuck slowed his jog and peered around the group. The tourists were staring at a couple standing together at the metal railing. The couple—a heavyset Latino man in his late twenties wearing a hooded sweatshirt and baggy jeans, and a woman about the same age, heavier still, in a tent-like sweater and tightly stretched nylon slacks—leaned against the railing at the edge of the canyon, their backs to the tourists. The two were the sort Chuck would have placed far from the park—in a suburban strip mall, maybe, or at least among the hordes of late-rising tourists who would pack the overlook later in the morning. But here they were, among the few who knew to get up early and catch a shuttle out along Rim Drive to take in the enchanting view of the canyon at sunrise.

Intrigued by the transfixed tourists and out-of-place pair, Chuck came to a stop. He stood, catching his breath, in his running sweats and T-shirt, hands on hips, as the man picked up a stray piece of gravel from a depression in the rough sandstone surface of the viewpoint and launched the rock, underhanded, out and over the railing. The woman sniggered as the stone disappeared where the leading edge of the canyon gave way in a series of narrow ledges. The tourists leaned forward as one, intent on the couple.

"Just missed," the woman said. "Try again."

The man turned and shot a smug look at the group of tourists. The breeze, coursing up and out of the canyon with the start of the day, swept a strand of black hair across one eye. He threw back his head, returning the strand to its place and revealing a scythe-shaped scar across the left side of his face. The long, ragged slash was pink as a slice of watermelon against his brown skin.

Chuck moved closer as the man retrieved another piece of gravel from the ground and lobbed it over the railing. Chuck halted between the tourists and couple, close enough to see that the man was targeting a chubby ground squirrel perched on a rock ledge a few feet below the edge of the promontory. The squirrel, easily as fat as the couple, was the obvious recipient of chips and candies thrown its way by scores of park visitors. The stone struck the squirrel a glancing blow on its shoulder.

"Got him," the man proclaimed.

The squirrel jerked at the strike from the small stone. Rather than run off, however, it rose on its hind legs and sniffed at the cool morning air, forelegs aloft, awaiting the food it was accustomed to receiving.

"Check it out, *pendejo,*" the woman said, smacking the man on his shoulder. "Ain't goin' nowhere." She stepped back and raised her phone, ready to take a picture. "Again," she demanded.

The man picked up another stone, bigger this time. Behind him, Chuck stooped and picked up a walnut-sized stone of his own.

No longer content to target the ground squirrel with underhanded tosses, the man reared back and let go with a hard, overhand throw. Chuck threw overhand, too, but with much less force. The man's stone struck the ledge to the right of the squirrel with a solid chock and caromed into the canyon. The sound sent the squirrel scurrying from sight.

Chuck's stone struck the man squarely in the back. The man's thick sweatshirt assured the chunk of gravel did no harm, but the stone's impact caused the man to jump. He whirled and glared at Chuck. The logo of the Isotopes, Albuquerque's minor-league baseball team, emblazoned the front of his gray sweatshirt. "What you think you're doing?" he spat.

Chuck eyed the man. "You don't like having rocks thrown at you?"

The scar on the man's cheek turned from pink to violet as a storm of emotions crossed his face. Confusion, then dawning recognition clouded by disbelief—then rage. He took a threatening step toward Chuck, who squared his shoulders. The man drew back his fist as he advanced, the woman following.

Chuck steeled himself. He used his long, solo runs these days to burn through "all the stuff eating at him," as Janelle put it to the girls. His morning runs were a help, but what Chuck really needed was exactly what this guy in the Isotopes sweatshirt offered.

The seconds drew themselves out as the man aimed a roundhouse at Chuck's nose. Chuck reminded himself not to go for the man's face in response, to avoid the battered knuckles that would result from such a blow. Acting on instinct and adrenaline, he rose on the balls of his feet, pivoted, and released. He threw his punch straight from his waist, using every bit of his coiled energy, which had built steadily in him for weeks now, despite his daily runs.

Before the man could complete his swing, Chuck buried his fist in the man's solar plexus, treating the blow as the final, all-out shot at the end of one of his workouts, the man's gut a stand-in for the heavy bag at the gym. Despite the man's sweatshirt and layers of fat, Chuck's blow found its mark.

It was good to know he still had it in him—the ability to defend himself, his honor, ground squirrels, whatever. It had been years since his last fight. He was north of forty, his sandy brown hair thinning, his blue-gray eyes covered by contacts, the pace of his runs slipping ever so slightly year by year. Regular workouts kept him fit, but age and gravity were taking their toll nonetheless, wrinkles pulling downward at the corners of his mouth, waistline gradually losing its sharp definition of youth, wrists aching after each workout from too many shots to the heavy bag over the years.

The man exhaled in a single, drawn-out *ooof* from the force of Chuck's blow. The man's hands dropped to his sides, his legs buckled, and he sank to his knees. Chuck had time to consider a follow-up punch before the woman came at him. Her eyes, framed by thick black makeup, were hot with fury. She lunged over the man and swiped at Chuck's face. His backward leap wasn't quick enough to avoid two of her long, red fingernails. They nicked his neck above his shirt, leaving parallel, inch-long cuts just deep enough to draw blood. The woman spun as she completed her swipe, losing her balance and toppling over the downed man. The two formed a tangled heap on the ground.

Chuck savored the sight of the collapsed couple before he returned to Rim Trail to resume his run.

Applause sounded behind him. He'd forgotten all about the Japanese tourists.

Cameras clicked and cheers burst from the group as he departed. The tourists would have a fine story to tell when they got home, wouldn't they? The American West, a place where even lowly ground squirrels are treated with respect.

He jogged off along the rim of the sunlit canyon, more than ready for the day to come, looking forward to watching Rosie dive into the pancakes he'd promised to cook up for breakfast.

Two

8 a.m.

No doubt Janelle would have spotted the fresh scratches on Chuck's neck even if he hadn't gone over to where she stood at the picnic table outside the camper as soon as he got back from his run. As it was, she returned his embrace only briefly before holding him at arm's length, eyes on his neck, eyebrows raised.

"Tree branch," Chuck said with a dismissive wave. Then he remembered their pact, her pact really, the one she'd made him swear to on their wedding day three weeks ago. The truth, she'd said. Always the truth between us. Nothing but.

He smiled. "Well, actually," he took one of her hands in both of his, "I punched this guy out, and his monster wife about ripped my head off."

The gold flecks in Janelle's hazel eyes glittered in the morning light as she returned his smile. "Look where you're going next time," she said, and went back to stirring pancake batter in a large plastic bowl, her quick hands making the work appear effortless.

She was a city girl, twenty-seven, on her first camping trip. She wore a sequined black leather jacket, electric-purple sneakers, and skinny jeans. Silver hoops dangled from her ears and a small jewel sparkled at the side of her nose. Her high cheekbones and dimpled chin were sharply defined by the early sun angling through the trees.

Other camps were coming to life around them, people emerging from tents and trailers scattered beneath the ponderosa pine trees that grew tall here in Mather Campground, half a mile south of the canyon rim at the east edge of Grand Canyon Village. The needle-covered ground was speckled with shade and sunlight. Already the chill of the high-desert night was nearly gone, giving way to the blazing August day to come. The smell of wood smoke and frying bacon drifted through the trees. Campers made their way on foot along the network of roads that led to bathrooms spaced throughout the campground.

Chuck put his arms around Janelle from behind and nuzzled the back of her neck. Her long, straight, dark-chocolate hair, pulled loosely into a ponytail, tickled his face. "Mmmm," he murmured. "Girls up yet?"

"You kidding? Late as we got here, I bet they'll go another hour."

He ran the tip of his nose along her cheek. She turned and kissed him hard, pulling the full length of his body against hers, then moved him backward a step with playful fingers that slipped under his shirt to tickle his stomach. "Coffee," she directed. "Then the pancakes, like you said."

"We've got an hour."

"Not for coffee."

They'd arrived well after dark, having made the seven-hour drive from the southwest Colorado mountain town of Durango across the Navajo Reservation in a single push. An archaeologist by profession, and founder and sole full-time employee of Bender Archaeological, Inc., Chuck had ticked off the sites he'd won contracts to survey and dig over the years as they'd passed them along the way: the Baptist Church expansion in Teec Nos Pos, the new Burger King on the west side of Kayenta, the enlarged Peabody Coal transfer yard at the foot of Black Mesa, and, along Highway 160 across much of northern Arizona, the two-year job that had kept him busy into July as things with Janelle had heated up, the right-of-way for a planned electric transmission line across the reservation to Phoenix from the Four Corners Power Plant in northwest New Mexico. Chuck's one-man firm had provided the required archaeological assessment, with digging, screening, and cataloging of unearthed artifacts as necessary, before construction at each site could begin.

They'd stopped along the way for Chuck to meet with Marvin Begay in the lobby of the Tuba City Quality Inn. Marvin was the young tribal official in charge of the transmission line contract, which included a specific focus on the ancient Anasazi Indians who predated the Navajo in the region by a millennium.

Chuck pulled his camp stove from the back of Janelle's pearl-gray mini-SUV, fired it up on the metal-mesh picnic table in the center of the campsite, and set water to boiling. He spooned French roast into his drip filter and poured in the steaming water, sending the heady aroma of fresh coffee straight to his brain. Before he could hand Janelle her filled mug, five-year-old Rosie came barreling out of the fold-out camper set up in the campsite's gravel drive. The camper's screen door slammed behind her as she charged barefooted across the site and piled into her mother's arms.

Janelle scooped her daughter up in a bear hug. "*Preciosa mia*," she whispered into Rosie's ear, as she did each morning.

"*Preciosa mia, tambien, Mamá*," Rosie recited back huskily.

Rosie's throaty rasp, particularly apparent first thing in the morning, channeled her grandfather's gravelly growl. Everything about Rosie matched Janelle's father. Rosie was squat and big-boned like her grandfather, and shared his wide face, deep-set eyes, and mischievous smile.

The girl's chubby heels dug into the small of Janelle's back. Animal-print flannel pajamas rode up her legs, exposing round calves. Matted brown hair stood out from the back of her head as if starched.

Rosie held on tight when Janelle lowered her to the ground, sliding down her mother's torso like a firefighter descending a firehouse pole until she came to rest seated in the dirt. Janelle stepped out of Rosie's circled arms, pulled her to a standing position, and patted her on her dusty backside in the direction of the camper. "Your clothes are on your bed, *m'hija*. Bring the hair brush when you come back out."

Rosie turned to Chuck, struck a pose with her hip jutted far out to one side, and gave him a circular wave. "Hey there, stranger," she said in a pitch-perfect impression of a smoky-voiced starlet from a 1940s Hollywood black-and-white.

Chuck grinned and returned Rosie's wave as she sashayed back across the campsite and reentered the camper. He turned to Janelle. "I thought you said we had an hour."

"Coffee." Janelle held out her hand. "Quick."

They sat sipping while Rosie bounced around inside the trailer, humming loudly as she got dressed. Chuck leaned back in his camp chair and relished the tang of the coffee at the back of his throat.

The meeting with Marvin Begay the previous afternoon had gone well. Marvin had been named Director of Anthropological Affairs for the Navajo tribe straight out of college three years ago, just weeks after his uncle, Robert Begay, had been tapped as the first-ever Native American chief ranger of Grand Canyon National Park. Chuck and his subcontracted assistant, Clarence, had completed the last of the fieldwork required by the transmission line contract a month ago, and the final report on their work was due to Marvin in two weeks.

The report would detail the scant evidence of past Anasazi presence Chuck and Clarence had discovered along the transmission line route. Chuck knew the rudimentary evidence he and Clarence had come across—a handful of potsherds, a few hunting points—wouldn't please Marvin. The tribal official had dropped several hints over the course of the contract that Chuck would do well to find something of value along the right-of-way to bolster the contention among a subset of young Navajos, Marvin included, that the Anasazi had been more culturally advanced than the current historical record indicated. To Chuck's relief, Marvin gave voice yesterday in Tuba City only to the same vague hints he'd made over the preceding two years. That enabled Chuck to offer equally vague assurances to Marvin in return and get back on the road with Janelle and the girls in less than an hour.

Chuck blew on his coffee and turned his attention to the day ahead. Everything about the last few days had been aimed at getting here—buying the used camper, outfitting it with gear from his garage, bolting a tow hitch to Janelle's car, and shopping for daypacks and hiking boots for her and the girls.

"I'm not sure I know how to do this," he confessed.

"Do what?" Janelle asked.

"Be a tourist here."

"That's why we came, Chuck."

A loud *thump* issued through the canvas walls of the camper as Rosie leapt from the sleeping platform to the floor.

Chuck smiled ruefully. "Our honeymoon."

"A few days. Just us. Before school starts. A chance for you to show the girls and me what it is you do out here for months on end, remember?"

Yes, he remembered. And yes, Janelle was right on all counts. This had been her idea, coming to the Grand Canyon, a place she'd never visited despite her whole life spent six hours away in Albuquerque. She'd insisted on camping, too, an entrée of sorts for her and the girls to Chuck's archaeological world, the epicenter of which was right here at the canyon.

The millions of tourists who visited Grand Canyon National Park each year did so for the incredible views of one of the most awe-inspiring geological wonders on Earth. But Chuck's fascination with the place was different. Though he bid for contracts all across the high desert uplift known as the Colorado Plateau, which stretched more than a hundred miles in all directions from the Grand Canyon, he bid hardest and lowest for contracts at the canyon itself—and every time he looked into the canyon's depths and felt his bones tingle with its long history of humankind, he knew why.

"It's great to have the chance to show you around," he said. "It's just . . ."

"It's just what?"

Chuck knew what he was supposed to do right now. It was his duty to explain himself, to work through the complexities of what he was thinking with his new wife. But how was he to do that when even the word *wife* remained foreign to him? How was he to open up to Janelle when he'd had a lifetime of working through things on his own, with no one else's opinions to consult or concerns to worry about?

"We'll do the rim today," he said, sticking to the basics.

"Fine." Janelle bit off the word.

He plowed ahead. "Grab some food and jump a shuttle out to Hermit's Rest."

Another thump sounded from inside the camper, causing the small trailer to rock atop its telescoped legs like a skiff bobbing on the ocean. This time the thump was followed by a high-pitched wail from seven-year-old Carmelita.

"Oops," Rosie said earnestly from behind the wall of canvas. "Sorry, *hermana*."

"Get away from me!" Carmelita screamed.

Janelle disappeared inside the camper to coo soothingly over Carmelita while Chuck, freed for the moment from the challenge of marital communication, centered the skillet over the larger of the stove's two burners and started in on the pancakes.

Three hours later, Chuck, Janelle, and the girls made their way through the village on foot, the girls scurrying ahead in their new boots, slender Carmelita several inches taller than Rosie, a wide receiver to Rosie's fullback. The girls' lacy blouses and matching red shorts blended easily with the colorful attire of the throngs of summer visitors making their way along the village walkways in the steadily rising heat of the day.

After stopping to pick up a picnic lunch of chips and sandwiches, they headed for the Central Village shuttle bus stop. The sun beat down on the metal roof of the bus as they settled into their seats and headed west on Rim Drive, the route of Chuck's early morning run. Fellow tourists filled the seats around them. Rosie collapsed against Chuck in the hard plastic double seat they shared, her eyes half closed in the heat. Carmelita sat slumped beside her mother a row behind Chuck and Rosie.

"This is sooooo boring," Carmelita declared, crossing her arms in front of her with an audible *harrumph.*

"Hush," Janelle warned, but her curt tone revealed her own discomfort.

Chuck realized, too late, that he should have directed Janelle and the girls to the cool confines of the South Rim Museum as the heat of the day came on. Janelle's after breakfast trip to the campground showers with the girls had taken well over an hour, far longer than he'd anticipated, yet it was he, as inexperienced tour guide, who had determined they should take the shuttle as midday approached. Now here they sat, trapped and broiling, the bus ride having just begun.

Should he suggest to Janelle that they stay on the shuttle when it reached the end of the out-and-back road and return to the village? Get to the museum as quickly as possible and come out this way again for sunset, after the heat of the day let up? Or was he better off sticking with the plan, not admitting his mistake?

The driver, dressed for the heat in a light-colored blouse and loose trousers, piloted the shuttle beneath the raised gate that kept private vehicles off Rim Drive. She steered the bus away from the village along the canyon rim. The depths of the canyon, visible to the right through breaks in the trees, were washed out by the harsh, midmorning sun. Mesmerizing at sunrise and sunset, the view of the canyon this time of day was a hazy muddle of weak reds, dusty tans, and indistinct browns bisected by the blurry gray ribbon of the Colorado River far below.

In a monotone as drab and colorless as the midday canyon depths, the driver delivered a stream of facts into a headset that carried her voice through speakers in the shuttle ceiling to her passengers: it was eight miles from the village to the end of the road at Hermit's Rest, the canyon was more than a mile deep at its deepest point, the volume of water in the river averaged fifteen-thousand cubic feet per second, enough to satisfy the residential needs of ten million people downstream in Phoenix and Los Angeles.

The shuttle rounded a bend and the first stop on the route came into view. Flashing lights at the stop jolted Chuck out of his heat-induced torpor. The paved pullout on the right side of the road was lined with park vehicles—three pale-green ranger patrol sedans, an ambulance, a fire-rescue truck, and the gleaming, white, government-issue Chevy Suburban driven by Chief Ranger Robert Begay—all with their blue and red emergency lights flashing.

The shuttle driver broke from her monologue long enough to interject, with a glimmer of animation, "As you can see, we won't be stopping at Maricopa Point this morning."

Chuck leaned past Rosie's slumped form to scan the rocky outcrop jutting from the canyon rim a hundred feet north of the line of vehicles. Just inside the railing at the far end of the point, where the promontory fell away straight down for more than a hundred feet, several park firefighters in heavy canvas pants, long-sleeved yellow shirts, and white helmets stuffed climbing ropes and ascending devices into large nylon duffels. Half a dozen rangers in standard park service uniform—dark green slacks, gray dress shirts with shiny gold badges, and broad-brimmed hats—stood in a loose circle around something resting on the sunbaked stone surface of the overlook.

The firefighters and rangers were gathered at the head of the promontory, a good fifty feet beyond where Chuck had buried his fist in the oversized gut of the guy in the Isotopes sweatshirt. That had been hours ago. No way, Chuck assured himself, was this scene related to his earlier altercation. Looking closer, however, he saw that the rangers surrounded a large, black, plastic sack half-enclosed in wire mesh. A body bag, that's what it was, encased in a tub-style search-and-rescue litter—and whoever was in the bag filled it to near overflowing.

Three

11 a.m.

Chuck squeezed his eyes shut. Could he have killed the guy he'd punched on Maricopa Point? As quickly as the question formed in his mind, he knew the answer. After all, his first fight very nearly had been his last.

He'd snuck into a Durango bar as a teenager and wound up drunk and shooting pool in the back room. In short order, he'd found himself down several hundred bucks to a gas-patch roughneck in worn jeans and a grease-stained T-shirt. Chuck displayed his empty pockets to the roughneck, who proceeded to jump him when he left the bar an hour later. A kick to his stomach ruptured his spleen; he'd required life-saving surgery. Chuck's broken nose, crooked to this day, was the visible reminder of the beating he'd taken that night.

What if something had ripped open inside the guy's gut when Chuck had punched him? Possible. Except the timing didn't fit. The guy would not have died right away. Any serious injury would have sent him to the hospital in Flagstaff, eighty miles to the south. But the ambulance and other emergency vehicles were still here at the scene, a good four hours after the confrontation.

Chuck sucked a breath through his compressed lips. He hadn't hit the guy hard enough to kill him. This was a coincidence, nothing more, the park vehicles, the flashing lights. Had to be. The rangers and firefighters were conducting a training exercise, that was it, and the body bag was filled with coils of ropes to provide ballast for the litter.

The shuttle bus trundled past the park service cars and trucks lined along the pullout. In breaks between the vehicles, Chuck caught glimpses of the park staffers gathered on the point before a screen of piñons and junipers blocked his view.

The bus slowed when it approached Powell Lookout, half a mile past Maricopa Point. Chuck spoke over his shoulder to Janelle, leaving no time for her to break in. "I bet I know just about everybody back there." He gestured out the rear of the shuttle in the direction of the point. "It'd be good for me to say 'hey,' see if somebody could show us around tomorrow, give us a behind-the-scenes tour." He stood as the shuttle bus came to a stop. "You three go on out to Hermit's Rest. I'll catch the next shuttle and meet you there."

"But—" Janelle began.

Chuck wagged what he hoped was a friendly finger to cut her off, then tousled Rosie's hair, as if ditching Janelle and the girls in the middle of the first day of their first-ever vacation together was the most reasonable thing in the world. He made his way down the aisle and off the bus and set off at a jog along Rim Drive beneath the scorching sun, careful not to look back as the shuttle pulled away behind him.

He slowed to a walk when the overlook came into view. He was sweating hard, the front of his shirt sticking to his chest. He pulled his baseball cap low over his eyes and hung his thumbs in the front belt loops of his jeans with fake casualness while he peered anxiously ahead.

The firefighters had finished stowing their gear and were hauling their full duffels to the fire-rescue truck. The rangers still encircled the body bag in the mesh litter. Chuck noted that the distinct form of a human body, not coils of ropes, pressed outward from inside the bag—the broad outline of shoulders, arms tucked at the sides of a large stomach, feet pointing upward. He stopped at the edge of the road. He never should have left the shuttle.

He took a step backward, but before he could make his getaway, a ranger climbed from an idling patrol sedan parked at the head of the line of vehicles.

"Chuck? That you? Christ, how long's it been?"

The ranger, tall and in his late forties, had a graying, bushy blond mustache. His wide stance supported a compact potbelly that pressed at the buttons of his shirt. He stood with his elbows cocked outward like the wings of a bird, his hands resting on the bulky sidearm belted to his right hip and extra magazine pouch strapped to his left. Purple splotches marked the ranger's face, the result, Chuck knew, of years of heavy drinking.

"Donald," Chuck answered. Ranger Donald Podalski had been assigned to oversee Chuck's work in the park on several occasions. Chuck indicated the firefighters and rangers on the promontory. "What's going on?"

"Guy took a tumble." Donald gave a descending whistle and imitated with his hand someone falling off a cliff. "Girlfriend says it was an accident, buuuut . . ."

Cliff-jump suicides weren't uncommon at the canyon, though it always amazed Chuck that such despondency could remain unaffected by the canyon's beauty. Accidental cliff falls were a regular occurrence at the canyon as well, one or two a year. Reported as suicide or accident, however, there was always the question whether a push might have been involved.

Chuck tugged his sweat-dampened shirt away from his chest. "Witnesses?"

"A bunch of Jap tourists, but they hardly spoke any English, and their guide, she was too freaked to do much translating. Doesn't sound like they saw much, anyway. The girlfriend was the only one close, taking his picture way out at the end of the point."

Chuck put a hand to the scratches on his neck. So. The guy in the Isotopes sweatshirt was dead—and, thankfully, Chuck's punch wasn't the cause. But had the girlfriend reported the fight with Chuck that had preceded the fall?

"Where is she?"

"Begay let her go." Donald pointed at one of the park staffers gathered around the litter: Grand Canyon National Park Chief Ranger Robert Begay.

Fiftyish, smoothly professional, always impeccably groomed, Robert had been handpicked by park service honchos in D.C. for the chief ranger post. His first year as head ranger at the park had overlapped with Chuck's most recent contract at the canyon, assessing and digging the site of a new solar latrine at Hermit Creek Backcountry Campground.

Like Donald and the other rangers, Robert wore park service slacks and shirt and a wide-brimmed Smokey Bear hat. The chief ranger was stout and broad shouldered. His sleek sidearm barely protruded from his hip. The hard kick of Donald's beefy .45 had surprised Chuck when he'd fired it with Donald at the park shooting range a few years ago, while Robert's slender handgun looked as if it would deliver its shots with the same silky efficiency with which he performed every aspect of his job.

"She just left," Donald continued. "Waited to make a visual when they got the body up to the rim, then took off. I went over to check it out." He made a face. "Guy's hamburger, but she didn't even flinch. Tough bird. She's supposed to stick around 'til the body's shipped."

"Flagstaff?" Chuck asked.

"Yep. Tomorrow, probably, by the time all's said and done. You know me though, always the last to know. They've got me on perimeter, like anybody's gonna sneak up on 'em. But hey," he aimed a thumb at the idling sedan, "I've got A/C."

"And 92.9," Chuck added. He moved toward Donald even as he struggled to come up with a way to justify making his escape.

"KAFF-FM, Flagstaff *Coun-try*," Donald crooned in agreement. He sat back against the hood of the patrol car. "What the hell are you doing here, anyway? What's it been? A couple years, at least. Figured you were all done with park contracts now that you're sucking on the tribe's teat."

Chuck ignored Donald's good-natured jab. "I'm with my wife and kids."

"Wife? *Kids*?"

Good. He'd managed to throw Donald. "Got myself one of those insta-families. All the rage these days."

"She cute, your new wife?"

"'Course she is." Chuck appreciated the opportunity to answer with complete conviction. "Knock-down, drop-dead gorgeous."

"I'd expect nothing less of you."

"There's plenty out there for you, too," Chuck said, covering territory he and Donald had gone over many times. "Get your butt out of your La-Z-Boy, throw away the bottle—"

"And run my ass off like you every day? Fat chance."

"Fat's what I'm talking about." Chuck eyed Donald's gut. The ranger had put on a few pounds since they'd last seen one another.

"Hey," Donald said defensively, covering his stomach with his hand.

"I was wondering if maybe you could show us around tomorrow. I said I'd find out."

"As if you knew I'd be here."

"You or somebody else."

"Like Rachel, maybe?"

Chuck shuddered. "I heard she transferred to the Everglades."

"She only lasted there for, like, six months. She's been back here quite a while now." Donald smirked. "Guess she forgot to tell you."

Chuck kept his tone even. "Guess so."

The ranger moved on. "These insta-kids of yours, any daughters?"

"Two."

"Teenagers?" Donald leered.

"Sorry." Chuck held out a hand palm-down at his waist. "Five and seven."

"Damn. How 'bout this wife of yours, any sisters?"

"Nope." Chuck couldn't hold back his smile any longer. "You never change, do you?"

"A little," Donald admitted, patting his belly.

Donald was divorced and likely to remain that way. The marriage rate for park rangers was near the lowest of all professions in the United States, and Donald was no exception. With its postings far from bright lights and big cities, the job attracted autonomous individuals set on their own paths through life. Fellow staffers in each national park served as a de facto family for most rangers, an ever-changing community gathered in the middle of nowhere by a shared love of the outdoors and by something else—the desire not to be sentenced to a life in suburbia "doing the deadly," as rangers referred to the nine-to-five, Monday-through-Friday routine. But the tradeoffs of park service life—working nights, weekends, and holidays far from hometowns, relatives, and lifelong friends—were significant, and they exacted a toll. Those tradeoffs certainly had taken their toll on Donald.

Chuck first met Donald upon winning his initial Grand Canyon contract to assess and dig the route of a proposed connector road out of the village to meet up with the park's South Entrance Road. That was twelve years ago. At the time, Donald was freshly split from his high school sweetheart; she wanted kids, Donald did not. Fed up with Donald's refusal to embrace parenthood by the time they'd reached their thirties, Donald's now ex-wife had decamped for their hometown of San Diego.

Donald was hard on the prowl when he and Chuck first met, trolling among female rangers and the unattached women who made up the bulk of the retail workforce in the village. Donald's playboy ways cooled as Scotch took over as his mistress of choice. For a time, Chuck considered confronting Donald about his drinking. But it never reached the point where it affected his on-the-job performance, at least not overtly so. If and when it rose to that level, Chuck told himself, he would act. In the meantime, he did what came naturally and kept his mouth shut.

Chuck glanced down at his own flat stomach. "You don't have to run your butt clear off, you know."

"A life of denial's not for me. Never has been." Donald returned his hand to the butt of his .45. "There are certain finer things in life that call my name. Far be it for me to reject them."

"You count French fries and pizza as 'finer things in life'?"

"Like I'm gonna gorge myself on caviar on what they pay me around here."

"Still on the 'oh, poor me' jag, are you?" Chuck had listened to Donald complain of living paycheck to paycheck for as long as he'd known him. "You've got benefits far as you can see. Health insurance, free housing, paid vacations, overtime. You name it, the government's throwing it at you. And still you're bitching about how broke you are?"

"You try getting by on what I make each month."

"There's nothing to spend your big bucks on out here. Look around. You see a Ferrari dealer anywhere? You should be drowning in money."

Donald studied the ground at his feet, causing Chuck to wonder what his friend might have added to his off-duty routine over the last two years—not that he was going to ask. How many evenings had the two of them hung out together in Donald's park service duplex while, night after night, Donald sipped himself into whisky-fueled oblivion? And never once had Chuck said a word. He wasn't about to start now, having run into Donald for the first time in more than two years, and with the full body bag waiting fifty yards beyond Donald's shoulder.

The rangers on the promontory were lining up on either side of the litter. "Looks like they could use your help," Chuck said.

Donald glanced back. "Right-o." He reached inside the patrol car and shut off the engine, then stepped to the sidewalk. "Gimme a call in the morning, I'll see what I can do. Where you staying?"

"Mather."

"Still the cheap bastard, huh? A hotel room's too nice for the new missus?"

"It's her idea. She wants to try camping."

"Sure she does," Donald said with a roll of his eyes. "By the way, this guy's girlfriend—" he gestured at the body bag behind him "—she's staying at Mather, too." He paused. "And Rachel's assigned to keep tabs on her."

"I'm taken, Donald."

"Never stopped you before."

"I'm *married.*"

"Never stopped you either, near as I can remember." Donald turned and headed for the point. "Call me," he said cheerily over his shoulder.

Chuck looked past Donald to the park staffers bent double at the sides of the litter, readying their lift—all but one, that is. Robert Begay stood unmoving, his dark eyes fixed on Chuck.

Chuck gave the chief ranger a tentative wave. Robert did not lift his hand in return. Though Chuck didn't know Robert well, their few interactions over the course of Chuck's work at the Hermit Creek latrine site had been amicable. Now, however, Robert's coal-black eyes burned with deep and unyielding suspicion.

Four

1 p.m.

Chuck held his position, his hand arrested in midair. When Robert neither moved nor broke his gaze, Chuck dropped his hand, spun on his heel, and headed away from the promontory, wholly unnerved.

Chuck made his living drawing the line between archaeological finds that were significant and those that weren't. In the field, truth was revealed through the gradual accumulation of many pieces of evidence, clues in the form of pressure flakes and hunting points, potsherds and bone fragments. Each discovered artifact, collapsed wall, or uncovered fire ring might disclose something critical to understanding the truths of the ancients. Or it might mean nothing at all. It was his responsibility to know the difference, and over the years he'd proven himself good at it.

When it came to the death of the guy on Maricopa Point, however, Chuck was left not with an accumulation of evidence, but only with Robert Begay's menacing gaze on the promontory.

Upon retreating from the point, Chuck caught up with Janelle, Carmelita, and Rosie at Hermit's Rest. Janelle greeted him with gritty silence. Carmelita glowered at Chuck, following her mother's lead.

They took refuge on a covered bench at the shuttle bus stop, the glare of the midday sun assaulting their patch of shade from all sides. No one spoke. Rosie swung her legs beneath the bench and shot surreptitious glances at Chuck while she nibbled on her sandwich. Chuck knew he could draw her into conversation with a single comment. He knew just as well what Janelle's reaction would be if he did that. He stayed quiet.

When they returned to the village, they walked straight to

the South Rim Museum. The girls turned slow circles on the varnished flagstone floor in the air-conditioned coolness of the museum's grand entry hall while Chuck worked through the questions arising from Robert's menacing look on Maricopa Point.

If the chief ranger suspected something, why hadn't he spoken with Chuck at the promontory? Why the silent stare-down? Perhaps, Chuck reasoned, it was actually good news Robert hadn't said anything to him. Maybe he was reading more into the chief ranger's look than was deserved.

Chuck led Janelle and the girls to a humidity-controlled glass case containing one of his discoveries selected for display in the museum's grand entry hall. He'd unearthed this one, a wide-bodied olla basket woven of long ponderosa needles, prior to construction of the new road connecting Grand Canyon Village to the South Entrance Road. A card next to the basket referred to its origin as *Ancestral Puebloan*, a new term gaining favor in the Southwest archaeological community—though Chuck still used the term *Anasazi*; most of the Navajos he'd worked with disliked the fact that the word *Puebloan* derived from the language of the Spaniards who'd invaded their lands five centuries ago.

Chuck aimed Janelle and the girls toward the glass case containing the second of his displayed Grand Canyon finds. Before they reached it, however, a bespectacled man in baggy khakis and a long-sleeved white shirt, head bent over a sheath of papers held in both hands, nearly ran Rosie over as he scurried through the hall. The man, and a gray-haired woman whispering into his ear as she hurried alongside him, had entered the hall from a side passage that connected the museum's display area with its administrative wing.

The man grabbed Rosie around her shoulders, as much to keep himself upright as to assure she didn't topple over. Papers cascaded to the floor. He brushed a thinning shock of white hair back over the top of his head before squatting to pick up the scattered documents. The woman crouched to help. Like the man, she was close to sixty, her face sun-browned and wrinkled. She wore a beige polyester pantsuit at least two decades out of date. Her graying hair was cropped close at the back of her neck and the top of her ears.

"Jonathan? Elise?" Chuck asked.

The couple looked up and broke into crinkly grins. "Chuck," they exclaimed in unison, rising with the collected papers. Jonathan embraced Chuck, and Elise patted Chuck's shoulder with a handful of paper.

Jonathan's bushy white eyebrows worked up and down at the sight of Chuck. "We heard you were here. So nice to have you in the park again."

Elise bent forward to the girls and confided in them, her face inches from theirs, "We call him our magician. Did you know that?" The girls stepped back, unsettled, but Elise merely leaned closer and warbled, "He digs up something amazing every time he sticks a shovel in the ground."

She straightened and focused her bright blue eyes on Chuck, who said, "Hours in, results out. That's all it is, Elise. You know that as well as I do."

"Actually," Elise said to the girls, "I don't know that. I just know that someday he's going to discover the ultimate of all discoveries for us, and our careers will be complete."

"Where are our manners?" Jonathan said. "Pray tell, Chuck. Who are these three lovely young ladies?"

At Chuck's introduction, Jonathan transferred the papers he'd gathered to one hand and bent to shake Carmelita's hesitantly proffered hand, then Rosie's outthrust one. Chuck explained to the girls, "Jonathan Marbury, Dr. Marbury, is chief curator for Grand Canyon National Park. And his wife Elise here, also Dr.

Marbury, is chief curator for the museum."

"The two chiefs," Jonathan crowed. "Actually," he told the girls, "we're the only curators in the whole park. They just call us chiefs to make us feel good." He winked.

Chuck tipped his head toward Janelle. "This is Jan, the girls' mother."

"Ah, of course, Jan," Jonathan said with a wide smile.

In response to Janelle's puzzled look, Elise said, "He's never heard of you before." She looked Janelle over. "But you certainly are lovely, I'll grant him that. Almost the equal of your girls."

Jonathan turned to Chuck. "Showing off your finds to your lovelies?"

"Of course he is, Jonny," Elise said. She raised her eyebrows at Carmelita and Rosie. "He's showing you his magic, isn't he?" She checked her watch. "And we should leave him to it." She directed an energetic shrug at Chuck. "Work, work, work, work, work, you know."

Jonathan turned to Janelle, Carmelita, and Rosie. "*Enchanté*," he breathed to the three of them.

"Shush, you," Elise said to her husband. She smiled at Janelle and the girls. "A pleasure." She leaned toward Chuck. "You're a lucky man, my friend." She herded Jonathan ahead of her down the museum's main corridor, waving the papers in her hands like semaphore flags to guide him in the direction of their side-by-side offices facing the display preparation room at the back of the museum.

Chuck turned to Janelle with an amused shrug. "They've been here forever."

"Funny," she replied, "they don't look anything like what I thought ancient Indians would look like."

"That pantsuit of hers? The height of fashion back in Anasazi times."

Chuck led Janelle and the girls to the case containing the

second of his displayed artifacts, this one an impressive double-ported urn he'd discovered a few hundred yards from the site of the new solar latrine. The urn's slender form was similar to that of the famous two-ported vases commonly used in modern Navajo wedding ceremonies—so similar, in fact, that Marvin Begay and other young Navajos insisted the tribe's renowned vases had to be derived from the work of the Anasazi potter who had crafted the sensuous urn now on display.

They moved on to the third and last of Chuck's discoveries displayed in the entry hall, an ornately decorated Anasazi turkey-feather burial shroud he'd found a decade ago at the bottom of a late-1800s mining debris pile where the national park's Backcountry Information Center now stood at the south edge of the village.

"I like the feather thing best," Rosie proclaimed, turning heads in the quiet museum. "It's pretty."

"You've got a good eye," Chuck praised her.

The skill of the Anasazi in the medium of clay was well known, while the shroud featured heretofore-unseen Anasazi mastery with needle and thread. As such, the shroud was the most impressive of Chuck's displayed artifacts, providing an even greater understanding of the Anasazi than did the double-ported urn.

"It's the most famous of my finds," Chuck told Rosie as he stood next to her in front of the glass case. "It led to all the work I've gotten with the Navajo tribe over the last few years."

"Wow." Rosie pressed her nose to the front of the case so that her breath fogged the glass. "Did they put you on TV?"

Chuck smiled. "Not yet. But quite a few papers and articles have mentioned it."

"That's how Chuck makes his living, *m'hijas*," Janelle explained to the girls as she bent over Rosie, peering into the case. "Your stepfather digs up these sorts of things so people can study and learn from them."

"He's a magician," Rosie whispered.

But Carmelita stiffened. "We already know what he does," she huffed. "Duh. That's why you made us come here." She folded her arms across her skinny chest and stalked away from the display case.

Janelle shot Chuck an apologetic look. She called after her oldest daughter, "You're right, *bonita. Perdoname, por favor.*" She put her hand on Rosie's shoulder. "The Grand Canyon," she murmured. "We're really here."

"The biggest hole in the Earth this side of the Mariana Trench," Chuck put in.

Rosie turned from the case. "There's a bigger hole than the Grand Canyon?"

"If you count what's underneath the ocean."

"Well, I don't."

Janelle gave Rosie's shoulder a squeeze. "Neither do I."

Rosie skipped out of the entry hall, trailing Carmelita beneath the exposed beams of the museum's main passageway. Janelle watched them go. She slipped her hand into Chuck's and looked up at him, her face alight with happiness. He lost himself in her gaze, just as he had countless times since they'd first met a few months ago. He wasn't sure what it was about her dancing eyes that had made him fall so quickly and completely in love with her, but he liked it all the same. Jonathan and Elise Marbury were right: Janelle was lovely.

For a few luxurious seconds, he basked in the delicious, schoolboy-like infatuation he felt for Janelle, until the growing pit in his stomach reminded him of the frighteningly hasty commitment he'd made to her and the girls. He turned his head away lest she see the anxiety in his eyes. What could she possibly see in him? he asked himself for the thousandth time.

All his adult life, Chuck had found peace in being alone—so

much so, in fact, that before Janelle had come along he'd regularly gone days at a time without speaking to anyone. He'd enjoyed his solitary life right up to the evening when, upon meeting Janelle at her parents' house, the calm in his head had been replaced by the combustive mix of ardor and trepidation that, at this point, was on the verge of driving him crazy.

He had no idea what he'd done to deserve this beguiling young woman who had materialized in his life, nor did he know how Janelle had come to trust him enough to allow him to join her in raising her two girls. He worried about missteps he might take that would result in his newfound joy vanishing, and wondered how, having experienced the thrill of his new life with Janelle and the girls, he could go back to his old life if that were to happen.

Deep down, he was convinced he risked scaring Janelle away if she ever realized how much he loved her. How could she not be frightened off when the love he felt for her was threatening to scare him away, to send him running from the museum this very instant?

Janelle tugged at his hand, and he forced a smile. "We're here all right," he said, his words guarded. He cursed to himself, knowing his uncertainty was visible in his eyes. "The Grand Canyon."

Janelle's eyes narrowed. Without a word, she let go of his hand and set off down the hallway after the girls.

Chuck gathered himself and followed. He would catch up with her and take her in his arms, tell her how fortunate he knew he was, how much he loved and cared for her. But he was still trailing her when she spun to face him in the middle of the corridor, causing other museum-goers to alter course as they passed. He avoided her eyes as he approached.

"Look at me," Janelle said.

He stopped in front of her and offered her an uneasy glance

before looking past her at Carmelita and Rosie, still making their way down the passageway.

"Look . . . at . . . me," Janelle repeated.

He did as told. Seconds ago, her mouth had been relaxed, her eyes warm and inviting. Now, every muscle in her face was tight, her eyes burning into him.

"I love what we've got going between us. You have to believe that," she said. "But I have to be sure you're with me on this. I already placed my trust in someone by mistake. You know that. I can't let it happen again. I *won't* let it happen again. Not to me, and not to Carm and Rosie."

Chuck opened his mouth, then closed it.

"Maybe I should have figured this out earlier—like, before we got married," Janelle went on, her voice softening. "But I'm doing the best I can here. And what I'm saying is, you have to be all the way in on this with me. No halfway about it. You don't deserve that. I don't deserve it." Her lower lip trembled. "And the girls . . . the girls . . . they don't deserve it either." Her voice shook. "I don't need a pretend husband, Chuck. I need the real thing. I can't stand by and let the girls grow close to you just to risk having you walk away from them."

"I—" Chuck began, but Janelle wasn't finished.

"There's a time limit on this thing," she said, her voice steadying. "I don't know how long, exactly. But there has to be, for the girls, for me. You have to come around for the three of us. All the way around. And you have to do it soon."

With that, she turned and headed down the corridor after her daughters.

Five

2 p.m.

Chuck shuffled down the passageway behind Janelle.

A time limit, she'd said.

She was headstrong, impetuous. She'd probably just been blowing off steam. Still, her comment filled him with dread because he knew she was right. Did he have it in him to do what she needed, what he himself knew he had to do, if their brand-new marriage was to last?

Rosie came charging back up the corridor. She darted around her mother, took hold of Chuck's wrist with both hands, and dragged him past Janelle toward a darkened doorway off to one side.

"You gotta see, you gotta see," she exclaimed gleefully, tugging him through the entry into a windowless, cave-like room lit only by black lights directed at luminescent specimens of hackmanite collected from Meteor Crater, a fifty-thousand-year-old, five-hundred-foot-deep asteroid-impact depression in the high desert east of Flagstaff.

Rosie pranced around the dark room, giggling at the way the cream-colored piping on her blouse glowed beneath the black lights. "Look at me!" she cried out.

Carmelita entered the room behind Chuck and Rosie. As she took in the spectacle of her sister dancing and spinning across the floor between the specimen cases, she smiled, her teeth shining as brightly as the luminescent rocks on display. "This is so cool," she said to Rosie. Catching sight of Chuck looking on, she clamped her mouth shut. Even from across the room, her disdain for him was evident. She turned her back on him and left.

This didn't surprise Chuck. Where Rosie had taken instantly

to him, Carmelita consistently turned a cold shoulder his way—perhaps wisely so, he chastised himself, given what Janelle had said to him in the museum corridor. Carmelita shared Janelle's striking beauty, same dark hair, heart-shaped face, and smooth olive skin. It was in her eyes that she differed most from her mother; where Janelle's were warm and inviting, Carmelita's tended toward cool and appraising, taking in the world without offering much in return.

Rosie took Chuck by the hand and bunny-hopped alongside him out of the black-lit room behind her sister.

After the museum visit, Chuck, Janelle, and the girls wandered with the crowds along Rim Trail, the strip of pavement that separated the village from the canyon. They escaped the blazing midafternoon sun by ducking into each of the several hotel gift shops that faced the trail and the gaping canyon beyond.

As they strolled from shop to shop, Chuck maintained a discreet distance between himself and Janelle, counting on the passage of time to dissipate any residual heat from her comments in the museum passageway even as the day's temperature kept climbing. He set himself to finding a gift for her in one of the shops. In the gift shop on the ground floor of Kachina Lodge, and again in the Bright Angel Lodge gift shop, he spotted some earrings he thought Janelle would like—though he wondered if she would see his present as too obvious an act of atonement.

Not daring to risk it, he abandoned the earring display and made his way to the safety of the camping gear section in the far corner of the store. There, among familiar displays of extended-reach lighters and LED flashlights, one item caught his eye: an old-school hatchet, silver, with a black rubber handle and hard plastic head cover. The hatchet, the last in the store, hung alone between foil packets of dehydrated strawberry ice cream and a row of digital compasses that pointed to true north at the press of a button. He slid the hatchet off its hangar rod; it was coated in a layer of dust. Hatchets were fast becoming relics of a bygone era. Rather than use one to chop kindling, it was far easier these days to start a campfire with a squirt of lighter fluid and the flick of a butane lighter.

He gave the hatchet an experimental swing. It was heavy and solid in his grip. He felt someone's eyes on him and glanced up in time to catch Carmelita watching him from a T-shirt display on the far side of the store. He smiled at her and slashed the hatchet through the air, bringing it to a sudden halt with a silent *thwack* when it struck imagined wood. Carmelita's eyes lit up. He thought she might smile back at him, but, catching herself, she pursed her lips and went back to studying the display of shirts.

The brief light in Carmelita's eyes was enough, however. Chuck paid for the hatchet and handed it to Janelle when the four of them regrouped across from the store.

"What's this?" Janelle asked, holding the hatchet away from her body with her finger and thumb, as she might a dead fish.

"A hatchet." Chuck grinned at her.

"I know, but . . ."

"I'm giving it to you for reasons of safety," he explained. He buried his grin, careful not to look at the girls. "It's indescribably sharp, a brutal and unforgiving implement of total devastation and destruction that's really for someone else. Some*ones* else." He paused, feeling the girls' eyes on him. "If you think they can handle it."

Janelle's face brightened in understanding. She wrapped her fingers around the hatchet's rubber handle and spoke gravely, even as her eyes sparkled. "I'm sorry, but I'm not sure I can allow this dangerous implement into our household."

The girls were on their toes, their eyes on the shimmering object now gripped firmly in their mother's hand. Chuck allowed the agonizing silence that followed Janelle's comment to play out for as long as he dared, his face set, smiling back at Janelle only with his eyes.

"Well, then," he said, taking the hatchet back. "I guess we'll just have to dispose of this in the simplest way possible." He turned to the girls. "Here goes nothing."

He reared back and made as if to heave the hatchet over the railing and into the depths of the canyon. Before he could complete his toss, however, Janelle laid a hand on his forearm and brought her face close to his. She was smiling openly now.

"Actually," she purred, "I kinda like things that result in devastation and destruction." Her fingers drifted down Chuck's arm and closed around the back of his hand.

From the corner of his eye, Chuck saw Rosie and Carmelita smiling along with their mother's obvious pleasure.

"Hmm," he said to Janelle. "Sounds like this implement is too hot for either of us to handle. We're going to have to come up with somebody else to carry it for us."

"Me, me!" Rosie hollered, her hand thrust into the air. "I'll carry it! It's not too hot for me!"

Chuck looked at Janelle, his brow furrowed, then back at Rosie. "I'm tempted," he told her. "I am. But you, all alone? I'm not sure. Don't you have someone you could share this duty with?" He slid his hand, still holding the hatchet, out of Janelle's grasp and raised the hatchet so that its metal handle glinted in the sunlight. "I believe this is going to have to be a shared responsibility."

Rosie looked confused. Then she beamed. "My sister!" she shouted. "Carm! She can help me!"

"Why, of course she can," Chuck said. He handed Carmelita the hatchet before she had a chance to refuse.

Carmelita feigned reluctance, but the gleam in her eyes betrayed her. She turned the hatchet over, its head protected by the plastic cover, as Chuck spoke to her in an Old West accent.

"You take good care of that instrument of destruction, little lady," he said with mock seriousness. "We aim to have us a camp-far this evenin', and we're a-gonna need that there blade to help make it fer us."

"A fire! Yea!" Rosie cheered at Carmelita's side. She turned to her sister, her eyes big and round. "Do you think you can do it, Carm?"

There was a beat of silence, long enough for Chuck to wonder whether Carmelita would reply, caught as she was between reassuring her little sister and maintaining the wall between herself and Chuck.

"Sure," she told Rosie. "I got this." Without looking at Chuck, she swung the hatchet through the air and brought it to a sudden stop with a silent *thwack* against an imaginary piece of wood. "See? Piece of cake."

She marched down Rim Trail, hatchet in hand. Rosie skipped alongside, chattering away.

"An ax?" Janelle said to Chuck as they headed down the trail. "You're trying to win the girls over, and you buy them an ax?"

"A chance to find out what you tied yourself and the girls into. That's why you wanted to come here, right?" Chuck gestured ahead at the hatchet hanging from Carmelita's hand. "For better or worse, that's my world right there."

Janelle dangled her thumb from the back pocket of Chuck's jeans and reached across her body to take hold of his upper arm with her other hand. "I guess you're right," she said, pulling him tight against her as they followed the girls along the trail. "I guess this is exactly what I tied us into."

Chuck glanced at her and was relieved to find that she was smiling.

Six

6 p.m.

A comfortable, early evening breeze, no longer hot though not yet cool, sifted through the trees. Carmelita and Rosie played in the camper. The plan was for Chuck, Janelle, and the girls to dine on the prepared meal of fried chicken and potato salad they'd picked up from a snack stand in historic El Tovar Hotel, then head over to the canyon rim for sunset.

Chuck sat in a folding chair in front of the campsite's ash-filled fire pit with a bottle of beer in hand, absorbed in his thoughts. Janelle sat next to him, her fingers tapping on the tiny keyboard attached to the Internet-enabled tablet computer balanced in her lap.

The fifteen-year age difference between Chuck and Janelle made for a gaping divide between them in any number of aspects—including their comfort levels with all things high tech. Chuck used plenty of technology in the course of his work, of course, relying on a digital transit, fluxgate magnetometer, and wheeled spectrometer to perform initial site assessments and determine how best to string grids and proceed with digs. He cataloged finds in spreadsheets on his laptop at the end of each field day, prepared reports and bids with the aid of ArchLogical software, and kept in close contact with contract administrators via text and email. His personal life, on the other hand, was decidedly low tech. Prior to meeting Janelle, his days away from work had revolved primarily around fly fishing the waters of the Animas River flowing through Durango, his nights around weekly poker games with a small circle of friends from his high-school days, and shooting pool an additional night or two a week with the same handful of buddies.

As his work grew more technological, Chuck had gone the

opposite direction when it came to the one pastime he was truly passionate about: elk hunting. Each autumn he scheduled the timing of his contracts to give himself a two week break, which he spent hiking through the high country north of Durango dawn to dusk in search of the elusive ungulates. He'd hunted with a high-powered rifle and scope for a number of years, until he'd grown uncomfortable with how easy it became to spot the movement of animals as far as half a mile away using his peripheral vision, a critical hunting skill, then close in and drop an unsuspecting elk with a five-hundred-yard shot. He took to hunting only with open sights, which required him to stalk within two hundred yards of an elk to make a reliable kill. After several more seasons, he increased the degree of difficulty of his fall hunts even more by switching from his 30.06 to a Civil War-era muzzle loader, which had a reliable firing range of only a hundred yards.

As he upped the challenge of his hunts over the years, Chuck remained committed to never wounding and losing an animal. Never again, anyway.

The first year he hunted elk, Chuck saw few tracks and not a single animal. He spotted elk his second year, but none were within range. During his third October hunt, he lined up a three-hundred-yard shot on a good-sized bull standing just below the top of a steep ridge.

Chuck steadied himself against the trunk of a tree and squeezed the trigger. He planned for the shot to drop several inches over the three-football-field distance to its target, but he didn't account for the added bullet drop resulting from the shot's uphill trajectory from his location at the foot of the ridge. That additional drop turned what should have been a clean kill into a shot that only wounded the bull. When the bullet clipped its ribcage below its heart and lungs, the elk stumbled, regained its footing, and charged up and over the ridge and out of sight.

Chuck tracked the bull until dark and resumed the search at dawn, following drops of blood, broken branches where the wounded animal had pushed blindly through thickets, and an occasional hoof print in dirt. Nearly eighteen hours after being wounded, the elk's meat by then was unsalvageable. Still, Chuck kept tracking the animal, unable to bear the thought of leaving the bull to a lingering death. Late in the morning, he broke from a stand of trees into an open meadow. A flock of magpies rose, squawking, from knee-high grass thirty yards ahead. At the spot where the birds had risen, he came upon all that was left of the bull: a shredded ribcage, a few stray bits of hide, and the animal's skull with a line of vertebrae attached to its base. The tines of the bull's antlers, protruding from the skull, pointed accusingly up at him from the grass. Scat from the pack of coyotes that had ended the bull's misery was scattered thickly around what was left of the animal.

Never again, Chuck swore that day. Never again, when presented with a shot, would he squeeze the trigger unless he knew with absolute certainty he would instantly end the animal's life. In the years since, by sticking to his pledge, Chuck had become an expert woodsman, capable of moving in complete silence across any terrain, alert to the slightest changes in wind direction, able to recognize the barest outlines of animals more than a mile away. He'd learned that the way to rise to the challenge of hunting ghost-like elk was to become ghost-like himself, and he'd never lost an animal since.

Chuck took a swallow of beer as Janelle tapped away at her computer beside him. Janelle's highly interactive social life was hardly ghost-like. She updated her Facebook page every few hours, and gossiped online and on the phone with her girlfriends all day, every day. Right now, with her daily, dinner-hour phone call to her parents still to come, she no doubt was divulging personal details of her first ever visit to the Grand

Canyon for all the world to see. She didn't hide from Chuck the leading role he played in her various communication streams these days, though when she tried to let him in on everything she posted about him online, he politely begged off having to listen.

His heart sank as his thoughts turned to Janelle's comments in the museum corridor. Was their marriage destined to end before it had a chance to begin? If so, Janelle would go back to Albuquerque. She would pick up where she'd left off, surrounded by family and friends. She'd be fine. So, too, would the girls. But what of him?

Suddenly he understood what it was that had driven Donald to drink in the years following his divorce.

Janelle must have felt Chuck's eyes on her. "Need something?" she asked, without looking up.

"Just enjoying looking at you."

She smiled and continued typing.

Chuck drained his beer. At least the hatchet had been a success. A piece of himself he'd shared with Janelle and the girls. And they'd liked it, hadn't they? That proved there was at least some sort of overlap between him and the three of them. He just had to dedicate himself to finding more of those points of crossover, that was all.

He pushed himself from his chair. "I'm gonna hit the john."

Janelle nodded without looking up, her fingers flying.

After visiting the bathroom, Chuck made his way through the campground row by row. Donald had said the woman from Maricopa Point was here at Mather somewhere. Chuck checked car license plates as he approached each campsite. Within a few minutes, he passed vehicles from Arkansas, Washington, D.C., Maine, and North Dakota. He passed two campsites with cars bearing New Mexico plates, but did not catch sight of the woman at either one. At a campsite at the far end of the campground, he spotted a ranger sedan parked in front of a large black SUV with gleaming chrome wheels.

Chuck scanned the site from behind a thin screen of brush. The patrol car blocked his view of the SUV's license plate. A uniformed ranger stood beside the park vehicle. Chuck recognized the trim athletic figure and blaze-orange hair of Rachel Severin, Grand Canyon National Park ranger and adventure race fanatic. And there, facing Rachel, was the woman from Maricopa Point, speaking angrily and jabbing the air with a pudgy, red-nailed finger. Behind her, a discount-store dome tent stood on the site's gravel tent pad. No other camping gear was in evidence.

The woman looked in Chuck's direction. Their eyes met through the brush, causing her to stop her rant in mid-sentence. Chuck froze, waiting for the woman to point him out to Rachel. Instead, the woman turned back to the ranger and resumed her diatribe.

Spooked, Chuck made for the nearest bathroom building. He ducked behind it and peeked back around the corner of the building in time to see Rachel climb behind the wheel of her ranger sedan while the woman kept right on with her tirade. Rachel pulled away from the campsite with a courteous wave to the woman, who glared after her, finally silent.

Chuck hurried across the campground as Rachel headed around the one-way loop leading to the exit. He reached the exit just ahead of Rachel and flagged her down. She stopped in the middle of the drive and looked up at him from her car window.

"Rachel," Chuck greeted her. Butterflies fluttered unexpectedly in his stomach.

"Donald said you were here."

"I—" he began. Why had he chased her down?

"Yes?" she urged.

"How you doing?"

"I'm not married, if that's what you mean."

Chuck blinked. What was he doing here? He should have known better than to go along with Janelle's idea that they take their first family vacation at the Grand Canyon—although, he realized, blanching, it was *he* who had hurried across the campground to chase Rachel down.

Independent, career-oriented women like Rachel had comprised virtually all of Chuck's romantic relationships over the years. And for the longest time, such women were all he had ever imagined wanting, partners who expected nothing more of him than the same surface companionship he took from them. The mutual desire to keep things simple had driven Chuck and Rachel apart on three different occasions. Each time they'd grown too close, they'd bounced away from one another like opposing magnets. The last time they'd spoken, Chuck had told Rachel he didn't think either of them were the marrying kind, and Rachel had agreed.

Then along came Janelle.

"She's really something," Chuck blurted.

Rachel shuttered her eyes. "I'm sure she is."

"I didn't mean—"

"You never do, Chuck."

"She's . . . She's . . . You're . . ." Chuck stuttered his way to silence, feeling as if he were drowning, as if he were last in a mile swim and Rachel was leading the way, far ahead, with her sure and steady strokes. She was smart, pretty, confident—everything logic told him he should desire in a mate. Their third and final breakup had come two years ago, just before Chuck had completed his work at the latrine site and left the park to begin the transmission line contract.

Rachel was waiting.

"Still competing?" he asked.

"I'm a few weeks away from hitting masters—" the masters

division of the adventure-racing circuit to which she devoted all her free time was for racers forty and over "—which means, barring injury, I should be looking at nationals next year."

Rachel's adventure races were held in places like Utah's red-rock country, the backwoods of Maine, and the high Sierra. The races lasted two to three days and nights, and involved rock climbing, whitewater kayaking, cross-country running, mountain biking, zip-lining, and any other outlandish outdoor pursuits race organizers could dream up. While serving as Rachel's one-man crew at a number of her races over the years, Chuck had come to appreciate the camaraderie between opposing teams and racers at the events, the odd juxtaposition of intense athletic competition waged deep in the backcountry, and the emotional highs and lows that were an inevitable part of such lengthy contests.

"Rachel Severin, national champion," he said. "Nice ring to it." Her green eyes glowed in response. "I saw you with that woman back there," he continued. "Looked like she was giving you a hard time."

"She wasn't too out of line, considering she's trapped here 'til morning. Gotta take it out on somebody."

"She can't leave?"

"Coroner's coming from Flag. Retired Air Force surgeon, just elected. Everything by the book. Wants to visit the scene before he accompanies the boyfriend's body back to town. Until then, Begay says she stays close."

Chuck recalled the man's Isotopes sweatshirt. "She's from Albuquerque?"

"Yep."

"The guy fell? That's what Donald said."

Rachel inclined her head. "Something to do with a fight. She says he was showing off, trying to save face. Climbed up on the railing, struck a pose, slipped. Big guy, like her. Never had a chance."

"The fight was between the two of them?"

"No. Him and some other guy. She says it was over before it began. Doesn't sound like there's much to it. This woman and her boyfriend, from the sound of things, their whole life was one big brawl."

"'Big' being the operative word."

"Zipper on the body bag blew out during the retrieval. Paramedics had to suture him back in just to get him to the top." Rachel's lips ticked upward in the start of a smile.

Chuck had forgotten how much he enjoyed being with her. He gave the roof of her car an amiable tap. "Good seeing you."

"You, too." She sounded as if she meant it. She accelerated a few feet, then stopped and stuck her head out the window. "Good luck, family man," she said, before ducking back inside and driving away.

He stood in the middle of the exit until an approaching car sounded its horn behind him, herding him out of the way. The evening sunlight winked out as a small cloud passed in front of the sun. Chuck dug his fingers into the palms of his hands as he headed across the campground toward Janelle and the girls, his thoughts returning to the woman from Albuquerque. Why had she ignored him when she'd spotted him spying on her? Why hadn't she told Rachel it was Chuck who had punched her boyfriend?

According to Rachel, Chuck's fight with the guy in the Isotopes sweatshirt was at least partly to blame for the guy's death. Chuck kicked at a pinecone lying in the campground drive. He knew one thing for sure: he had to get away from here. He shouldn't have agreed to come to the canyon. There was no rush for Janelle to learn the details of his profession; she'd get to know all about what he did for a living as she got to know him.

He stopped.

Janelle didn't really know him yet, did she? As fast as everything had happened between them, how could she? And, when it came right down to it, Chuck knew just as little about her.

It was far too soon for Janelle to judge the strength of their marriage. How could either of them measure their true commitment to each other at this early stage? That was the reasoning he would present to her as soon as they were back in Durango. She would agree that they should give themselves enough time to fully get to know one another, and things between them would smooth out.

He resumed walking. He had to get away from the canyon with Janelle and the girls, get back to the new life they were still in the process of creating for themselves in Colorado. No excuse he could come up with would convince Janelle to break camp this evening and drive back to Durango through the night, but he'd be able to come up with something by morning that would require their departure—maybe a sudden need to finish the final report on the transmission line project sooner rather than later for Marvin Begay.

Yes, that excuse would work when he trotted it out over breakfast tomorrow. All he had to do was make it through tonight.

The girls were seated side by side at the picnic table eating dinner when Chuck returned to camp. Rosie's cheeks were shiny with chicken grease. She bounced up and down in excitement at his appearance. Even Carmelita, looking up from wiping each of her fingers fastidiously with a paper towel, brightened at his approach.

Janelle waved him over to where she sat in her camp chair. "My folks are so glad we made it," she told him. She held up her phone, beaming. "Dolores and Amelia, too," she added, naming her closest friends in Albuquerque.

Chuck took in Janelle and the girls. This would work. Sunset in a little while, a good night's sleep followed by a second round of pancakes in the morning, then, upon checking messages, he would announce that Marvin had moved up the delivery date for the final report, and Janelle would agree to head for home. Once they were back in Durango, they would have the time and space their still-developing relationship needed. The girls would start school. Janelle would finish moving into Chuck's house. And he would do whatever it took to prove himself to her.

As for what had happened this morning on Maricopa Point? That was done, finished.

"And guess what," Janelle announced with a wide smile, her phone now clasped between her palms. "Clarence is joining us. He's on his way right now!"

Seven

7 p.m.

Chuck glanced away in an attempt to hide his dismay. Why hadn't Janelle checked with him first?

She leaned forward, trying to catch his eye. "What's wrong?"

"Nothing." Chuck looked back at her. "Really."

So much for the truth, always the truth, between them.

"It was his idea, Chuck. He's so excited for me. For us. He asked if he could come. Of course I said yes. He's my brother."

"And my brother-in-law."

"And your assistant. Is that what this is about?"

"Was my assistant. The fieldwork's finished."

"What's the problem then?"

"I told you. No problem." Which was, to a certain extent, the truth.

Chuck had enjoyed working with Clarence Ortega more than any other subcontractor he'd hired over the years. Twenty-four months on the transmission line project, the longest contract Chuck had ever worked, and Janelle's brother had been with him the whole time.

Clarence had been a fresh graduate out of the University of New Mexico School of Anthropology who'd been smart enough to follow up the résumé he'd sent Chuck with a personal phone call. At Chuck's side, as the two worked their way section by section, month after month, along the transmission line right-of-way across the Navajo Reservation, Clarence had proven himself to be hardworking, eager to learn, and acceptably, if not entirely, reliable.

As had Chuck in his early twenties, Clarence partied too long and too hard on a number of weeknights over the course of the contract. He'd arrive at the worksite an hour or two late on those occasions, uncharacteristically soft-spoken, clearly hung over, and not worth a dime productivity-wise. Clarence hadn't racked up enough of those unproductive days for Chuck to make an issue of them. Besides, Chuck enjoyed having Clarence around. The young man was friendly and easygoing. He got along well with Chuck and, notably, with young Navajos across the reservation as well.

Clarence mixed easily with the twenty-something Navajos, many chronically unemployed, who filled the rez towns along the transmission line route, hanging out in fast-food joints and crowding the impromptu flea markets held several days a week in every reservation community. While working for Chuck, Clarence often spent his weekends just across the border from Arizona in the mid-sized city of Gallup, New Mexico. The primary gathering spot on the rez for young tribal members was a few miles southeast of Window Rock, the Arizona town that served as the official capital of the Navajo Nation.

"My Latino people been mixing it up with Indian folks 'round here for more than four hundred years," Clarence said with a laugh when Chuck gave him a hard time about his late-night wanderings. "I'm just keeping the tradition alive."

Archaeological digs on the reservation often fostered accusations of grave robbery and cultural theft, which made Clarence's off-hours role as an unofficial goodwill ambassador for Bender Archaeological a significant plus. Clarence's informal public relations work on the reservation was particularly beneficial given the unusually long timeframe of the transmission line contract. It made good business sense, then, for Chuck to cut Clarence some slack on the rare occasions the young man's off-the-clock fun limited his on-the-job performance.

Not until this past spring had Chuck accepted Clarence's long-tendered offer to swing through Albuquerque and meet his parents, Enrique and Yolanda. Janelle stopped by her parents' small stucco home in Albuquerque's South Valley the same evening Chuck showed up for dinner, and Chuck's life had been on fast-forward ever since.

Carmelita and Rosie looked up at Chuck from the picnic table as he stared out across the campground. No way could he convince Janelle to return to Durango tomorrow morning with the girls' Uncle Clarence set to arrive here tonight. If Chuck announced that Marvin Begay had moved up the deadline for the final transmission line report, Janelle would suggest, logically enough, that Chuck work on the report in camp on his laptop while she, the girls, and Clarence explored the South Rim on their own.

Chuck took a deep breath. Any way he looked at it, he was trapped at the canyon for at least another day. The best thing he could do, he supposed, was get used to the idea. He exhaled. Everything would be all right. The woman from Albuquerque had chosen not to point him out to Rachel when she'd had the chance. She would leave in the morning to accompany her boyfriend's body to Flagstaff. After that, Chuck would be in the clear.

He summoned a smile and slipped behind the girls. "Hear that? Your Uncle Clarence is coming!" He tickled each of them in turn. Rosie shrieked in delight, laying her head back against Chuck's chest. Even Carmelita managed a giggle as she curled her shoulders away from him.

"We gotta eat," he said to Janelle, waving her over to the table. "Sunset's in forty-five minutes."

They left camp at a brisk walk fifteen minutes later and arrived at crowded Grandeur Point just west of the South Rim Visitor Center as the last of the sun's rays set fire to the farthest walls of the canyon. The topmost ramparts of Shiva Temple, a wedding-cake-layered butte rising a vertical half-mile from the bottom of the canyon, shone like a Roman candle in the last of the day's sunlight.

Chuck positioned Janelle and the girls against the overlook railing and used Janelle's phone to snap pictures with Shiva glowing behind them. Rosie jumped from one foot to another. Carmelita held her mother's hand and displayed a timid smile.

When an elderly man with a heavy German accent offered to take a picture of the four of them together, Chuck handed him the phone and found it easy to slide behind Janelle and the girls at the railing and grin over the tops of their heads. He accepted the phone back from the German man, draped an arm around Janelle's shoulders, and looked out over the canyon. Around them, dozens of tourists spoke in reverent tones in all sorts of languages as daylight gave way to dusk. The setting sun splashed the cliffs of the North Rim with orange and red, and shadows smoldered deep in the purpling canyon below the pulsating cliffs, the Colorado River a thin dark curl at the bottom of the gorge.

The four of them headed back to the campground after the last of the sun's rays left the canyon. Chuck tucked his hand around Janelle's waist as they ambled alongside one another while the girls skipped ahead. This was everything he had imagined married life could be, though he'd always thought of it with friends and acquaintances in mind, not himself. As he'd told Rachel two years ago, 'til-death-do-you-part never had been part of what he'd pictured for his future, not after his upbringing, if it could be called that, as a lonely only child with a mostly absent mother and entirely absent father. Yet here he was, barely four months after meeting Janelle, and he couldn't dream of being any happier than he was at this minute.

Yes, there was still the stuff that was eating at him, to use Janelle's terminology. And there was her time limit comment earlier today in the museum. But all that was muted this evening. Maybe the death of the guy he'd punched had something to do with it, the finality of the bulging body bag. Chuck was ashamed to think how eager he'd been to confront the guy on Maricopa Point. But he was through with all that now. No more looking for fights. That version of himself didn't fit with being a committed husband to Janelle and parent to Carmelita and Rosie. He pulled Janelle close as they walked, happy to find that, for the first time since he'd stood beside her and pronounced a shaky "I do" to the Albuquerque City Hall clerk twenty-some days ago, he had no qualms whatsoever about his life's recent radical change of course.

When they got back to camp, Janelle phoned Clarence while Chuck picked up the hatchet and called the girls over. He made a show of removing the plastic head cover.

"It's super sharp," he warned Carmelita as he handed her the hatchet. This time, she took it from him without hesitation. "Now that the cover's off, this is the real deal."

She shot him a pointed look, identical to one of Janelle's. "I'm good," she replied. "Seriously."

Janelle watched while talking on the phone with Clarence, her eyes wide with concern, as Chuck fetched firewood from a box beneath the camper and wadded up pages of newspaper. The girls stayed close to him as darkness closed in around them.

Chuck took the hatchet back from Carmelita and demonstrated how to strip thin slices of kindling from one of the chunks of split cedar he'd brought from Durango.

"See?" he said as he leaned the piece of wood against the metal wall of the fire pit and angled a gentle stroke down its side. A reddish-hued sliver peeled from the chunk of wood and the air filled with the pungent aroma of cedar. He flipped the hatchet in his hand and held it out to Carmelita by its handle. "Take it easy. It's not about blunt force. The idea is to let the sharpness of the blade do the work."

Carmelita took the hatchet while Rosie, on her toes, looked on.

"Can I do it, too? Can I? Can I?" she begged.

"Afraid not," Chuck told her.

"Awww."

"For now, Carm will have to take your cuts for you." He turned to Carmelita. "All set?"

She nodded, dead serious. Chuck steadied the chunk of cedar and stepped back.

"Spread your feet so there's no chance of hitting your leg if you miss," he instructed.

She took a couple of practice swings, then let the hatchet fall so gently against the piece of cedar that the blade didn't even bite into the wood. She shot an embarrassed look at Janelle, who raised her eyebrows in nervous encouragement, still talking to Clarence on the phone.

Carmelita licked her lips and lifted the hatchet for another try. She swung the hatchet downward with a little more force, breaking a small piece of kindling free from the chunk of cedar.

"Yippee!" Rosie cheered.

"Now you're getting it," Chuck said.

Carmelita set herself again and took several light chops at the chunk of wood, her confidence growing with each blow. Over the course of a few minutes, she reduced a third of the piece of cedar to a pile of kindling. Chuck showed her how to arrange the kindling pieces and larger chunks of firewood in a pyramid over the wadded-up newspaper in the center of the fire pit. He helped her put a lighter to the base of the pyramid. The flames licked upward, illuminating her face.

"You did it, Carm!" Rosie squealed, dancing around the fire.

Carmelita crouched in front of the flames and held out her hands to the growing warmth. "Yeah," she said softly. "I did."

"Way to go," Janelle praised Carmelita, lowering her phone.

"And she's still got all ten fingers," Chuck said.

"You didn't tell me my daughters would become ax-wielding pyromaniacs if we came here."

"Daugh-*ter*," he corrected, pointing at Carmelita. "She's a natural."

Carmelita straightened her back but did not look up from the flames.

"Agreed," Janelle said. She set her phone on the picnic table. "He's two hours out. Almost to Flagstaff."

"Good to hear." Chuck found himself looking forward to Clarence's arrival. He'd missed working with him since the completion of the fieldwork portion of the transmission line contract a month ago. Janelle's brother had been fun on the job; he'd be just as fun here at the canyon.

Before bedtime, the girls enjoyed their first-ever marshmallow roast, during which Rosie slimed her hair with a long string of melted white sugar. The sliming precipitated a trip with Janelle to the hot-water tap in the sink of the nearest bathroom. Just as Janelle and Rosie returned to camp, Carmelita said that she, too, needed to visit the bathroom.

"You can't be serious," Janelle said in response to Carmelita's ill-timed announcement.

"You don't need to go with her," Chuck said, gesturing at the well-lit bathroom building little more than a hundred feet away. "She's seven. She's a big girl." He pointed at the fire. "She proved it."

Carmelita's eyes grew large at Chuck's proposal. "Can I, *Mamá*?"

Janelle looked from Carmelita to Chuck and back. "I guess," she said hesitantly. "Straight there, straight back, got it?"

"Got it," Carmelita said with a solemn nod to her mother. Then she looked at Chuck for reassurance.

"I meant what I said," he told her. "You're a big girl. You can handle it."

She nodded again, this time to herself. Chuck held a flashlight out to her from his seat by the fire. She dusted her hands on the sides of her striped sweat pants and looked out at the darkness. Then she accepted the flashlight and set off. Janelle watched the beam of light bob away up the gravel road.

"Oh, Chuck," she said, her voice small.

She reached for him from her chair. The fire crackled and popped. A tendril of wood smoke drifted between them. Chuck took Janelle's hand in both of his. How incredibly brave—or foolhardy—she was. Her life as a single mother in Albuquerque had been fine—decent apartment, steady job as an office receptionist, built-in babysitters in her parents—yet she'd sacrificed it all for a lifelong bachelor who didn't know a thing about raising kids, or how to be involved in a fully committed adult relationship either, for that matter. Late last month, she'd left her friends, her family, her whole world behind in New Mexico to embark on an entirely new life for herself and the girls in the mountains of southwest Colorado, far from everything and everyone she'd ever known. Now here she was, trusting the well-being of her oldest daughter to a man she'd known only a few months. If Chuck was nervous about his new life with Janelle, then Janelle had every right to be terrified of her new life with him.

"*No te preocupes, esposa mia,*" Chuck told her. He liked using bits of Spanish with her, just as she did with the girls. In this case, the word *esposa* didn't feel as odd coming off his tongue as the word wife had with Donald earlier in the day.

Carmelita returned to camp, her eyes alight at her accomplishment. Janelle hugged her oldest daughter to her before leading both girls off to bed. Carmelita and Rosie were asleep in the camper by the time their uncle drove up half an hour later.

Clarence emerged from his dented hatchback with a bottle of tequila in hand. "Time to celebrate," he announced, coming around his car. He hitched up his baggy jeans and waved the bottle so the golden liquid glinted in the firelight. "Whew, that's a long drive."

"You oughtta be good at it by now," Chuck said.

Every weekend throughout the transmission line contract, Clarence had driven at least as far as Gallup, if not all the way home to Albuquerque.

"Four weeks off makes a big difference," he replied.

Clarence was stocky and broad-chested like his father and Rosie. He shared their throaty tone of voice as well. His large set of white teeth gleamed when he laughed, which was often. His ruddy face and round cheeks reminded Chuck of Santa Claus—if, that is, Santa sported raven-black hair to his shoulders, wore a thick silver stud in each ear, and had a thing for Navajo girls and mezcal tequila.

Janelle rose from her seat beside the fire to hug her brother.

"Lemme at you, Sis," Clarence said, wrapping her in his arms. Then he reached out to fist-bump Chuck. "*Jefe.*"

"Something to eat?" Chuck asked.

Over the course of their two years of fieldwork, Chuck and Clarence had spent most weeknights in motel rooms in whatever nondescript reservation town was nearest the section of right-of-way they were working. They'd slept out, Chuck in the enclosed bed of his pickup truck and Clarence in the rear of his hatchback, when the windswept towns that passed for civilization on the rez were a long drive away.

"I grabbed a burger in Gallup," Clarence said. He gave the nearly full bottle a shake. "This is what I've been looking forward to, and you guys have to join me."

"One shot, that's all," said Janelle as she sat back down. "I'm half asleep as it is."

"It's a celebration, is what I'm saying. My sister, my boss, happily married. Who'd've ever thought?"

He returned to his hatchback and dug around inside until he came up with three shot glasses. He lined them on the roof of the car, filled each in turn, and carried them to the fire.

"The two of you took off for Durango and never gave me a chance to say this," he told Janelle and Chuck, handing out the shots and raising his glass. "Here's to both of you. Three weeks in, and may it be three centuries."

"Centuries?" Janelle fluttered her eyes at Chuck over the top of her glass. "I'm not sure he'd want me three hundred years from now."

"Yes, I would," Chuck said. "Three hundred. Three thousand. Three million."

Her eyes glittered in the firelight. He shivered with pleasure as their glasses clinked. He downed his shot, gasping as the alcohol burned its way to his stomach. He set his glass on the picnic table and tossed another chunk of wood on the fire, sending a shower of sparks into the night air. The three of them settled back in their chairs around the flickering flames.

"How're things at home?" Janelle asked her brother, as if her daily calls to her mother and father didn't keep her fully up to date.

Clarence, who lived in an apartment above the garage behind his parents' house, offered news Janelle probably knew: the latest plan to drive Albuquerque's drug gangs from the city, a neighbor recently diagnosed with cancer, another who'd won a thousand bucks in the lottery.

It wasn't long before Chuck's eyelids began to droop. A glance at Janelle showed she was fading as well. It had been a full couple of days. A full three weeks, for that matter.

"Bedtime," Chuck said, standing up. "Come on." He pulled Janelle up beside him.

"'Night," Janelle said to Clarence as Chuck led her to the camper.

"'Night, Sis," Clarence replied, remaining by the fire.

Chuck handed Janelle the flashlight and held the screen door open for her. He turned to Clarence. "All set?"

Clarence indicated his hatchback. "Bed's already made."

Chuck cradled Janelle in his arms as they fell asleep on the platform opposite the girls in the camper. He slept late the next morning. Like Janelle, he'd had only the one shot of tequila, but the pleasant evening must have had a calming effect on both of them because it was past eight when he slipped outside, leaving Janelle breathing evenly behind him, her head buried in her pillow.

The day was sunny and already warm. He rotated his upper body in a few leisurely stretches, finding that he had little desire to take off on his morning run. Instead, he fired up the camp stove. He finished making coffee just as Janelle joined him at the picnic table in low-cut jeans and a sleeveless top. He poured her a cup while she yawned and kneaded the back of her neck.

"Where's Carmelita?" she asked sleepily, taking her mug from Chuck.

"Inside." Chuck poured his own cup and pointed at the camper. "Isn't she?"

Janelle shook her head.

"I've been up a while," Chuck said with a frown. "Fifteen or twenty minutes."

Janelle looked around the quiet campsite. She set her mug on the picnic table and ducked inside the camper only to re-emerge seconds later. "Rosie's there, that's all," she said, her voice strained.

She circled the camper, checking the windows of her mini-SUV and Clarence's hatchback and looking all directions. Chuck followed, coffee cup in hand. She set off toward the nearest bathroom, the one Carmelita had visited on her own the night before. Chuck set his mug on the table and jogged to catch up.

Janelle turned to him. "No. You stay here."

She walked a few more paces, then broke into a run.

Back at camp, Chuck peered into Clarence's car. Clarence

lay diagonally across the folded rear hatch area in his sleeping bag, his eyes closed, the bottle of tequila, half-empty, tucked beside him. Chuck double-checked Janelle's car next, convinced she'd overlooked Carmelita curled up inside reading a book. But both the front and rear seats were empty. He turned a full circle. Where was she?

The campground was full of noise and motion, campers cooking, washing dishes, collapsing tents, and walking to and from the bathrooms, unaware of the frigid rush of fear now coursing through Chuck's veins.

Janelle emerged alone from the women's bathroom. She took a couple of steps in the direction of camp, then turned and disappeared inside the men's half of the building. She came out seconds later, still alone, and ran toward camp.

"Carm!" she called. "Carmelita!" she yelled again, drawing stares from neighboring campers.

Chuck met her at the edge of the campsite. "She's gone, Chuck," Janelle said, her voice shaking, her eyes filled with alarm. "Carm's gone."

Thursday

"A descent into the Cañon is essential for a proper estimate of its details, and one can never realize the enormity of certain valleys, till he has crawled like a maimed insect at their base and looked thence upward to the narrowed sky."

— John Stoddard
John L. Stoddard's Lectures, Vol. 10, 1898

Eight

8:30 a.m.

Fire blazed suddenly in Janelle's eyes. She slapped Chuck hard on the side of his face. The *pop* of her palm echoed across the campground. Chuck stumbled backward, putting a hand to his stinging cheek.

"You let her go last night," Janelle snapped. "'You're a big girl,' you told her. Well, she isn't, Chuck. She isn't!"

The flames receded from Jan's eyes as quickly as they had come. She collapsed against Chuck's chest. Before he could put his arms around her, she shoved herself away from him.

"Where is she, Chuck? *Where is Carmelita*?"

Chuck's eyes darted around the campground, searching for a glimpse of Carmelita's wispy frame. Janelle needed strength. Encouragement. She needed a good cop, a proclaimer of positive thoughts.

"She's around here somewhere," he said. "She's gotta be. Where could she possibly have gotten off to?"

"Farther today than she ever would have yesterday, no thanks to you."

"Which is why she's somewhere nearby, just out of sight," Chuck countered. But Carmelita, proud though she'd been of her solo trip to the bathroom, never would have awoken this morning and purposefully set off somewhere out of sight of camp. Doing so simply didn't fit her cautious nature. Might she inadvertently have wandered somewhere beyond their view? That, at least, was a possibility worth investigating.

"Expanding circles," Chuck said, naming a basic archaeological work method. He pointed in the direction opposite the campsite of the woman from Albuquerque. "You loop that way. I'll swing the other. We'll meet back here in a few minutes."

Chuck went just far enough on his loop through the campground to catch sight of the Albuquerque woman's campsite. It was empty, the tent and large black SUV gone. He returned from his unsuccessful search to find Janelle pounding on her brother's hatchback. Clarence's haggard face appeared in the car's sloping rear window. He pulled on his pants, crawled out, and stood unsteadily, rubbing his eyes.

"Have you seen Carm?" Janelle demanded.

"What?"

"Have—you—seen—Carm? Since last night?"

"Um, sorry, Sis. No." Clarence looked to Chuck for help. "What's going on?"

"Carm's wandered off somewhere," Chuck told him.

Clarence's eyebrows lifted. "That's not like her."

Janelle took hold of his shoulder. "Which is why I'm trying to get your attention."

"You checked your car?" Clarence asked.

She dropped her hand and nodded.

"What's missing of her stuff?" Clarence asked her.

"What do you mean?"

"I mean, what'd she take with her? What's she wearing?"

Chuck looked at his assistant, impressed. Clarence had nailed the first two rules of site study.

The first: *Don't just do something, stand there.* That is, think things through. Ask questions. Get answers. Don't begin the initial survey of an archaeological site, much less digging, without a plan.

And the second: *Begin at the very beginning, that's a very good place to start.* Complete the full site assessment first, set up grid units based on the best sense of what's underfoot, then excavate each unit in turn, beginning with the one that holds the most promise and working outward from there.

Chuck led the way to the camper. The air inside was stale

and musty. The lighting was dim, diffused by the camper's canvas walls. Clothes, toys, and sleeping bags were strewn across the sleeping platforms, while sneakers, sandals, and boots were scattered on the floor—a compact version of the upheaval that had come to Chuck's small house in Durango when Janelle and the girls arrived three weeks ago.

Chuck turned a half-circle, uncertain where to begin. Janelle stepped past him and kicked at the shoes on the floor.

"She's wearing her hiking boots," she said. "The new ones."

She slid Rosie, still asleep in her bag, to the rear of the girls' sleeping platform and clawed through clothes, dolls, stuffed animals, electronic toys, and children's books. She came up with the red shorts and blouse Carmelita had worn the day before. She lifted Carmelita's silky yellow pajamas from the jumble of clothing and toys and held them to her chest, her eyes closed.

"She's wearing her sweats, the ones she had on last night," Janelle said, turning to Chuck and Clarence. "Her favorites."

Clarence stepped to the edge of the girls' sleeping platform. "With the stripes? The blue ones?"

"She slept in them. She and Rosie were tired, didn't want to change."

"There's a jacket and pants, right?" Clarence pushed Carmelita's empty sleeping bag aside. He and Janelle began rummaging through everything on the platform.

"What's this?" Janelle asked, dropping the pajamas and picking up a piece of white paper previously hidden by Carmelita's sleeping bag.

She squinted at the sheet of paper in the dim light. Her hand and the paper shook. Two words were penned on it in large, plain block letters: "NO COPS."

Clarence snatched the paper from Janelle's hand and flipped it over. Other than the two large words, it was blank. The three of them stood around the piece of paper in stunned silence.

Rosie chose that moment to poke her head from her sleeping bag. "Uncle Clarence!" She kicked her way out of her bag and leapt into Clarence's arms.

Clarence handed the sheet back to Janelle and clasped Rosie to him. Looking over her shoulder at Janelle and Chuck, he unleashed a string of Spanish curses.

Rosie leaned away from him. "What did you say?"

"*Nada, bambina.*" He put a finger to her lips. "*Nada importante.*"

Chuck took another look at the paper in Janelle's hand. It had to be some sort of prop made by Carmelita while the girls played in the camper yesterday afternoon. But a glance at Clarence told him otherwise. Clarence's face was drained of color, his eyes haunted.

Chuck turned to Janelle—the look in her eyes matched her brother's. Janelle knew what Clarence knew. Her eyes told Chuck something else as well: Carmelita had been kidnapped.

A hole opened inside him, black and bottomless. *Carmelita. Kidnapped.*

Janelle dropped the sheet of paper to the girls' sleeping platform, put a fist to her mouth, and ducked outside. Chuck and Clarence, carrying Rosie, followed. Janelle bent double at the side of the camper and vomited, her hands on her knees. Chuck rested a hand on her back, his own stomach churning.

"What's wrong, *Mamá*?" Rosie asked.

Janelle straightened and swiped her mouth with the back of her hand. She looked at Clarence, who looked straight back at her. Only then did she turn to Chuck, her eyes steely with determination.

"Tag," she said grimly. "You're it."

Chuck stared at her, bewildered.

"Miguel," Clarence said, his voice hard.

Janelle kept her eyes trained on Chuck.

"Miguel," she repeated.

Nine

9 a.m.

Chuck waved his hands in front of him and took a step backward. "Wait a minute. Wait just one minute."

Janelle had told Chuck little about Miguel Gutierrez, the father of Carmelita and Rosie. Chuck knew only that Miguel was a small-time drug dealer a few years older than Janelle, that he'd hooked up with her while she was a community college student, that the two had never married, and that Miguel had disappeared from the lives of Janelle and the girls shortly after Rosie's birth five years ago.

"What is it the two of you know that I don't?" Chuck demanded. Rosie's eyes darted from her mother to her uncle and back. Chuck reached over to rub her shoulder, but she ducked away from him and buried her face in Clarence's neck. Hurt, Chuck turned to Janelle. "Talk to me," he said, his words clipped.

"He always made threats," Janelle said. "From the very first. 'I'll kill you if you leave.' Then, after Carm was born, 'You leave me, you'll never see your little girl again.' I was so scared. Of course I never left. How could I?" She looked plaintively at Chuck. "It was Miguel, finally, who left us. He swore Rosie wasn't his. He was broke all the time. People were after him." She paused. "It was so good when he was gone. *Mami* and *Papi* were, like, the best. These last five years, I've finally gotten to know what it's like to be alive." Her voice cracked. "And then you . . ." She raised a hand toward Chuck's face, but he backed away from her.

"How long's it been since you've seen him?" he demanded.

"The day Rosie was born." Janelle lowered her hand, her face pale.

"You haven't *seen* him," Chuck urged.

"He calls. Out of the blue. Usually when he's wasted."

"Any more threats?"

"Yes," she said softly, her eyes downcast.

"When was the last one?"

"A few weeks ago." Her voice was barely audible.

"What'd he say?"

Rosie reached from Clarence's arms for her mother. Janelle traded Clarence the sheet of paper for Rosie and balanced her youngest daughter on her hip. "*Preciosa mia*," she whispered in Rosie's ear, tears streaming down her face.

"*Preciosa mia tambien, Mamá*," Rosie replied mechanically, wiping away her mother's tears with the flat of her hand.

Chuck asked Janelle, "You were with him for what, four years?"

"Three. Just three."

"You had one baby with him, then you went ahead and had another."

"I was different back then. A different person. I blamed *Mami* and *Papi*, but it wasn't their fault. They worked so hard. But they were all over me, like every minute. I needed space, my own life."

"And this Miguel," Chuck muttered, "he gave you that."

"I was nineteen and pregnant by a drug dealer," Janelle said. "And I was so sure I knew what I was doing."

"So you just kept doing it," Chuck said, stone-faced.

"I'd been so sheltered." She glanced at Clarence. "We'd been so sheltered. I quit college. I'd only been going part time anyway. I was going to make my own way in the world. At least, that's the way I thought of it. But I knew it wouldn't last. It couldn't."

Clarence said, "Not in the South Valley."

"People kept disappearing," Janelle said. "The ones Miguel worked with. Prison, back across the border. One day they'd be playing with Carm on the floor of our apartment. The next, it was like they'd never existed. There were so many close calls.

The pressure was always on. One day, when I was pregnant with Rosie, I looked at Carm, really looked at her—she was a toddler by then, just learning to walk—and I knew what I was doing was wrong. Just like that, like flipping a switch. I waited until Rosie was born. Miguel came to the hospital. Refused to touch her. His phone rang, some deal he had going. Rosie was in my arms. Carm was with my parents. I told him to get out, and he did."

She looked straight at Chuck, her eyes shining. He looked straight back. This was why he'd fallen so hard for her. Just as she'd been as a new mother, she was her own person today. Stubborn, strong-willed, devoted to her girls. God, she was beautiful, even now, even in the midst of all this.

The muscles in Chuck's jaw loosened. It finally made sense, what had attracted Janelle to him. It was the same thing that had drawn her to Miguel: Chuck presented her and the girls with a new world, one far different than the circumscribed world of Albuquerque's South Valley. Maybe, just maybe, she wasn't as different as she claimed from the impulsive coed she'd been eight years ago—except this time around she'd done a far better job of choosing her man.

Chuck pictured Carmelita's pride-filled eyes, so like her mother's, when she'd returned to camp from her trip to the bathroom last night. *Carmelita.* That's who this was about, and seconds were ticking by.

"You said he threatened you the last time you talked to him," Chuck said to Janelle.

"He needed money. I told him to forget it."

"That was it? Nothing more specific?"

"He said he'd get me, the girls. But he always says that."

"Why do you still speak to the guy?" Chuck asked, an edge to his voice.

"It's safer," she said flatly. "For the girls."

"Okay," Chuck said, backing off. "This Miguel, do you have

any pictures of him? On your computer, your phone?"

"I got rid of them when he left. Every single one."

"Is he fat?"

"Not really. Or he wasn't, anyway, last I knew."

Clarence tapped the collar of his shirt. "He has matching tattoos. Chinese letters running along each of his collarbones."

"One side says 'peace,' and the other, 'beauty,'" Janelle said bitterly. "He got them right after we met, to impress me."

Clarence looked at Chuck. "Why are you asking? Think you saw him?"

"I don't know a damn thing at this point," Chuck said.

Clarence held the "NO COPS" sheet of paper up before him. "The only good thing about this is, if it *is* Miguel, then Carmelita's okay."

Janelle nodded stiffly. "He wants money. He won't hurt her."

Chuck looked from Janelle to Clarence and back. Janelle had just said Miguel had threatened the girls in the past. How could she and Clarence be so sure of Carmelita's safety now? There had to be something else going on here.

"Carmelita?" Rosie asked in alarm.

"Hush, baby," Janelle told her. "Your sister's with her father." Then she rounded on Chuck, bristling. "You're the one who made her so independent last night. She woke up this morning, went off to the bathroom on her own—"

But Chuck was having none of it. "Maybe if I'd known. Maybe if you'd told me."

Janelle looked away. She spoke under her breath. "I didn't want to think about it."

"Did he know about us?" Chuck asked her. "That you'd taken the girls to Colorado? Could he have followed us here?"

"He always knew what was up. He knew about the time Carm broke her arm when she was four. He kept tabs."

"Was he still dealing, last you knew?"

Janelle shifted Rosie on her hip and shrugged. "He said he'd moved to prescription drugs mostly. Said it was easier. I don't think he's capable of anything else."

Clarence growled, "Except kidnapping his own daughter."

Gravel crunched on the campground road. Chuck turned to see Robert Begay's white Suburban headed their way. Chuck, Janelle, and Clarence faced the Suburban as it rolled to a stop at their campsite, Janelle sliding Rosie from her hip to stand next to her.

Chuck studied Robert as he stepped out of his car. Yesterday the chief ranger had refused to acknowledge Chuck. Now here he was, with Carmelita having just gone missing, showing up for a personal visit. What was going on?

Chuck knew Robert to be the product of two worlds, *Diné* and *bilagáana*, Navajo and white. The chief ranger had been raised off the reservation in suburban Phoenix and had graduated from Arizona State University. His brown face, high forehead, thick lips, and dark eyes bespoke his full-blooded Navajo ancestry, while his straight-ahead manner of speech and willingness to tackle park problems head on, rather than in the communally circuitous way of the *Diné*, were products of a life lived in the *bilagáana* world.

Robert's badge gleamed on his chest. He retrieved his wide-brimmed hat from the passenger seat of the Suburban and adjusted it on his head. After checking his reflection in the driver's side mirror, he approached the campsite. At Chuck's introduction, Robert touched his brim at Clarence and tilted his head to Janelle and Rosie. He spoke to Chuck, his tone inscrutable. "You were at Maricopa Point yesterday."

Chuck gave Robert a tight smile. "Is this some sort of interrogation?"

"You could say that."

Chuck swallowed. "You saw me out there," he said evenly. "Mind telling me why you showed up?"

"Mind telling me why you're asking?"

"A man is dead. Another, gone from the park for a good long time, just happens to appear at the scene."

"You're saying you're just doing your job."

Robert did not reply. His eyes were still and watchful.

Because Chuck's work at the Hermit Creek latrine site had overlapped with Robert's first months as chief ranger at the park, Chuck knew him to be smart, capable, and unfailingly professional. Moreover, Chuck had heard Robert's stature among the park's staff had only risen in the two years since.

Chuck chose his words with care. "You know me, Robert. Curiosity's part of my job description. My wife and girls and I passed Maricopa on the shuttle. I doubled back to see what was up."

"You knew the overlook was closed."

"I was looking for Podalski, to ask about a personal tour of the park. We're here as tourists."

Robert nodded. It appeared he'd received the same report from Donald. "Just that and curiosity, then?"

"You mean, why I was there?"

Rather than answer, Robert waited. He was good at that, his Navajo side coming to the fore. Taking advantage of the pause, Chuck determined his course.

The woman from Albuquerque had recognized him last night. It made sense, given the chief ranger's unannounced appearance, that she'd told Robert as much. Chuck's leveling with Robert about his having been at Maricopa Point would simply confirm what the chief ranger already knew. Plus, there was the outside chance Chuck's coming clean might somehow help in tracking down Carmelita. But Chuck wasn't ready to tell Robert about his involvement, however tangential, in the death of the woman's boyfriend.

"Curiosity," Chuck repeated with a nod. Then he zigged.

"There was quite a crowd. I couldn't see what was going on. What if you'd found the A. Dinaveri?"

Ten

9:30 a.m.

"The A. Dinaveri?" Robert scoffed. "You've gotta be kidding."

Chuck mustered all the false enthusiasm he could. "You know the calendar, the dates. A lot of people think this could be the year." He turned to Janelle. "The A. Dinaveri is a necklace thought by the one-and-only Arturo Dinaveri to have been left by the Anasazi Indians in a secret shrine somewhere along the South Rim a thousand years ago, about the time the Anasazi disappeared from the Colorado Plateau. Dinaveri was a famous Italian archaeologist who worked at Chaco Canyon in the 1950s. You know where that's at, north of Albuquerque, right?"

Janelle's tight nod made clear her frustration at the delay in getting on with finding Carmelita. When Clarence cleared his throat to speak, she wheeled on him, her eyes flashing.

"According to Dinaveri," Clarence said, showing off his own archaeological know-how despite Janelle's obvious irritation, "the Anasazi hid a necklace in the shrine as an offering to Chirsáuha, the Anasazi god of fertility said to live under the river at the bottom of the canyon."

Robert raised a skeptical eyebrow. "Dinaveri just wanted to make his time at Chaco look worthwhile."

In Italian archaeological classification, the A. in A. Dinaveri stood for *articulo*, although everyone in the Southwest archaeological community, Chuck included, assumed that in Dinaveri's famously self-inflated mind the A. stood for Arturo as well. How Dinaveri had come up with the idea of a hidden shrine at the South Rim from his study of the Anasazi at a site far from the Grand Canyon had been subjected, over the decades, to much ridicule.

"It makes a great story though," Clarence responded, avoiding Janelle's acidic glare. "Myth says the Anasazi people first came to the Earth's surface from beneath the river."

Chuck gave Janelle a look of understanding and brought the story to a close. "Dinaveri's team discovered a shadow calendar at Chaco, one that tells time by directing the sun's rays between lined-up slabs of sandstone. Dinaveri claimed the calendar indicated Chirsáuha was due to lead a reemergence of the Anasazi to the Earth's surface here at the Grand Canyon sometime about, well, now."

"I can't believe you, of all people, believe Dinaveri's drivel," Robert said.

Drivel was the right word for the Italian archaeologist's brash prediction. But at least all the talk of the A. Dinaveri had steered the chief ranger away from discussing Chuck's appearance at Maricopa Point. "Your nephew believes it," Chuck said.

"Marvin?" Robert grunted. "That's his problem. Yours, too, I guess, long as you're still working for him."

"Final report's due in a couple of weeks."

"Still enough time to find the A. Dinaveri for him," the chief ranger replied dryly.

"It's supposed to be hidden right here under your nose."

"Doesn't exist. You know it and I know it."

"Someday, Marvin'll know it, too. Meantime, I'll make sure to leave the possibility open in my final."

"Spoken like someone who wants another contract to come his way."

"Look, I'm sorry," Janelle broke in, "but Rosie really needs some breakfast."

"Yessireebob," Rosie proclaimed from Janelle's side. "I'm hungry!"

"I apologize, miss," Robert said to Rosie. He addressed Chuck with mock formality, "Mr. Bender."

Chuck dipped his head in return. "Chief Ranger Begay."

Robert walked to his Suburban. He turned to Chuck as he opened the door. "Girls," he said, his tone measured.

"What's that?"

"You said *girls*, plural, on the shuttle with you and your wife yesterday."

"Oh. Right." Chuck had introduced only Rosie to Robert. "Carmelita," Chuck said after a second's hesitation. "Carm. Rosie's sister." He waved vaguely in the direction of the camper.

Robert waited, unmoving, next to his car. It was Rosie, finally, who broke the silence. "My sister is with her daddy," she told Robert. She did a little dance, her arms above her head. "Uh-huh, uh-huh, uh-huh."

The chief ranger scanned the campsite from one side to the other until his eyes came to rest on the camper. "Well, okay then," he said slowly. He looked at Janelle. "I hope you and your girls enjoy your visit."

He tossed his hat on the passenger seat, climbed in, and drove away.

Chuck turned to Janelle and Clarence. They'd lost precious minutes dealing with Robert's visit; it was time they came up with a plan. "Should we have told Robert?" he asked. "Do we go to the police?"

The two shook their heads.

"The paper, the 'NO COPS,'" Janelle said. "Miguel means it." She took Rosie by the shoulders and pointed her in the direction of the picnic table. "He's used to getting what he wants."

"He's not stupid either," Clarence told Chuck. "Dude's never been busted. Not once. He's got a clean sheet, far as I know. Everybody around him has done time. But Miguel? Not so much as a parking ticket."

"He always bragged about how hard he worked to keep things quiet," said Janelle. "He was a master at staying in the background, getting other people to do the dirty work for him, letting everyone else take the heat."

"If he's so smart," Chuck said, "why was he broke when he called you? Why is he reduced to coming all the way out here and kidnapping his own daughter for money?"

Janelle and Clarence exchanged looks. Clarence gave Janelle a small nod.

"I've never known a more jealous person," she told Chuck. "He put a knife to a guy's throat once just for looking at me the wrong way. And he's vindictive, always saying he never forgets anyone who wrongs him, how it might take years, but he'll get them back."

"You think he's coming after you?" Chuck asked. "After all this time?"

"No. He won't hurt me on account of the girls. It's all part of his messed up sense of *familia*, his Latino honor. I'm their *mamá*. He can't hurt me, and he won't hurt the girls, so . . ."

Chuck's eyes widened as he remembered what Janelle had said before Robert's arrival at the campsite: "*Tag. You're it.*"

"So I'm fair game," Chuck finished for her.

"I'd bet everything I had on it," Clarence interjected. "He knows all about you by now. Probably has the Bender Archaeological website memorized."

"But why Carmelita? Why not just track me down, put a gun to my head, and be done with it?"

"Because that would be too easy?" Clarence pondered aloud. "No. There's more to it than that." He looked at Chuck. "Miguel Gutierrez is mean. And I mean mean, as in e-*vil*. You have no idea how happy I was, my parents were, when he left. Every time I'm with the girls, I think how lucky they are to be rid of him. But I can't help having visions of him showing up again sometime. I know how bad he must want to hurt Jan, especially now that she's so happy." He shuddered. "I agree you're fair game, but I think he just can't help going after Jan, too, sticking the knife into her even while he convinces himself he's not."

"You're getting pretty deep here, Clarence."

"Yeah, but I'm certified, remember?"

Chuck smiled at what had been an ongoing joke between the two of them throughout the transmission line contract. Clarence had teased Chuck mercilessly for getting an archaeology degree from tiny Fort Lewis College to do what Chuck did for a living: assess, dig, screen, report; assess, dig, screen, report; contract after contract, year after year. In contrast, Clarence claimed, his degree from Albuquerque's renowned University of New Mexico School of Anthropology in anthropological archaeology gave him license to do much more.

"I'm an archaeologist and an anthropologist," he boasted. "I've got a brain and I'm certified to use it." Which had led to Clarence's telling an imagined story about virtually every hunting point and potsherd he came across.

"Bag it and move on," Chuck had admonished him each time. "We're doing a job here, not making a movie."

But Clarence never could let go. "I wonder . . ." he would begin, holding up his latest discovery. "What if . . ." he would continue, outing himself as just the sort to believe in the A. Dinaveri—not because the idea of the necklace made any logical sense, but because the possibility made such a good story.

Chuck doused his smile as quickly as it had come. "Okay. We've got a crazed maniac who has kidnapped Carmelita to somehow get at me and Jan at the same time." He faced Clarence. "So tell us, swami, what's he going to do next?"

"One: he'll take good care of Carm. She's having fun right now. I'm sure of it. I bet she doesn't even know she's been kidnapped. Two: this is going to come down to money, one way or another. Everything else aside, that's how Miguel measures himself. He's going to make you pay. First in cash. Then, but only then, and only maybe then, in blood."

Chuck thought about the guy he'd punched, who'd fallen to his death off Maricopa Point. "Is Miguel a monster-SUV type? Big, showy, and bad-ass?"

Clarence took a moment, considering. "Could be by now, I suppose. But he was into sportier stuff before." He turned to Janelle. "The Miata. *¿Recuerdas?*"

"Two seats," Janelle explained to Chuck. "That's what he had, we had, when Carmelita was born. He refused to get anything else. If I wanted to go anywhere with her, I had to go by bus or borrow somebody else's car."

Chuck dug the toe of his shoe into the ground. It didn't sound as if Miguel was the guy he'd tangled with on the promontory.

Rosie twisted back and forth beside the picnic table. "I said I'm hungry!"

Janelle went to her, and Chuck stepped away from the campsite.

Did Janelle and Clarence know that all national park rangers were trained and deputized as full-on law enforcement officers? That they were, for all practical purposes, cops? Betting the answer was no, he pulled his cell phone from his pocket and scrolled to the number he wanted.

Eleven

10 a.m.

Janelle sat at the picnic table, Rosie eating a banana beside her. Clarence sat across from them, gripping a cup of coffee so hard his knuckles were white. Chuck hovered at the head of the table. Miguel was about to call, Janelle and Clarence claimed, any minute now.

Chuck had suggested calling the girls' father rather than giving him the chance to initiate contact, but Janelle and Clarence nixed the idea, arguing that Miguel wouldn't answer anyway, that it was better to let him make the first move. Besides, Janelle had explained, Miguel changed phones so often she had no idea what number to call.

"We should let *Mami* and *Papi* know," Janelle said to her brother.

Clarence drummed the side of his coffee cup with his fingers. "Agreed."

Chuck frowned. "You'll scare them to death."

Janelle picked up her smartphone in its jeweled case.

Enrique and Yolanda Ortega, the only babysitters the girls had ever known, lived for Carmelita and Rosie. That fact alone, Chuck supposed, gave them the right to know what was going on with their oldest granddaughter.

Janelle punched in the call home, spoke tersely in Spanish for a couple of minutes, then turned to Clarence when she ended the call. "You heard, didn't you? They're coming."

"They're *what*?" Chuck broke in.

Janelle looked up at him from the picnic table. "They're coming here, to the canyon." She placed her hands palm down on the table and pressed them so hard into the metal-mesh tabletop that her arms shook, as if that action would somehow return Carmelita to her.

"When?" Chuck asked.

"Now. Right away." She folded her hands away in her lap.

"What if Miguel's on his way to Albuquerque with Carm?" Chuck asked. "It'd be better to have your folks there."

"No. He'll hole up here with her. Carm will go along with whatever line he's feeding her, but only as long as he stays at the canyon. She'll go ballistic if he tries to take her away anywhere. His whole idea will be to make this happen fast, get what he wants and get out."

"You sound like you know what you're talking about."

Janelle hesitated.

"He's done this before, hasn't he?" Chuck prodded.

"Yes," Janelle said, her meek, one-word answer explaining why she wasn't absolutely beside herself with worry, why she was willing to sit here and wait for Miguel's call.

Chuck gave her time to continue.

"It was right after we got together," she said, speaking softly. "His cousin's daughter, Shanti. She was a little older than Carmelita, eight or nine. It happened so fast, it was over before I even knew about it. He made a quick five hundred bucks. His cousin never found out it was him. I don't think Shanti ever knew what was going on either." Janelle looked at the tabletop. "The only person I ever told was Clarence, nobody else."

Chuck groaned, but Clarence came to Janelle's defense. "Like you've never done anything in your life you're ashamed of."

Chuck glanced away, thinking of how he'd goaded the guy on Maricopa Point, and of the ultimate result of what he'd set in motion. "Okay," he said, turning to Janelle. He waited until she looked at him. "You agree with Clarence? That this time it's about more than just money?"

"Yes."

Unless, Chuck realized, it had in fact been Miguel he'd

punched in the gut—in which case the woman from Albuquerque was running things on her own now, and money would be her sole focus.

But the pieces of that puzzle didn't fit. For one thing, someone had come inside the camper while they'd slept to leave the "NO COPS" note—and likely to lure Carmelita away as well. Miguel, from what Chuck now knew of him, could conceivably have pulled off such a feat. But not the woman from Albuquerque. If nothing else, the lightweight camper would have swayed so much at her step that Chuck and Janelle surely would have awakened.

No, this was Miguel's doing. The girls' father must have come into the camper armed and ready to be caught—perhaps *looking* to be caught, looking for the opportunity to face off with Chuck in some sort of perverse showdown.

There was only one thing that could explain Miguel's willingness to take that sort of risk. "He still loves you, doesn't he?" Chuck said to Janelle.

"Yes," she replied, her eyes downturned.

Clarence confirmed: "And everybody in the South Valley knows it."

"Can't say as I blame him," Chuck told her.

She sobbed silently, her shoulders shaking. She rose from the table and buried herself in Chuck's arms. He held her close and watched as Donald's ranger sedan approached through the campground and pulled to a stop at their campsite.

Janelle peered over her shoulder at Donald's car, then up at Chuck in confusion, sniffling and wiping her nose.

"Ready for your tour?" Donald called over to them as he climbed out.

Janelle stiffened. "What's he talking about?"

Chuck waved at Donald, who saw Janelle and wisely remained at the side of his car.

"Look at this as an opportunity," Chuck told Janelle, holding her at arm's length. "Donald knows every nook and cranny on the South Rim."

"You think we're going to go off on some joyride when Carmelita's just been kidnapped?" Janelle asked in disbelief. "Besides, what makes you think Miguel's crazy enough to be out in the open somewhere with her?"

She was correct, of course. Chuck never should have arranged the tour with Donald this morning. But from what he'd learned, he was certain the phone call from Miguel would come to him, not Janelle. Despite the additional stress he knew he was putting on his and Janelle's already strained relationship, his overriding goal was to free himself of Janelle and Clarence before Miguel's call came through. That way he could deal with the girls' father on his own, the way he preferred.

"Donald doesn't know anything about what's going on. We're waiting for Miguel's call. We might as well poke around some in the meantime." Chuck patted his phone in his jeans pocket. "Call me the instant you hear something. I'll do the same."

"You're not coming with us?" Janelle asked incredulously.

"It's me he wants. We all agree on that. And if it's me he wants, it's me he'll get." Janelle stared at Chuck, her eyes wide, prompting him to continue quickly. "I agree he's keeping Carm here at the park somewhere, that he hasn't left. Let's poke around, see what we can find. I'll work the village on foot. I can cover lots of ground that way. But you shouldn't be alone, especially with Rosie. Better to go out with Donald."

"What if she comes back or Miguel brings her back while we're gone?" Janelle asked.

"This won't take long. I'll keep swinging by here. We can't just sit around and do nothing, Jan. Carm deserves more than that from us."

Chuck motioned Donald over before Janelle could object

any further. He made introductions and explained, after sending Rosie to Janelle's car to fetch her cap, that Rosie's sister was still asleep in the camper. He told Donald he was staying behind to look after Carmelita and work on the transmission line report. "I'm on final for the tribe," he said. "They're making lots of noise."

"For the first time in history the Navajos are in a hurry for something?"

"Marvin Begay's the contract administrator. The elders have him on a short leash."

"And he's leaning on you to prove himself."

"More or less."

"Using others to make himself look good. Sounds like his uncle."

"I'm just doing my job."

"Aren't we all?"

"And yours, this morning, is tour guide."

Janelle scowled at Chuck as she climbed into the back seat of Donald's sedan with Rosie. With a glare of his own, Clarence joined Donald up front and they drove out of the campground. Chuck pulled his phone from his pocket. He was anxious to find out if Rachel knew the whereabouts of the woman from Albuquerque, but his phone rang before he could make the call. The incoming number, listed as an Unknown Caller, began with New Mexico's 505 area code.

"You're alone now," the caller said, a statement, not a question. The voice was unrecognizable, a synthesized computerization made possible by some sort of smartphone app.

Donald had driven away less than a minute ago. Was Miguel somehow monitoring the campsite? Or was the timing of the call just a coincidence?

"Put on your boots," the computerized voice commanded. "You're going for a hike."

"Where to?"

"Catch the shuttle to Hermit's Rest. Call when you get there."

"If you think I'll just—"

But the caller was gone.

Chuck looked around uneasily. The campground appeared as before, campers going about their business, no sign of Carmelita, no sign of the woman from Albuquerque, no sign of anything out of the ordinary.

Chuck climbed inside the camper. He rooted around among the girls' toys and clothes but came up with nothing more of interest. He slumped on the edge of the sleeping platform. Bowing to the demands of some unrecognizable voice didn't suit him. But what choice did he have?

He swiped at dust motes afloat in a shaft of sunlight angling through a slit in the canvas wall.

"Wait a minute," he said aloud.

He *did* have a choice. He could walk away. In fact, walking away was exactly what he should do.

Chuck preferred American-style boxing to any other form of fighting. Straight-ahead, take-matters-into-your-own-hands pugilism had been a mainstay of his workouts for as long as he could remember. But there was another way to fight, the Eastern method of feint and counterattack embodied in the disciplines of Judo, Tai Kwan Do, and Karate. The Asian technique of meeting an opponent's strength with weakness never had appealed to Chuck. Yet that was precisely what this situation called for, wasn't it?

He looked at his hands in the shaft of light. His knuckles were knobby and misshapen from years spent pounding the light and heavy bags at the gym. The blue veins that cobwebbed the backs of his hands had become increasingly pronounced over the years as he'd imagined himself, day after day, punching not the workout bags but the face and body of the father he'd never met.

The best way Chuck could assure Carmelita's safety, the

very best way, was to let Miguel win. Carmelita's kidnapping was about punishing Chuck for taking Miguel's place in Janelle's life. Chuck had simply to remove himself from her life, and the struggle with Miguel would be over. Janelle would be free to pay off Miguel, and Miguel would release Carmelita.

By taking himself out of the situation, by walking away, Chuck would accomplish the return of Carmelita to Janelle more quickly and safely than any other option. But if he walked away now, there would be no coming back. If he let Miguel win this first time, there would be no second, because Janelle never would take Chuck back into her life. This guy she was still getting to know who had cleared out as soon as the going got tough? Why should she?

Besides, even if Janelle did take Chuck back, Miguel would come after him again, and again and again, for as long as Chuck and Janelle remained together. If Chuck wanted a future with Janelle and the girls, he had to deal with Miguel now, or he would have to deal with him later. It was one or the other.

Chuck balled his hands into fists, thinking of how Janelle had clung to him just a few minutes ago as her tears had flowed. She was counting on him—*him*—to win Carmelita's release. He pushed himself to a standing position from his perch on the edge of the sleeping platform. It was true he was still getting to know Janelle, still coming to terms with the idea of their quick courtship and quicker marriage. But it was also true that he was deeply in love with her all the same. The last thing he could do, the very last thing, was walk away from her—and from Carmelita and Rosie.

"The deal with being a parent," a friend once told Chuck, "is that the instant your kids are born, you find out you're perfectly willing to step in front of a speeding truck if that's what it takes to keep them safe."

Chuck looked around the camper at the girls' scattered belongings. He had been their stepfather for only three weeks, but already he was fully prepared to do whatever it took to make sure Carmelita and Rosie were safe, including, in this instance, stepping in front of an oncoming truck driven by Janelle's ex.

He set about assembling his daypack, pulling together everything he might need from the storage compartments beneath the camper's bench seats as he considered what, in all likelihood, lay ahead. The computerized voice had said he was going for a hike, and Chuck had a strong suspicion where he was headed.

Twelve

11 a.m.

Chuck walked straight to the Central Village shuttle bus station, prepared to duck from sight at any glimpse of Donald's patrol car. An hour later, he stepped off the Rim Drive shuttle at Hermit's Rest into the rising heat of the nearly cloudless day, his daypack slung over his shoulder.

Rather than call Janelle before leaving camp, he'd left a note in the camper with the vague explanation that he was off doing Miguel's bidding. He'd reasoned he was protecting Janelle, and Rosie, too, by acceding to Miguel's demands on his own and not letting Janelle know where he suspected he was headed. Besides, he'd reassured himself, cell phone service below the canyon rim was extensive these days; when the time came to let her know specifically what he was up to, he would call.

With the busy midmorning hours past, the cliff top viewpoint at Hermit's Rest was nearly deserted. Only a handful of tourists braved the midday heat to snap pictures of the murky canyon depths and the North Rim off in the hazy distance. Other than Chuck, no other hikers were preparing to set off into the canyon as afternoon approached.

Chuck stood beneath the small roof that capped the end-of-the-road information kiosk, putting off the call Miguel had directed him to make when he arrived at the trailhead. A large map on the kiosk's information board showed the routes of the two primary trails, Hermit and Boucher, that descended into the canyon from the road's terminus at Hermit's Rest. He knew both trails well, having hiked them numerous times over the course of his work at the Hermit Creek latrine site two years ago.

The combined Hermit/Boucher trail plunged off the edge of the canyon for a mile and a half. Then the routes diverged.

Hermit Trail angled north and dropped deeper into the canyon, paralleling the ridgeline that separated the Hermit and Monument creek drainages. Boucher Trail, meanwhile, curved west along a broad sandstone bench to Dripping Spring and the abandoned home site of prospector Louis Boucher, the original hermit of Hermit Basin. From Louis Boucher's home site, Boucher Trail descended along the west side of Hermit Basin until it met up with Hermit Trail at Hermit Creek Backcountry Campground.

The Santa Fe Railroad had constructed Hermit Trail in 1898 as an alternative to Bright Angel Trail, a private and expensive toll route into the canyon prior to the creation of the national park in 1913. Though Hermit was the best-maintained trail in the canyon during its years of operation by the railroad, it fell into disrepair in the decades following the establishment of the national park and the subsequent opening to all comers of the more central Bright Angel Trail. Nowadays, the eight-mile stretch of Hermit Trail to Hermit Creek campground was rocky and unmaintained, providing an arduous but direct route to the string of campsites along the perennial waters of Hermit Creek deep in the inner canyon.

Louis Boucher built Boucher Trail in the early 1890s, a few years prior to the construction of Hermit Trail by the railroad. Though the route to Hermit Creek campground via Boucher Trail was several miles longer than via Hermit Trail, the meandering Boucher Trail was not nearly as steep, providing a reasonable alternative to Hermit Trail for backpackers descending to the backcountry campground, with the added benefit of water replenishment at Dripping Spring along the way.

"You're not planning to head into the canyon right now, are you?" said a stern voice at Chuck's side.

A swarthy young man in ranger garb had taken up a place next to Chuck in the shade of the information board. The man, in his early twenties, had close-set eyes, tightly coiled black hair, and thick eyebrows that almost came together above the bridge of his large nose. His uniform lacked a ranger's badge. Its absence marked him as what full-time park staffers derisively called a "student ranger," one of the recent college graduates from around the country who rotated through the park as part of the Student Conservation Association's National Park Service Academy. The young man held his arms an inch or two out from his sides to show he was ready for whatever Chuck might bring at him.

Chuck opened his mouth to reply. Then, thinking of his altercation with the guy on Maricopa Point, he went back to studying the map in front of him.

"*Sprechen sie Englisch*?" the student ranger insisted.

"*Ja*," Chuck answered.

The student ranger shifted his weight from one foot to the other. "No—go—walk—canyon—hot!" he proclaimed, louder this time, breaking off each word.

Chuck kept his eyes on the map, his mouth shut. He knew from his many ranger friends that park rangers, student and otherwise, were attracted by their nature to the orderly world of rules and regulations promised by park-service work. All of Chuck's ranger friends disliked the fact that hikers could choose for themselves when to set off into and out of the canyon. Indeed, Grand Canyon rangers regularly argued in favor of a ban on midday hiking in the canyon during summer months, though the ban never had been imposed.

"Look at it this way," Chuck said each time the subject came up. "People stupid enough to hike in the canyon in hundred-degree heat get what they deserve."

"Except we're the ones who have to save their sorry asses," came the response. "People call up, say they're a little overheated, and would we please send a rescue chopper for them? Oh, and by the way, they've got dinner reservations at El Tovar, so could we get a move on?"

"But you charge them for it," Chuck would rejoin. "It's called job security."

At Chuck's side, the student ranger sounded off again, this time nearly yelling in his ear, "You—understand? No—canyon—now!"

Chuck tensed. Rather than whirl and lay into the young man, he rolled his shoulders and rocked back on his heels. "Got it, thanks," he said. He walked away before the student ranger could say anything more.

Chuck grunted to himself as he headed down the rocky trail away from the information board. The young man was right. Chuck should not be setting off into the canyon this time of day in the middle of the summer. The temperature was easily in the nineties at the canyon rim. That meant inner-canyon temps were well over a hundred, dangerously hot, and it wasn't even noon yet.

When he was out of the student ranger's earshot, Chuck ducked into a patch of broken shade beneath a trailside piñon and punched the return call button on his phone.

"You're there?" came the same disembodied computer voice as before.

"I'm on the phone with you, aren't I?"

"Start down into the canyon on Hermit/Boucher." The person at the other end of the line pronounced the French surname of the old hermit correctly, *boo-shay*. "Call again from each trail junction."

"Should I call from Waldron junction or the Hermit/Boucher split?"

Little-traveled Waldron Trail descended from farther west along the canyon rim to meet up with the combined Hermit/Boucher trail just above where the two trails diverged. The trail junctions were less than a quarter mile apart.

"Don't be smart," came the quick reply, followed by the rustling of a map. Chuck awarded himself a point.

"Hermit/Boucher," the computerized voice said.

"I don't know how long my phone battery will last."

"Our conversations will be short. Long as you don't call anyone else, you shouldn't have a problem. And one more thing: there's nothing to be gained by lying about your location. We'll be tracking you."

Chuck looked out from beneath the tree. A handful of tourists stood at the overlook railing. A few more made their way to and from the bathroom. A half dozen or so, finished sightseeing, sat on the sheltered benches at the edge of the shuttle bus turnaround waiting for the next bus back to the village. No one appeared the least bit suspicious.

"Anything else?" Chuck asked.

"Enjoy your hike."

The line went dead.

Chuck put away his phone and stepped back into the sunlight. The student ranger glowered at him from the information board, his arms crossed. Chuck gave him an informal salute and headed down the trail.

The heat set to work on him within minutes. The pocket of air trapped between his scalp and baseball cap grew oven-hot beneath the blazing sun. Sweat barely gathered on his brow before it evaporated, leaving a grainy film of salt on his skin. Before pulling on his hiking socks and boots in the camper, Chuck had slathered the soles of his feet with petroleum jelly—the lubrication would keep his soles from blistering and peeling off in the intense heat. The jelly turned to squishy liquid as he walked. He sloshed down the trail, his boots twin buckets of hot grease, the air around him thick with the oily smell of an auto repair shop.

He sipped a mouthful of water every few minutes from a

tube leading to a three-liter bladder stowed in his pack. Already, time was working against him. No matter how much he drank, he could not maintain his body's minimum level of hydration in the extreme heat of the inner canyon.

Though crowded with day-hikers and backpackers at the beginning and end of each day, the trail was deserted now, the silence broken only by the accusatory *rach-chat-chat-chat* of cicadas buzzing from trailside tree branches. A steady breeze, hellishly hot, blew upward from the superheated depths of the canyon, scorching Chuck's lungs.

He considered explaining to the computerized voice the insanity of venturing into the canyon in the middle of a day as hot as this, but he knew any request to wait until evening to make the descent would be summarily rejected. He'd known what he was in for when he'd loaded up at camp. In addition to the three-liter bladder he was steadily draining, another was stowed in the bottom of his daypack. The question was whether the combined gallon and a half of water was enough to get him to Hermit Creek, where he could cool off, drink his fill, and replenish the two bladders.

But he wasn't headed to Hermit Creek, and he knew it.

In all the time Chuck had spent at the Grand Canyon, he'd never hiked the inner canyon in the middle of a hot summer day. He had, however, floated a raft down the Colorado River through the canyon during a searing July a decade ago. The torturous heat would have been incapacitating had it not been for the cold water beneath his raft. The river ran a refrigerator-like fifty degrees after it was freed from the base of seven-hundred-foot-tall Glen Canyon Dam upstream. The river water through the canyon was so cold, in fact, that an additional hazard to canyon backpackers, along with heatstroke and cliff fall, was death by drowning. Upon reaching the bottom of the canyon, unsuspecting hikers regularly took what they believed would be refreshing dips in the river, only to be shocked by the frigid water and swept to their deaths—though for Chuck, hiking nearly a vertical mile above the river, such a fate was the stuff only of dreams.

He rounded the last of the trail's initial switchbacks off the canyon rim and came to a quarter-mile section of trail known as the Chalk Stairs, a series of steps chipped more than a century ago by the Santa Fe Railroad's trail-building crew into a half-mile-wide slab of sloping limestone along the route previously laid out by Louis Boucher. At the time of their construction, the steps provided a secure means of descent for mule-borne tourists down the pitched slab of white rock to the broad, flat bench of tan Coconino sandstone beyond. But a hundred years of erosion had worn away the steps, resulting in a sloped ditch filled with marble-sized pebbles that made for treacherous footing.

The sun's rays reflected off the expanse of limestone, bumping up the temperature a few degrees. Chuck's body temperature rose along with the air temperature as he edged his way down the hazardous section of trail. He doffed his cap and wiped the long sleeve of his hiking shirt across his broiling brow. If Miguel were trying to kill him, this descent might well do it.

Waves of heat rose from the surface of the limestone and bounced off the legs of his lightweight hiking pants. His sunscreen-coated face and hands, the only portions of his skin exposed to the sun, were puffy and stiff.

At last, he left the expanse of sloping limestone and followed the trail, now smooth and flat, across the top of the Coconino sandstone layer, past the Waldron Trail junction, toward the place where, a few hundred feet ahead, the leading edge of the Coconino layer fell away into the canyon. There, the Hermit/Boucher trails divided. Boucher Trail headed west along the top of the sandstone layer while Hermit Trail angled north, dropping through a rare break in the Coconino and into the inner canyon.

Low yucca, a few prickly pear cacti, and a smattering of chest-high creosote bushes sprouted amid scattered rocks. Otherwise, the area around the trail junction was a desolate Mars-scape of scattered boulders and shimmering sand.

Chuck hit redial on his phone as he approached the trail split. One ring. Two. Finally, the computerized voice: "We've got you at Hermit/Boucher."

"How's Carmelita?"

"She'll be fine—as long as you keep moving."

Before Chuck could respond, the muffled report of a gun blast sounded directly behind him.

Thirteen

Noon

Chuck dropped his phone and dove for cover behind the nearest creosote bush. He knelt, trembling, behind the scant protection of the bush's spindly branches. He swung around, quickly ascertaining that the closest real cover was several hundred yards away, where a small stand of piñons clung to a north-facing slope below the canyon rim.

Nothing moved in the direction of the piñons—but the sound of the gunshot had been far closer than the stand of trees. He drew a stream of air past his dry tongue, fighting for control. He held his position, unmoving, his knees hot in the burning sand.

No follow-up shot came. No sign of an assailant. In fact, as with Chuck's own predicament, there was nowhere in the immediate vicinity for an assailant to hide.

Chuck mentally replayed the sound of the shot. It had come from behind him and, though explosively loud, had seemed somehow stifled.

He sat back on his haunches and slapped a hand to his forehead, unzipped his daypack, and looked inside. Sure enough, slimy white goo was sprayed across the interior—melted yogurt expelled in the explosion of a previously unopened bag of yogurt-covered pretzels he'd brought from camp. The steadily rising heat had built the pressure inside the vacuum-sealed bag until, like stepping on a balloon, the bag had exploded with the concussive force of a gunshot, spraying melted yogurt and bits of pulverized pretzel throughout the pack's interior, and sending Chuck scrambling for cover.

He climbed wearily to his feet. The heat was playing games with his head. How long until it affected his physical abilities as well?

He zipped his pack closed and retrieved his phone. "Still there?" he asked.

"Continue down the trail," came the computerized voice. "Hermit, not Boucher. Call when you reach the ridgeline."

"I know where you're sending me."

"Of course you do." The caller hung up.

Chuck shoved the phone back in his pocket. Miguel was proving himself every bit as smart as Janelle and Clarence claimed him to be. Somehow, the girls' father knew the canyon trail system and the correct pronunciation of Boucher. And he knew where to send Chuck, and why.

Chuck had told a number of people about his discovery over the course of his career. A dozen, maybe more, almost all of them early on. He'd been young and full of himself when he'd first dropped hints to others about his find. The Southwest archaeological community had been different back then, freer, more open. Chuck and his peers had shared secrets with one another they never would today, not after what had transpired in the years since.

First, the cannibalism dispute. When human coprolite—fossilized feces—containing human DNA was found at two Anasazi sites on the far northeast edge of the Colorado Plateau, many experts took the findings as proof the Anasazi had practiced widespread cannibalism during the closing decades of their collapsing society. Others rejected that conclusion as demeaning and overly simplistic. Little more than two hundred years ago, they pointed out, Massachusetts whalers lost at sea in lifeboats had drawn lots to determine who among them would be killed and eaten so the rest could survive long enough to reach land. As far as those experts were concerned, such heartrending decisions didn't make cannibals out of eighteenth-century Anglo-Americans any more than the recent coprolite findings made cannibals of the Anasazi.

Close on the heels of the cannibalism debate was the bust by federal agents after a three-year sting operation of the so-called Bland of Brothers, a group of grave robbers from the small town of Blanding in southeast Utah who pillaged Anasazi burial sites and sold their takings on the black market. The purported leader of the Bland of Brothers turned out to be none other than Blanding's town doctor, a revered family practitioner who lived in a sprawling house on a ridge overlooking town.

The physician was said to have led the grave robbers, not for the money he made from the backcountry digs, but for the thrill of the find. It was said he also robbed Anasazi graves to demonstrate his contempt, shared by many in southeast Utah and across the Colorado Plateau, for the government officials charged with overseeing the federal lands that comprised almost ninety percent of the massive desert uplift. When the feds swooped in on the members of the Bland of Brothers with search warrants in hand, the plunder discovered in the doctor's basement alone—baskets, jewelry, sandals, pots, burial shrouds, even skeletal remains—was valued at well over a million dollars on the black market. The physician and a second member of the group committed suicide in the months leading up to their trial, while several other group members were sentenced to lengthy prison terms.

The cannibalism controversy and Bland of Brothers bust focused unaccustomed attention on the Southwest archaeological community. True to the introverted nature of many archaeologists, those working across the Colorado Plateau provided few quotes to media types sniffing around after the two stories, and clammed up among one another as well. In the wake of the dual controversies, Chuck stopped boasting of his Grand Canyon discovery to his fellow Southwest archaeologists. These days he did the work each contract required of him, submitted his report, took a few weeks off if his schedule allowed, and got going on his next contract. What happened to his reports and the artifacts that came with them was no longer his concern.

Along with dropping hints about his discovery to fellow archaeologists, Chuck wrote a number of research papers early in his career based on discoveries he made while working various contracts. One, published in the *Journal of the Archaeological Southwest*, detailed his discovery of several black-slipped Mesa Verde pots near the Navajo town of Chinle in east-central Arizona. Chuck pointed to the large size of the pots, found far south of the Anasazi population center of Mesa Verde, as indication the Anasazi had traded heavy goods over greater distances than his fellow Southwest archaeologists previously believed.

Another of his papers, accepted after extensive review and published in the prestigious *Journal of the Americas*, covered his discovery of bits of vibrant, blue-green Yucatan turquoise at several dispersed sites across the Colorado Plateau. Chuck proposed in the paper that his findings indicated the Anasazi Indians and the Indians of the sophisticated Mayan culture on the Yucatan Peninsula far to the south had interacted on regular occasions as trade partners despite the thousands of miles separating their societies. He'd even gone so far as to posit that future researchers might one day discover DNA evidence of Anasazi/Mayan commingling.

Chuck's scholarly work leaned unabashedly toward supposition, offering the sort of conjecture considered unacceptable in today's Southwest archaeological world. Current articles in Southwest archaeological journals were expected to include extensively detailed data sets and numerous corroborating findings. Today's research papers on the Anasazi were aimed at closure, at proving obscure findings beyond doubt—that most Anasazi flint-knappers were right handed, or all Anasazi sandals were fixed at the sole with a particular type of slipknot. The result was an overall decline in broad archaeological inquiry that, as far as Chuck was concerned, drained much of the fun out of the field.

It was as if all big-picture thinking related to the Anasazi was forbidden, prompting Chuck to wonder how long he could keep doing what he was doing if the only reason he did it was for a paycheck. He'd considered more than once in the last few weeks, in fact, whether his growing career disillusionment might have played a role in how speedily he'd committed himself to Janelle and the girls.

Janelle.

He looked out across the canyon. It was well past noon. The tour with Donald would be over by now. She and Clarence, along with Rosie, would be back in camp and beside themselves with worry. Or maybe they had good news to report. Maybe they'd tracked down Carmelita somehow, meaning Chuck could turn around and head back up to the canyon rim. Either way, it was long past time for him to check in.

Janelle answered his call on the first ring. "Where are you?" she asked breathlessly. "Your note said not to call, but—"

"I'm doing what he wants," Chuck said.

"And leaving us in the dark."

"I know what he's after. I'll give it to him, he'll give us Carm, and we can all go home. This'll all be over in few hours. You just have to sit tight."

"Sit tight?" she asked. Her voice squeaked.

"What'd you do, Jan?"

"I . . ."

"Talk to me, Jan."

"He said 'no cops.'"

"*Janelle.*"

She spoke in a rush. "I posted it on my Facebook page."

"You did *what*?"

"She's my little girl, Chuck. Last thing I'm going to do is sit around and do nothing."

"But *online*? What were you *thinking*?"

"He said no police. Fine. But he didn't say anything about anybody else. It was your idea—you said we should be doing something for Carm, and that we should keep our eyes peeled. There's zillions of people here, they've all got their computers and their smartphones, and they're all online, like, all the time."

"You updated your Facebook page to say, 'Oh, guess what, LOL, my daughter's been kidnapped at the South Rim of the Grand Canyon'? You know what you've done, don't you? You've sent out an amateur Amber Alert. How long do you think it's going to be before the police find out?"

"I don't care if they find out. Don't you see? He said 'no cops,' in that *we* weren't to go to the police. But if it reaches them indirectly, well, okay, fine. Besides, I didn't say 'kidnapped.' I just put up a picture of her and said we think she's wandering around the village somewhere, and if anybody spots her, would they please post back." She paused. "It might force his hand, you know."

Chuck bit his lower lip. Maybe she was on to something. "It might help," he admitted grudgingly. "Show him you mean business."

"He'll be checking my page. I know he will."

Chuck's phone beeped, signaling its reduction in battery strength from full to half power. "I gotta go. You hear anything, call me. I'll do the same. A few hours, I'll be back, and we'll get this over with."

"Promise?" The ache in Janelle's voice went straight to his heart.

"Promise."

Two miles farther down Hermit Trail and another thousand vertical feet deeper in the canyon, Chuck wondered whether he'd be able to keep his promise. The air temperature was over 110 now. The ground temperature, far higher, broiled his lubricated feet. Though he was drinking water as sparingly as possible, he'd already depleted his first three-liter bladder and started in on his second.

He followed the deserted trail as it angled across the face of the ridge separating Hermit and Montezuma basins. The trail topped out on the ridgeline between the two drainages at a commanding viewpoint, then cut back across the west face of the ridge, continuing its plunge into Hermit Basin and on to the backpacker campground at the creek.

An unrelenting wind blasted Chuck as he reached the ridge-top viewpoint. Particles of dust rode the harsh breeze, carrying the gritty feel of absolute desiccation. He looked longingly down and to his left at the green slash of vegetation marking the course of Hermit Creek's perennial waters. There would be no wind where the deep, side-canyon walls protected the creek. His nostrils filled with the imagined odors he knew awaited him there—the tangy scent of wild mint, the syrupy-sweet smell of tamarisk, the mineral aroma of wet sand. Openings in the brush along the creek were campsites for backpackers. The new latrine sat well away from the waters of the creek in the center of the open plot he'd assessed and dug.

Chuck turned away from the alluring greenery below. He pulled his phone from his pocket and punched in his call.

"We've got you at the ridge," the disembodied voice said without preamble. "You're close now, aren't you?"

"Yes."

Here at the open viewpoint, the connection was clear and static-free.

"You know what you're to get."

"I don't have enough water. I'll never make it back out of the canyon."

"Sure you will. Besides, you don't have any choice. Carmelita's counting on you." The line went dead.

Chuck cursed. The odds that he could make it back up to the

canyon rim without replenishing his water supply at the creek grew longer with each parched gust of wind. He was nauseous and lightheaded. Of all the canyon's killers, heatstroke topped the list, and he was well on his way to reinforcing that statistic.

Hermit Creek was four trail miles deeper in the canyon. With a delay of less than five hours, he could descend to the creek, refill his water bags, and return safely to the ridge after the heat of the day passed.

Or he could do as the caller directed.

His destination lay only a few hundred yards away. And in truth, the delay caused by dropping down to Hermit Creek would be much greater than five hours. The final shuttle of the day from the end of Rim Drive back to Grand Canyon Village departed at 8:30 in the evening. If he visited the creek, he would miss the last shuttle and be forced to walk the eight miles back to camp along the closed road late into the night.

He pictured Carmelita looking to him for reassurance before setting off through the dark to the Mather Campground bathroom. He couldn't leave her to face the coming night alone.

He would not descend to Hermit Creek. He would complete the retrieval here and now, and he would make it back out of the canyon this afternoon. As the caller said, he had no other choice.

Fourteen

2 p.m.

Chuck allowed himself one last yearning look at the greenery along Hermit Creek before turning to face the rugged ridge in front of him. The steep, cactus-studded east side of the ridge was a case study on the near impossibility of off-trail passage in the inner canyon, where every step had to be carefully considered lest an ankle be turned or a leg ripped open by a jagged rock or the hooked thorn of a barrel cactus. Rattlesnake bite was a constant off-trail concern as well, while slips and falls away from the canyon's maintained trails could be instantly or, in the absence of help, gradually fatal.

The off-trail route across the face of the ridge was one he'd traveled a number of times, though he'd made the traverse only when mentally sharp in the coolness of spring or fall, not as he was now—sluggish and unsteady in the middle of a brutally hot summer day. He adjusted his pack, wavering in the heat.

How had the kidnapper known where he was? "*We've got you at the ridge*," the computerized voice had said. And who was the "we" the voice had referred to?

Chuck faced due north. At his back, the ridgeline separating Hermit and Monument basins descended precipitously from the South Rim. Ahead, the ridge climbed upward in a series of encircling cliff bands to form a flat-topped knuckle of rock and desert scrub known as Cope Butte. The ridgeline fell away again, on the far side of the butte, the final two thousand vertical feet to the Colorado River at the bottom of the canyon.

Twenty years ago, as a solo backpacker taking advantage of a long fall weekend off from his studies at Fort Lewis College, Chuck had stopped to rest and take in the view from this very spot. The trail had been crowded with other backpackers that day. Chuck visited with several of them until the call of nature sent him scrambling away from the viewpoint and down into the Monument Creek drainage in search of a place out of sight of the trail.

His search proved unexpectedly difficult. It took two hundred yards of arduous scrambling along the face of Cope Butte to reach a spot far enough around the east side of the butte to be screened from the trail. It was from his precarious perch there that he spotted a depression in the center of the topmost cliff band encircling the butte's summit massif. The small, cave-like opening was tucked into a south-facing fold in the cliff, 150 feet above where he stood and another three hundred yards around the east side of the butte.

Chuck was adept at recognizing likely locations of abandoned Anasazi ruins based on criteria presented by his Fort Lewis professors: south-facing to catch the winter sun, built into or at the foot of cliff walls to avoid storms and provide good defensive positioning to fend off invaders, and close to perennial water sources. The cavity high on Cope Butte met the first two of those three criteria, but it was far from both the perennial waters of Hermit Creek to the west and the intermittent waters of Monument Creek to the east. Furthermore, its location halfway up the vertical cliff band meant reaching the alcove would have been difficult for the Anasazi, though a ladder of tree limbs and yucca-cord lashings could have overcome that problem.

Chuck had just read *The Man Who Walked Through Time* on the recommendation of one of his professors. The book was an autobiographical account by famed distance hiker Colin Fletcher of Fletcher's 1962 journey along the 150-mile length of the inner Grand Canyon on foot and largely off-trail. In it, Fletcher described coming across numerous small Anasazi structures built into the cliff walls of the inner canyon, many far from water sources. The structures Fletcher discovered were uniformly a few feet high by a few feet wide and constructed of tightly stacked rock mortared into place. Each featured a single opening that could be sealed shut with a thin slab of sandstone.

Similar ruins, found by the hundreds across the Colorado Plateau, were assumed by Arturo Dinaveri and other early Southwest archaeologists to be granaries used for the storage of maize. But Fletcher disagreed after he climbed inside the first of those he found. Upon lying down inside the structure, he discovered its interior dimensions were a good fit for his reclining frame, while the opening in the structure aligned with his line of sight, giving him an expansive view of the inner canyon from where he lay inside, protected from inclement weather.

After Fletcher overnighted in that first ruin, he found and examined others in the canyon. All, like the first, provided a perfect fit for his body, and all their openings were positioned to offer sweeping views to someone reclining inside. Fletcher grew convinced that the small stone structures, when not filled with corn, had served as one-man bivouac sites for Anasazi scouts on the lookout for nomadic invaders.

Chuck had wondered if the alcove high above him on Cope Butte might harbor just such a ruin. While the depression itself was well hidden, certainly the view from the mouth of the cavity would be as expansive as any in the canyon. He was captivated by the remoteness of the alcove as well. Its location halfway up the cliff band virtually assured it had never been visited in modern times, if ever.

Armed with little more than the recklessness of youth, Chuck had set out to see if he could reach the depression. Two and a half bands of cliff ranging in height from forty to sixty feet separated him from it. He inched his way up a cleft in the first cliff band to reach its top, then worked his way around to the butte's north side. There, he came upon a tight, three-walled chimney that cut into the second cliff band from bottom to top. After wrapping a length of rope around his waist to use in descending from the cavity, provided he managed to reach it, he left his backpack at the base of the second cliff, wedged himself into the chimney, and climbed upward. From the top of the chimney, he scrambled back around the summit massif to a point directly below the alcove.

The cavity was nearly within reach above him. However, thirty feet of cliff wall separated him from the floor of the alcove, and on first glance, the cliff appeared impossible to scale without the aid of climbing devices. When Chuck searched the wall, looking for linked breaks in the face of the rock, he spotted a series of cracks, ledges, and handholds that just might provide a route to the depression.

A hand jam into a fist-wide crack got Chuck five feet off the slope, which angled steeply downward away from the base of the cliff. A series of quick, hand-over-hand moves enabled him to grasp a small ledge a few feet higher. He mantled himself upward, achieving a precarious standing position on the narrow ledge while maintaining his balance by clinging to protrusions above it.

He was nearly two-thirds of the way there. Above, a few small outcrops provided the only holds between him and the bottom lip of the cavity. Once he left the relative security of the ledge, he would have no choice but to keep moving until he reached the floor of the depression. If he slipped or ran out of arm strength before he reached the alcove . . . well, the mystery of the alcove overrode those concerns.

He took hold of a pair of small outcrops above his head and hauled himself off the ledge. Quickly, he brought his feet even with his waist, pressed his toes to the rock face, and lunged upward. He grasped a small protrusion three feet higher with his left hand, only to find that the top of the outcrop sloped away from the face of the cliff. Even as he grasped it, nearing the extent of his strength, his fingertips began to peel from the hold.

He was more than twenty-five feet up the cliff face, a few feet below the floor of the cavity. If he lost his purchase, he would plummet to the slope at the bottom of the cliff and tumble to his death at the boulder-strewn base of the butte. Yet retreat was not an option; the holds below him were too tenuous to enable him to descend unroped to the narrow ledge.

Terrified, he redoubled his slippery hold on the outcrop and pulled himself higher in an all-or-nothing play for the lip of the alcove. His boots maintained their place on the face of the cliff and he clung to the protrusion just long enough to extend his right hand to the floor of the cavity. He exhaled with relief as his fingers closed over the lip of the depression. He hauled himself up and over the lip and into the alcove and collapsed in the shaded mouth of the depression, his eyes closed and his cheek pressed to the alcove's flat sandstone floor. Gradually his breathing slowed, and he raised his head and looked around.

Tucked at the back of what proved to be a low-roofed cavern extending fifteen feet into the face of the cliff was a granary-like structure unlike any Chuck had seen. The rock structure, five feet high from floor to ceiling and spanning the entire eight-foot width of the rear of the cavern, presented workmanship of unbelievable quality. The structure's mortarless front wall, constructed of chunks of rock chiseled to fit so closely together a gnat couldn't squeeze between them, was an exquisite length of jigsaw puzzle in the medium of stone.

Chuck's boots kicked up small clouds of dust as he duck-walked to the sandstone wall. The wall appeared even finer upon close inspection than it had from the lip of the cavern. He touched the chiseled chunks of fitted sandstone with trembling fingertips, then turned his attention to the structure's entrance, a sandstone-slab door featuring a knob, something he'd never known the Anasazi to have used in any other instance.

The doorknob was made of a leather strap wrapped around and around itself to form a ball. The two ends of the strap disappeared through a hole chiseled in the oval door. Chuck pulled gently on the knob. The strap crackled but did not break. The door, two feet high and a foot and a half wide, slid easily from its slot. A lip lining the inside of the doorframe fit the single-piece door precisely. The ends of the leather strap that formed the knob were tied around a stick snugged against the door's back.

Chuck set the sandstone-slab door aside and crouched in front of the opening. The interior of the walled-off space at the back of the cavity, roughly six feet deep, was dim and shadowy. No light shone through chinks in the wall; the structure was as tight as when it first had been constructed. He inhaled through his nose, sampling the air inside and finding it musty and free of moisture. Whatever lay within was still dry, not ravaged by mildew and rot over the course of all these years.

He leaned into the small room at the rear of the alcove. When his eyes adjusted to the semi-darkness, he nearly fell to his knees before the astonishing pair of objects sitting in front of him on two carefully arranged stacks of round river rocks.

Fifteen

2 p.m.

Two decades after first reaching the alcove, standing on the ridge with Cope Butte rising ahead of him, Chuck fought the growing fogginess in his brain. How did Carmelita's kidnapper know his exact location? He ran a mental inventory of the contents of his pockets and pack. The only technological device he had with him was his cell phone.

That had to be it.

Miguel knew how to disguise his voice using some sort of high-tech computer application—the same technological know-how enabled him to track the location of Chuck's phone.

Every time Chuck had boasted about his Grand Canyon find over the years, he'd been careful to describe its location in vague terms, saying only that it was somewhere below Hermit's Rest between Hermit and Monument basins. There was no reason to alert Miguel to the alcove's exact location now, he decided. After peering up and down the empty trail, he tucked his phone out of sight beneath a waist-high boulder near the viewpoint. He left the trail and made his way across the rugged east face of the ridge.

He worked his way to the top of the cleft in the first cliff band. From there, he continued around the steep slope to the chimney that led to the top of the second cliff band on the north side of Cope Butte. As he had the first time and each visit since, he wedged himself into the three-sided break in the forty-foot cliff and climbed upward. Though the three tight walls were shaded, they were hot to the touch. Moving fast, he reached the top of the chimney in little more than a minute. He paused to shake the burning pain from his hands before traversing back around the slope to the east side of the butte's summit massif.

A length of mottled-brown climbing rope, invisible from more than a few feet away, dangled from the mouth of the cavity to the base of the cliff. The desert-camouflaged rope held when he gave it a yank and leaned away from the cliff, putting his full weight on it.

Chuck left his original length of rope after his first descent from the alcove twenty years ago. He'd left a new rope in place of the preceding one each visit since. The last time he'd visited the cavern had been while working the latrine site at Hermit Creek more than two years ago—two-plus years of sun, wind, and rain having their way with the exposed length of rope now hanging before him. Of the three elements, sunshine was the most damaging. Day in and day out for the last two years, the sun's ultraviolet rays had struck the rope's nylon fibers, rendering them increasingly brittle and prone to breakage.

Chuck leaned back to study the route to the depression thirty feet above him. He'd barely managed his only unaided climb to the alcove as a wiry college kid twenty years ago, and he did not have the specialized climbing gear necessary for a protected solo climb to the cavity. His only option was to trust the rope. He gave it one more tug, took hold of it with both hands, and started climbing.

The bare rock wall, exposed to the sun, was blistering to the touch. He clasped the rope to his chest and used his feet to bear as much of his weight as possible, taking hold of outcrops only when necessary. While clinging to the rope and taking a short break halfway up the face, he heard the telltale *pop-pop-pop* of individual fibers giving way where the rope turned ninety degrees downward at the lip of the alcove.

Spurred upward by the sound of the failing rope, he reached the cavern seconds later and knelt on its floor, catching his breath and rubbing his singed fingertips together. He was dizzy and disconcerted in the stifling heat, but he was sweating heavily, which meant he wasn't fully dehydrated.

The stone structure at the rear of the cavity appeared as it had when he'd first seen it, the intricate front wall, the sandstone-slab door with its leather knob. And there, still in place where he'd tucked it at the side of the closed door, was the dried grass stem that would have fallen to the floor of the alcove unnoticed had anyone opened the door since his last visit.

Chuck made his way to the rear of the cavern. Carmelita's kidnapping notwithstanding, he was eager, after all these years, to lay hands on his discovery.

Though he'd always known he would disclose his find to the world someday, he'd put off doing so year after year, enjoying the secret, and recognizing that the news would change his life forever—akin, certainly, to the way the life of Waldo Wilcox, an elderly Utah rancher, had been disrupted after the rancher had disclosed the existence of extensive ruins left by Fremont Indians, contemporaries of the Anasazi, along Range Creek in south-central Utah.

Range Creek Canyon, encompassed within the boundaries of the rancher's large private holdings, contained dozens of undisturbed Fremont ruins, a fact the rancher kept secret for more than half a century. Only with mortality staring him in the face did he tell officials of the artifact-filled canyon's existence, after which he sold his ranch to the government, fearing the destruction he expected would come to the canyon if he left it to others to stumble upon after his death.

The sale of the ranch with its heretofore unknown trove of artifacts made national headlines. Within months, archaeologists and treasure hunters overran the formerly secret canyon, leading the rancher to voice his regret at ever having told anyone about it.

Chuck had no specific need to publicly unveil the existence of his discovery for its protection. Its remote location in a national park guaranteed it never would stand in the way of development. Nor was anyone else likely to follow Chuck's arduous route up the face of the remote butte just to peek inside the cavity. But Chuck knew his find would prove so transformative to current Anasazi scholarship that it demanded revelation. It was that knowledge as much as anything else, he suspected, that had led him to drop hints about his discovery at the start of his career, as if he knew, on some subconscious level, that if he bragged about the wondrousness of his find enough times to enough people, he'd eventually be required to tell the world of its existence by a gathering of forces beyond his control. Now, twenty years later, those forces had gathered.

Chuck slid the stone door from its slot and set it aside. He slipped on his headlamp, leaned inside the small room at the rear of the cavern—and there they were: two massive Anasazi pots resting, altar-like, above the dusty floor on matching stacks of river rocks.

Other Anasazi vessels, similar in size to the black-slipped Mesa Verde pots Chuck had unearthed near Chinle, were no more than two feet high by a foot across. Anything larger, when filled with grain or water, would have been impossible for even the strongest Anasazi to transport. Yet the twin clay storage jars in the granary were nearly double that size. Each was almost three feet high, at least a foot and a half across at its widest point, and a good fourteen inches across at its base. The pots were urn-shaped, with openings at their tops of perhaps twelve inches capped by slabs of fired clay formed into perfect circles.

Though the immensity of the pots was unheard of, it was their exterior decoration that made them truly incredible. Intricate paintings and carvings, none more than a quarter-inch high, covered every square inch of the vessels. The paintings were black, while the carvings showed up as the dark gray interior of the pots against their white-slipped exterior.

Like traditional Anasazi urns with their repeated geometric designs generally an inch or two high, the two vessels in the granary featured horizontal rows of geometric designs and artistic renderings. But each row of artwork on these vessels was only a fraction of an inch high, first a row of painting, then a row of carving, then another row of painting. Though only a few millimeters tall, the designs and pictures on the pots were startlingly detailed, and no two were repeated. Tiny squares, circles, ovals, trapezoids, and lines interwoven like rope. Miniature paintings of deer, cougars, snakes, frogs, birds, and desert rams, of bows and arrows, spears, and human stick figures, of Kokopelli, the flute-playing jester of Anasazi lore, playing his instrument while standing upright, leaning far forward, leaning back, seated, and lying down. Depictions of cliffs, mountains, canyons, trees, cacti, and streams, countless representations of the sun and moon, and tiny pinpricks of stars.

As he did each time he laid eyes on the pots, Chuck wondered how many hundreds or thousands of hours must have gone into their creation. How could the potter's imagination have been so fertile as to cover the two urns with literally thousands of pictures and geometric designs without a single repetition?

Handprints and fingerprints on preserved pots indicated most Anasazi potters, like most modern Native American potters, were women. But everything Chuck's fellow Southwest archaeologists suspected of Anasazi women—that they were task-oriented, primarily concerned with completing the job at hand—didn't fit with the pots here in the small room at the back of the cavern. The beautifully decorated vessels in the alcove notwithstanding, everything the archaeological world knew about the Anasazi indicated that life for the ancient Indians of the Colorado Plateau had been short and brutish. The prevalence of child graves at Anasazi burial sites indicated a high infant mortality rate. For those who reached adulthood, the average Anasazi lifespan was less than thirty-five years. The unending hard work required to survive resulted in bent and twisted spinal columns for most adults, whose teeth were worn down to shapeless stumps by the time they reached their mid-twenties as a result of their grit-laden diet based on sandstone-ground maize flour.

Many archaeologists believed the Anasazi had spent their entire lives working every day, dawn to dusk, before collapsing in exhausted heaps at night. The spiritual rooms known as kivas found in most Anasazi villages and the fine craftsmanship of items such as the burial shroud Chuck had found in the mining debris pile on the South Rim belied that assertion somewhat, while the amazing pots sitting before him blew that idea away entirely. The huge, painstakingly painted and carved urns would provide Marvin Begay and his fellow young Navajo believers with what they sought—incontrovertible proof of the Anasazi people's heretofore unacknowledged cultural progression.

The question still remained, however: as fine as the two pots were, why had an ancient potter or group of potters spent so much time crafting them? The answer, without doubt, was that the urns contained objects even more fantastic than the vessels themselves.

Sixteen

3 p.m.

Chuck lifted the lid from the nearest pot and set it aside. Kneeling, his head against the room's low roof, he aimed the beam of his headlamp into the pot and, as always, gasped. Dozens upon dozens of turquoise necklaces lay curled one against another like nested snakes, and the artistry of the necklaces captured in the beam of his light was, like the decoration on the pot that contained them, orders of magnitude beyond that of any other Anasazi finery ever discovered.

At least twenty of the necklaces, nestled against one another at the top of the pot, were visible in the light of Chuck's headlamp. Assuming the urn was filled with necklaces, the vessel contained perhaps two hundred in all. Every necklace Chuck could see in the light of his headlamp was meticulously crafted. They shone with every shade of turquoise imaginable, from the translucent ocean-blue of Sonoran Desert turquoise to the tortoise green of Mojave Desert turquoise and every shade between. Like the designs on the pots, each necklace was unique, differing in size and style from its neighbors. In essence, every necklace in the pot was an A. Dinaveri, in and of itself.

For the first time in all his visits to the alcove, Chuck caressed the topmost necklace with his fingertips. Barely daring to breathe, he slipped his fingers beneath the necklace, lifted it from the urn, and admired it hanging from his fingers in the light of his headlamp.

The necklace was comprised of well over a hundred individually carved turquoise beads strung on an eighteen-inch loop of tightly woven yucca cord. Each bead fit snugly against its neighbor. The beads were small at the top of the necklace and grew successively larger until the two sides of the loop reached the necklace's most amazing feature, a pendant fashioned from a single, enormous piece of turquoise.

The pendant, the size of Chuck's palm and shaped like an oversized teardrop, was chiseled and polished to a smooth sheen that glittered in the light of Chuck's lamp. The face of the pendant was inscribed with tiny depictions of the sort that adorned the exteriors of the pots, more than a hundred minuscule inscriptions in all, none of them repeated. Every necklace in the pot featured a similar large pendant fashioned from a single chunk of turquoise, and every pendant, unique in shape and form, was as meticulously inscribed as the one dangling from the necklace Chuck held.

Together, the vessel and its contents displayed artistic sophistication light years beyond any Anasazi craftsmanship discovered to date—and that wasn't even taking the second vessel's contents into account. The second urn contained no jewelry, nor was it filled to the top. Rather, the pot was half-filled with saucer-shaped stone disks about two inches across, their faces inscribed with repeated geometric patterns of triangles, crosshatches, rectangles, and squares.

Had Arturo Dinaveri been its discoverer, the Italian archaeologist surely would have declared that the alcove, with its necklace- and disk-filled urns, was the hidden shrine constructed by the Anasazi at the Grand Canyon in honor of Chirsáuha, the Anasazi god of fertility. Chuck, however, was convinced he'd discovered not an Anasazi shrine but an ancient Anasazi bank. Following years of internal debate, he'd settled on the belief that the necklace-filled pot was an Anasazi version of Fort Knox, with the necklaces serving as a sort of gold standard for the disks in the second pot. The disks, he'd concluded, were a form of currency, though because disks like those in the second vessel had never been discovered elsewhere on the Colorado Plateau, he speculated that the collapse of Anasazi society had occurred before the banking system had been initiated.

Whatever their true purpose, the urns and their contents would trigger decades of impassioned debate in the Southwest archaeological community, and they would provide welcome evidence of advanced Anasazi culture for Marvin Begay and his fellow young Navajo believers. Chuck would unleash all of that as soon as he unveiled his discovery to the world.

He slipped half a dozen of the topmost necklaces into individual Ziploc bags he'd brought from camp. He sat back, ogling the necklaces lined in front of him on the stone floor of the alcove. Just the raw turquoise in one or, at most, two of the necklaces would be enough to win Carmelita's release. With Carmelita safe, he would turn the remaining necklaces over to Jonathan and Elise Marbury and let the debate over the necklaces, disks, and pots begin.

He swiped at the yogurt-slimed interior of his daypack with a bandana, collected the six bagged necklaces in a single nylon sack, wrapped the sack in a hand towel he'd brought from camp for padding, and settled the bundle in the bottom of his pack. He replaced the lids on the pots and re-fitted the sandstone door in its frame. After switching out the dangling length of rope with a fresh length, he stuffed the old rope in his pack, wrapped the new rope over his shoulder and around his waist, and stepped backward out of the cavity.

He broke out in a feverish sweat and nearly vomited the instant the full sun struck him upon leaving the shade of the alcove to rappel down the face of the cliff. It was three o'clock, the hottest time of day. The air temperature in the inner canyon had to be a few ticks above 110 by now, perhaps above 115. He unwrapped himself from the rope at the foot of the cliff and made his way woozily along the steep slope to the north side of the butte. Every breath he took burned his lungs. His feet bubbled like sausages in his boots.

He down-climbed most of the three-sided chimney in the second cliff band without incident until, five feet from the bottom of the second cliff, he slipped and plummeted to the rocky slope at the base of the chimney. He hit the ground hard and tumbled downhill, his arms and legs flailing, grabbing at cacti and brush and gouging a large ragged flap of skin from the palm of his left hand. His chin slammed into a rock before he managed to bring himself to a halt. He rose, shaky and confused, and stumbled around the base of the butte, making for the east face of the ridge, his chin aching and his gouged hand dripping blood. He banged his shins into low rocks along the way, raising welts through the light fabric of his pants.

He sucked greedily at his second bladder of water, unable to control his thirst, as he staggered back around the butte. The large dose of liquid did him good. His mind cleared as he descended the cleft in the lowest cliff band and made his way across the face of the ridge to the point where Hermit Trail topped out between the Monument and Hermit Creek drainages. He headed up the empty trail without pausing, willing himself onward, intent only on the few feet directly ahead of him.

Refreshed by the water, he clicked off a quick mile. Then he began to slow. The petroleum smell of the hot grease in his shoes rose into the air and filled his nostrils, sickening him. The sun beat on his back and reflected off the trail into his face.

He took another deep draw of water. The soothing liquid flowed through the plastic tube into his mouth. The tube gurgled and his mouth filled with stale air—his second bladder was dry.

Hermit's Rest was three miles and 1,500 vertical feet above him, the temperature was pushing 115 degrees, and the sun was more than four hours from setting. The numbers didn't work. There was no way he could make it out of the canyon this afternoon, in this heat, without more water. Yet there was nothing he could do but keep going. He was too far up the trail to turn back for Hermit Creek. Dripping Spring was even less accessible on the far side of Hermit Basin. His nearest salvation was the drinking fountain at Hermit's Rest.

He could almost taste the stream of clear water arcing from the fountain, wet and cold. Time passed with agonizing slowness. Other than the constant buzz of cicadas, the day was silent. His thoughts grew increasingly unfocused as he wandered up the trail. His lips cracked and his mouth turned to sandpaper.

"Jan," he said aloud, his tongue thick and heavy. "Carm. Rosie."

The trail remained empty of other hikers—although, he realized suddenly, he wasn't actually on his own in the depths of the canyon. Like anyone else foolish enough to attempt hiking the inner canyon in the murderous heat of a mid-summer day, all he had to do was call 911 for help.

He fumbled in the right-hand pocket of his hiking pants for his cell phone. The pocket was empty. He shoved his left hand into the opposite pocket, grimacing as he tore back the flap of skin on his injured palm, but that pocket was empty as well.

Then he remembered. He'd plodded right past the boulder where he'd hidden his phone. His stomach fell. The phone was too far behind for him to retrieve. There was nothing he could do but trudge upward, one faltering step after another.

He'd known all along he couldn't pull off this hike. But he'd set off anyway. What had he been thinking? He couldn't remember. Couldn't remember much of anything. Couldn't think in linear fashion. Wasn't sure where he was, only that he was on a trail and that the heat literally was killing him.

He poked the open wound on his palm every few steps to jolt himself toward some degree of consciousness. Sweat no longer gathered on his forehead; he was too dehydrated for that. He was a curled brown leaf skittering aimlessly along the ground, driven onward in fits and starts by the scorching, inner-canyon breeze.

The trail angled uphill, then leveled. He squinted, his eyes dry and blurry behind his sunglasses, his contacts sticking now and then to the backs of his eyelids. There at the side of the trail was the wooden sign marking the junction of Hermit and Boucher trails. A mile and a half and a thousand vertical feet to go.

He could make it. He had to make it.

He passed the junction without stopping. His feet were on fire, his hands dead weights at his sides. His head lolled forward. The sun pounded with the force of a sledgehammer on the back of his neck.

He barely noticed the sign marking the Waldron Trail junction. One step. Another. Another.

He stopped every few feet. Each time he halted, he took a few rasping breaths, concentrated on the stretch of trail just ahead, and willed himself to resume walking. One unsteady step. Two. Three. Another halt.

The sun reflected with blowtorch-like heat off the canted face of white limestone where the worn Chalk Stairs climbed upward. He lurched up the pebble-filled gully until he slipped on the small stones gathered in the eroded trail and pitched forward, slamming his elbows and forehead on the sloping rock.

He sat up, bruised and dazed, in the middle of the expanse of blazing white stone, his head throbbing. How had he gotten here? He couldn't remember. Barely knew who he was. But sitting was nice. Far preferable to standing. And if sitting felt so good, wouldn't lying down feel even better?

He flopped backward awkwardly on his daypack, his face to the sky. The hot sun soothed his battered chin and eased the pain where he'd slammed his elbows and forehead on the rock. The worn steps were unexpectedly comfortable. The hot stone surface didn't bother him. It felt fine, in fact.

He'd always heard freezing to death was the best way to go. You just went to sleep. Now he knew dying of heatstroke wasn't so bad either. You just evaporated.

He took off his cap and sunglasses and tossed them away, giving himself up to the canyon. He tried to unbutton his shirt, but his fingers were too swollen and clumsy. He shifted in a failed attempt to work the pack out from beneath his back only to find he was content as he was, tangled in the pack's shoulder straps, lying half on his side.

Janelle. He'd done what he'd had to for her. At least he could be proud of that.

Carmelita. He'd finally begun to win her over with the hatchet and campfire.

He could have been a good father to Carmelita. And to Rosie. He would have been a good father to the girls—unlike James Anthony Bender, whose last name Chuck shared despite the fact that James Bender had left Durango a few weeks after Chuck's birth and never returned, leaving Chuck to a childhood of bouncing around Durango with his waitress/bartender mother from low-rent apartment to trailer park to by-the-week motel room. A month before Chuck's high school graduation, his mother took off for Southern California with the latest in her string of straggly-haired boyfriends. Chuck worked his way through Fort Lewis College over the course of the next six years, sometimes managing only a single class per semester.

Like everyone in Durango, he'd grown up hearing the many stories of the Anasazi who'd populated the region long before the arrival of Navajos and Utes and, later, European settlers. An Intro to Anthropology course early in his college career turned him on to the welcome notion of losing himself in the study of the long-ago Anasazi. A couple of years later, one of his professors told him she saw in his single-minded pursuit of his degree the potential to one day run his own business. Chuck held fast to her suggestion. He embarked on his career as a solo contract archaeologist upon graduating, and prided himself on having made a decent living over the years while being accountable to no one but himself.

The sun beat down on the Chalk Stairs just as it had on the hot sunny day just over a year ago when Chuck had tracked down his father, having decided the time had come to unleash a lifetime's worth of resentment on the man who'd shirked his parental responsibilities. It had been easy for Chuck to find the man who shared his genes. He ran an online search based on information provided by his mother that turned up a current address for one James A. Bender in El Paso. Chuck climbed into his truck and drove south from Durango through New Mexico and on across the Texas border. There, despite his every expectation to the contrary, the rage he'd long harbored for the father he'd never met turned to pity the instant he saw the broken man who answered his knock.

Chuck's father lived in a small, fourth-story walk-up in a weather-beaten apartment building in downtown El Paso a few blocks from the Rio Grande. The apartment was furnished with castoffs, and Chuck's father, bowed and skeletal, turned out to be a castoff himself.

James Bender ushered Chuck into a stuffy living room. Chuck introduced himself as the stooped man in loose slippers shuffled across the room and collapsed into a sagging easy chair. An ashtray next to the recliner overflowed with cigarette butts. The apartment reeked of cigarette smoke. A bottle of cheap bourbon sat on a worn coffee table in front of a daybed along the near wall. An ancient television trumpeted the jeering audience of a daytime talk show. Latino pop music thumped through the walls.

Chuck sat on the edge of the daybed opposite his father. James Bender's translucent skin was taut over the top of his skull, which was bald save for a few stray hairs above his ears. His eyes, the same blue-gray as Chuck's, were rheumy and sunken deep in their sockets. He clung to the arms of his easy chair with claw-like hands, as if holding his head above water.

With surprising energy, he launched into a bitter diatribe aimed at Chuck's mother. She was an arrogant woman, he proclaimed between hoarse breaths. Pig-headed. She had left him no choice but to leave Durango and never look back.

Chuck drew in his cheeks. Granted, his mother was no paragon of respectability. She was a smoker and drinker who'd never managed to get ahead financially. She'd raised her hand at Chuck more times than he could remember. But she'd never struck him. And, tenuous though their life together had been, she'd always kept a roof over their heads and some sort of food on the table.

Chuck cast his eyes around the cramped apartment and filled his lungs with the odor of his father's bleak existence. He crossed the room and rested his fingers on the back of one of his father's bony hands. Veins spread cord-like across it, identical to those that snaked across the backs of Chuck's own hands. He bent close and looked his father in the eye. "I'm glad to see you, to know you're alive," he told him.

James Bender looked at Chuck with moist, red-rimmed eyes that were blank and lost. He said nothing in return.

"Goodbye, Pop," Chuck said, using the term of endearment he'd always imagined he'd have used as a boy with the father he'd never known.

He straightened, left the apartment, and drove home. Every month thereafter he sent a check to El Paso that was dutifully cashed until, just six weeks ago, the envelope came back unopened. When a phone call to the El Paso County Department of Health and Human Services disclosed his father's death, Chuck slipped the returned check in a folder marked "Pop" and tucked it at the back of his filing cabinet.

In the weeks since his father's death, Chuck had come to appreciate all the more the kind reception Janelle's parents, Enrique and Yolanda, had extended him since the first day he'd happened into their daughter's life. As he lay on his back in the middle of the deserted Chalk Stairs, hot stone searing the backs of his legs, he wondered idly why he'd been so reserved in response to the elder Ortegas' warm welcome.

Enrique and Yolanda had grown up across the Mexican border in Juarez. The two fell in love as teenagers, immigrated, and made their way north to Albuquerque, where Enrique secured a city street-crew position through connections with members of the extended Ortega family already living in the city. He and Yolanda built their house together, concrete block by concrete block, nights, weekends, and holidays, on a barren lot in Albuquerque's crime-ridden South Valley that they picked up for next to nothing before Janelle and Clarence were born. They gave their two children non-Latino names and did all they could to shield them from the gang-infested neighborhood that surrounded their home. When Janelle got pregnant and dropped out of college, the Ortegas redoubled their efforts with Clarence, hiring tutors and pushing him to excel in high school and finish college.

Enrique worked his street crew job for more than twenty-five years, straight through to the day his knee was crushed by a front-end loader. His years of heavy construction work cost him more than just a working leg; he was in his early fifties, barely a decade older than Chuck, but he appeared much older with his weathered face, gnarled hands, and stooped shoulders.

These days, Enrique and Yolanda got by on Enrique's moderate disability payments along with the money Yolanda earned by rising before dawn each day to make breakfast burritos, which she sold to friends and neighbors. Janelle's mother was nearly as slender as Janelle, just over five feet tall, always on the move, with an ever-ready smile and long, gray-streaked black hair she wore circled in a bun at the back of her neck.

Had Chuck been given the opportunity to choose his parents, he'd happily have selected the Ortegas. Now, as he stared up at the blinding sun from the sloping limestone, he clung to his fading vision of Enrique and Yolanda, and of their daughter and granddaughters.

Janelle. She'd said yes to him without hesitation.

Rosie. The firecracker.

Carmelita. Icy cool.

He closed his eyes. The sun danced beyond his eyelids, red and leering.

He never should have hiked into the canyon. He'd known better, but still he'd set off. For Janelle. For Rosie. And for Carmelita.

His arms fell to his sides. His legs shook, then quieted. He lay, unmoving, as consciousness ebbed from him like water draining from a pool.

Seventeen

5 p.m.

Chuck choked and sputtered, coughing blood. Liquid trickled down the back of his throat, thick and dark red in his mind's eye. He gagged. Spat weakly. Clawed his way to a sitting position, eyes still closed. Felt something pressing at his back. Tried to shove it away.

He heard voices. A voice. Found he could take in a word or two at a time.

". . . heat . . . ridiculous . . . can't believe . . ."

The voice was familiar. More liquid filled his mouth, welcoming this time. So what if it was blood? It was delicious. He gagged again. Managed to swallow. Took hold of whatever was pouring the liquid into his mouth: a bottle. Grasped it with both hands and pressed it greedily to his lips. Water, that's what it was. Not blood after all, but water, blessed water.

Chuck opened his eyes. His head spun, then cleared. He looked around him, regaining his senses and remembering. He was seated on the Chalk Stairs, his legs splayed before him. The sun, dropping in the western sky, still blazed down on him. The air temperature remained sizzling. He'd been out for an hour, maybe two.

Someone's hand pressed at his back, steadying him so he could drink.

He rotated his head woodenly and found himself staring into the accusatory eyes of the uniformed student ranger he'd left at Hermit's Rest a few hours ago. He maintained his grip on the young man's proffered bottle and drank deeply. Life flowed back into him with each swallow.

The student ranger replaced Chuck's hat on his head and his sunglasses over his eyes, centered his daypack on his back, and helped him to his feet, catching him when he toppled sideways. Wasting no time, the young man tucked his empty bottle in his own daypack, snugged his arm around Chuck's waist, and set off slowly up the trail with Chuck held securely at his side.

"You saved my life," Chuck croaked, barely managing to stay upright and hobble up the sloping limestone.

"Nah. Somebody would have found you later this evening. They probably would have had to chopper you out by then—which would have cost you a fortune, I might add—but you'd have been okay."

"I can't believe—" Chuck began.

"Don't worry about it," the young man cut in. "I figured you'd make it to the creek all right."

"I didn't go to the creek."

"No kidding. I'm just glad I saw you coming out. Stumbling is more like it. I watched you from the rim. You were hanging in there 'til you went down. It was clear you weren't getting back up."

"Ran out of water."

"'Course you did."

"Too hot."

"I told you that." The young man's tone was surprisingly mild.

"For a student ranger, you're not so bad."

"We prefer interpretive-ranger-in-training."

"Better yet, you got a name?"

"Conover. Hansen Conover."

"Hansen? What kind of name is that?"

"I just walked a mile and a half into the canyon in this heat to save you from your own stupidity, and you're hassling me about the name my parents gave me?"

"No, no. You can go by whatever name you want. I'm just glad to be alive and talking."

Chuck was making his way up the trail under his own power by the time he and the student ranger, Hansen, reached Hermit's Rest an hour and a half later. The sun was low in the sky and the trailhead was busy with backpackers preparing to descend into the canyon as the day gave way to evening. It was 6:40. The frequency of shuttle buses slowed from every thirty minutes to every hour as the end of the day approached. The next shuttle wasn't due until 7:30. He hadn't checked in with the caller or Janelle since noon.

Hansen saw Chuck checking his watch. "I'm on my way back to the village," he said, pointing at a white, park-service pickup truck parked at the far side of the shuttle turnaround. "Want a lift?"

"Another lift, you mean?"

As Hansen drove, Chuck chugged water from a gallon jug stored in the passenger compartment of the pickup. He was rehydrated by the time he climbed out of the truck at the campground entrance. The cut on his palm burned and the bruises on his head, elbows, and shins throbbed, but the nausea and lightheadedness that had plagued him in the canyon were gone.

The campground was shadowed with the onset of evening. He headed across it, angling between sites where families were gathered at picnic tables preparing dinner. The smell of grilled hamburger filled the air.

Ahead, Enrique's shiny blue pickup, two ranger patrol sedans, and several private cars were parked next to Janelle's mini-SUV and Clarence's hatchback in front of the campsite. A crowd of twenty or so people stood around the picnic table at the center of the site, shaded from the last of the day's light by the campground's tall ponderosas.

Chuck's legs wobbled beneath him. He needed food and rest. The last thing he wanted was to face Janelle in front of all these people. But what other option did he have?

Heads swiveled his direction as he got closer. The group around the table was made up primarily of people he didn't know, middle-aged men and women—recruits, presumably, from the alert Janelle had posted online. In their plaid shirts, button-up blouses, high-waisted shorts, and sensible walking shoes, they clearly were tourists, their faces lined with concern, their eyes wide at Chuck's banged-up appearance. Enrique stood on the far side of the table. He wore a work shirt and jeans. Yolanda, wearing a floral-print blouse and dark slacks, stood in front of her husband. Donald was there, talking on his cell phone. Rachel was there, too. Both were in uniform.

Chuck recognized two women, Dolores and Amelia, Janelle's best friends from Albuquerque, huddled together at the edge of the group. Like Janelle, they were in their late twenties. Along with Enrique, Yolanda, and Clarence, the two were key pillars in Janelle's Albuquerque support network. Dolores was short and, if such a thing was possible, skinnier than Janelle. She wore black, form-fitting yoga pants that flared at the calf above her high-heeled leather sandals. Her sleeveless yellow shirt hugged her tiny breasts and toothpick-thin torso. Her makeup was flawless, her bob-length hair flipped and styled.

Amelia was as big and round as Dolores was short and skinny. Below her midriff blouse, Amelia's enormous waistline muffin-topped over a pair of wide, white-denim shorts. Her shiny black hair, teased and sprayed, rose several inches from her forehead before sweeping backward, helmet-like, to her shoulders.

Chuck wasn't surprised by the pair's arrival. But that didn't mean he was happy to see them. Janelle, Dolores, and Amelia had been tight since their school days in Albuquerque's South Valley, where Dolores and Amelia still lived. Chuck knew Janelle's friends had supported her throughout her trials with Miguel and in her years of single motherhood since. But as Chuck and Janelle grew closer, Janelle confided that Dolores and Amelia had expressed plenty of concerns about him, questioning his age, his long-established bachelorhood, his lack of family ties, and the fact that his job kept him on the road so much of the time.

Janelle's friends scowled at Chuck from across the table. Clearly, they held him responsible for Carmelita's disappearance.

Janelle detached herself from the group and ran to him. He tensed, but she wrapped her arms around him and pulled him close.

"We—" she said, her voice catching. "We were afraid you were—"

He loosened her grip and held her out from him. "I'm sorry I didn't call. The phone . . ."

Janelle raised her fingers to his face. She touched his scraped chin, then the hard knot on his forehead. "They've been calling here instead," she said, lowering her hand. "That voice." She shuddered. "Rachel said there was no way you could survive down there on a day like this."

"She was almost right." Chuck checked out the group gathered around the table in the waning light. All eyes were on the two of them. He looked back at Janelle. "He still has Carmelita?"

She nodded, her face drawn.

"What's he been telling you?"

"To wait and see if you show," she said. "If not, then Plan B, whatever that is."

"What's Plan A?"

"They haven't said."

"They?"

"He. She. I don't know."

"It's Miguel. It has to be."

"Should be."

"It's computerized," Chuck insisted. "His voice."

"There's something about it, though. It doesn't sound like him. His cadence or something."

Chuck thought of the twin cuts on his neck. "You think it could be a woman?"

"It just doesn't sound like Miguel, that's all."

"And these people?" Chuck said of the group. "From your posting?"

Janelle shrugged. "They know she's not just missing, that there's more to it than that. It's been too long. Donald's the only one who knows the whole story. He figured it out pretty quick while he was showing us around. He forwarded my Facebook posting to some sort of online bulletin board they've got here at the canyon. He's a talker. Likes his phone. Knows how to get things out of people." She squeezed a strand of her hair tightly between her fingers. "He's agreed not to tell the whole story to anyone else—except this Rachel of yours."

Chuck ignored the look Janelle directed at him. "They haven't told any other rangers?"

"They say they haven't. I've explained to them about the note. But they're saying they can't wait much longer. Donald already has people looking everywhere for us. Maids, cooks, janitors. Rachel's helping him run dispatch. She knows what she's doing, I'll give her that much." Janelle gave Chuck another look, this time more accepting.

"Sounds like you've got a lot going on."

She shoved the strand of hair behind her ear and drew herself up. "I know you said we shouldn't do anything. But Donald and Rachel insisted."

Chuck dipped his head. "You're right. They're right." He pointed at his daypack, still on his back. "The good news is I've got what he wants. I just need to check in with him." Then he frowned. It wasn't going to be that simple, was it?

All day he'd been reassured by the belief Carmelita was safe, at least relatively so, with her father. But Janelle had just said the computerized voice might not be Miguel's after all. Chuck reached behind him and rested his hand on the bottom of his pack where the necklaces were stowed. How was it that a small-time drug dealer from Albuquerque knew so much about Chuck's discovery in the canyon, and about the canyon's trail system, too? The truth was, Miguel couldn't know. Not on his own. Which meant someone else had to be involved, either working with Miguel, or instead of him, someone who knew the canyon well.

"What happens if somebody sees something?" Chuck asked.

"There have already been, like, ten reports. They've been sending people to check, but nothing has panned out."

"You haven't put it on the Nightly News yet?"

The corners of Janelle's eyes tightened. "I know Miguel. We squeeze him, he might call the whole thing off. He likes his low profile."

"You just said you don't think it's him on the phone."

Her face collapsed. "I just want my little girl back," she said, her eyes filling with tears.

Unable to summon a reassuring reply, Chuck turned Janelle by the elbow and they walked to the group gathered around the picnic table. The group parted to let them approach the head of the table. He felt Rachel's eyes on him. Across the table from her, Enrique stood stiffly behind Yolanda, his gelled hair combed across his high forehead. "*M'hijo*," he implored Chuck, his salt-and-pepper mustache trembling. "Anything?"

"We're getting there, Enrique."

"Getting there?"

"We pay, they let her go."

Enrique uttered a string of Spanish curses, echoing Clarence's morning outburst.

Chuck raised a hand and looked around the group. "We'll do what they say. No police. Not until we're in the clear. It won't be long now. Everybody understands that, right?"

Chuck glanced at Donald, now off the phone. Janelle was right about his being a talker. The question was whether Donald was capable of keeping things under wraps long enough for Chuck to trade the necklaces for Carmelita, assuming it wasn't too late already.

"We give them what they want and they give us Carm," Chuck continued. "Then everyone goes home."

Dolores spoke up, an edge to her voice. "Jan says what they really want is you."

Chuck put a hand to his banged-up chin. "They almost got me already."

"Don't you think you should let the rangers handle this?"

"I'm not sure what—" Chuck began, but Dolores cut him off.

"You've been at this all day, right? And you've gotten nowhere so far."

Janelle raised a hand to quiet her friend. "We should—" She stopped when her phone chimed. She fished it out of her pocket, checked it, and held it out to Chuck, her eyes pleading.

"Are you there?" came the computerized voice.

"It's me," Chuck said, walking away from the group. "Chuck."

"About time." A pause. "What's with your phone? You haven't been answering."

Would the caller admit to knowing Chuck's phone was still deep in the canyon? Or was his phone programmed in such a way that it gave its location only when he used it to make a call? "My battery," he said. "I told you."

"And this online crap. Facebook, chat rooms."

"That wasn't me. Besides, your note said no cops."

"So you decided to tell the whole world instead."

"I told you, it wasn't me. And no cops have been told."

There was a lengthy silence. Chuck detected what sounded like a sigh of frustration. Then, "Use the phone you've got now. You're back in camp?" The question was deductive, lacking the assurance with which the caller had pronounced Chuck's location earlier in the day.

Good, Chuck said to himself. There was still a little something the kidnapper wasn't sure of.

"You have what you were sent for?" the voice continued when Chuck didn't respond.

"Yes."

"Excellent." In spite of the computerization, the sudden animation in the caller's voice was unmistakable. "Okay. Ten o'clock. Just you, nobody else. At the BIC."

The caller pronounced the abbreviation for the Backcountry Information Center as a word, *Bic*, with a hard c, as did all park personnel.

Eighteen

7:30 p.m.

"She's okay," Chuck reported to the group. "Long as we keep this thing to ourselves. We're getting close."

Yolanda reached behind her for Enrique. He squeezed her shoulder. "What do you have in mind?" he asked.

Chuck knew he couldn't get away with simply telling those gathered at the table to do nothing. Besides, there was the outside chance they could prove valuable in advance of the exchange. "We fan out, do some looking."

Janelle clucked in disapproval. "We tried that this morning."

"Not with twenty of us spread all over the place." Chuck looked her in the eye. "You're the one who wants to put the pliers to him. This is our chance."

"Chuck's right," Rachel said to Janelle. "The phone call points to the girl still being somewhere nearby. They've got to be getting nervous by now." She turned to Chuck. "You're thinking group text, aren't you?"

"That's exactly what I'm thinking."

The first adventure race Chuck had attended with Rachel, deep in Washington's coastal rainforest, had been a disaster. Poor trail directions led numerous racers to become lost along the backcountry route. One racer fell to his death from a cliff after straying from the course during the second, rain-drenched night of the competition. In the aftermath of the tragedy, officials determined the primary problem had been lack of trail marshals along the racecourse. But it wasn't feasible to station dozens of marshals along the lengthy courses. Instead, the officials instituted a new rule that essentially turned all competing racers into course marshals. Racers carried GPS-capable cell phones during all competitions and checked in with race marshals by text at regular intervals throughout each race, making use of the group's growing body of knowledge to keep all racers on course. Rachel likened the process to flying birds. In the same way one bird's movement rippled instantly through the flock and enabled them to change direction as one, so too did the flow of group texts enhance the ability of all competitors to stay on course throughout their contests.

Chuck took in the disparate group gathered around the picnic table: the concerned tourists, Enrique and Yolanda with their fear-filled eyes, Rachel and Donald displaying steady resolve, Janelle and Clarence exchanging glances of disquiet, and Dolores and Amelia, their jaws set. Hard to imagine all these people working so closely together that they could change direction as one, but worth sending them out before the exchange nonetheless. Between the nearly two dozen of them, who could say what they might see and report before ten o'clock?

"We'll head out on foot," Chuck said. "We don't want a bunch of people driving all over the place, making a big scene. Everybody will have a specific location. Donald, can you assign spots around the village for people to monitor?"

"Sure," Donald replied.

"Look for anything out of the ordinary," Chuck told the group. "I'm to meet them at ten. Anything we spot before then can only help."

"Everyone should go out in pairs," Rachel put in.

"But we have to be unobtrusive," Chuck said. "The idea is to be eyes and ears out there, not mouths."

An older man in a short-sleeved dress shirt, pleated shorts, and brown loafers raised his hand.

"I'm here at my wife's insistence," the man said in a reedy voice, touching the sleeve of a gray-haired woman standing next to him. "And I have to admit, I'm a bit ill at ease right now." He looked from Rachel to Chuck. "I'm a retired district court judge."

Chuck felt Janelle grow rigid at his side as the elderly man continued.

"There's obviously a lot more going on here than you're telling us. But that's a-okay with me, and, I think, with the others as well." The man looked around the table. "I just feel it's my responsibility, our responsibility, to be sure you're not putting any of us at risk with what you're asking."

Chuck drew in a breath. "Fair enough."

The retired judge touched the tip of his tongue to his lips. "Okay then. My sense is that we've got some sort of family squabble going on here involving the missing little girl whose picture my wife showed me on her computer. I just want to be assured that a resolution to this dilemma is forthcoming, as you've indicated."

Rachel replied before Chuck could answer. "That's correct, sir. Which is why we—" she glanced at Donald "—are willing to help work through this problem outside of normal, park-service channels."

"You must know you're risking your career in so doing, dearie," the elderly judge said to her.

"A little girl's well-being is at stake," Rachel responded. "*That's* what is driving my decision-making process at this point, regardless of any potential risks to my career. And, I might add, you're taking quite a risk yourself in calling me 'dearie.'"

The judge's wife smiled and dug her elbow into her husband's side. The old man chuckled. "Right you are, dear—er, ma'am," he said. He clapped his hands together. The sound echoed across the campground just as the rap of his gavel must once have filled his courtroom. "All right then. I'm a married man. I know when I've been beat."

He looked across the table at Chuck, who surveyed the group of tourists. There were plenty of squared shoulders; a middle-aged couple turned to one another with grave nods. Before meeting Janelle and the girls, Chuck's loner self would have scoffed at the idea of sending a group of strangers out on a mission such as this. Yet here were these people, brought together by nothing more than Janelle's online posting, willing to head out into the coming night on Carmelita's behalf based on nothing more than the judge's broad-brush assumption that what they were doing was for the best. Chuck was deeply impressed. Within minutes of setting up the group text account between group members' phones and sending the tourists off to various outposts around the village, however, he was entirely unimpressed.

Nonsensical reports of questionable activity began pouring in via group text shortly after the tourists dispersed from the campsite.

"Mother and son at market," came the first text. "Locked and loaded?"

Whatever that meant.

"Behind dumpster," came another report, with no further information.

Then, a minute later, from the same number, "Just somebody having a smoke."

And so the texts flew: someone locking up Kolb Studio, a group of college-age kids piling out of a van in front of El Tovar, even a report that the drip irrigation system had come on at Thunderbird Lodge.

Chuck chided himself as he made his way along a darkened village walkway toward the Backcountry Information Center. So much for his bright idea. But at least the tourists were keeping themselves occupied. He set Janelle's phone to vibrate, shoved it in his pocket, and gave up trying to follow the unending stream of meaningless texts that proved, yet again, why he preferred to go things alone.

Chuck had insisted he be allowed to follow the explicit

instruction of the computerized voice that he make the exchange on his own. He'd brooked no compromise when Janelle wondered aloud whether giving in to the caller's demand was in Carmelita's best interest.

"He wants me, just me. That's what we'll give him," Chuck had responded. "We're almost there. If he tries to pull anything, *then* we go to the police."

Janelle had tried to convince Chuck to stay at the campsite until closer to ten o'clock, but he wanted to reacquaint himself with the terrain surrounding the information center in advance of the exchange.

Ten years ago, the site had been an open meadow at the south edge of the village. The contract Chuck won to assess, dig, and screen the meadow for the park service in advance of the Backcountry Information Center's scheduled construction had been his second at the Grand Canyon. The new information center would provide long-overdue office space for staffers who oversaw the park's booming backcountry activities—rafting, hiking, backpacking, and mule riding—while a paved lot around the center would supply overflow parking for backcountry users, village visitors, and guests of Maswik Lodge to the west.

Jonathan and Elise Marbury recognized that the required dig would be sensitive, given the meadow's visible location south of the lodges, eateries, and gift shops lining the canyon rim. Aware of the headline-grabbing allegations of cultural theft that might result if the wrong crowd heard about the dig, the park's husband-wife curator team selected Bender Archaeological for the contract because of Chuck's reputation for keeping his work low profile.

Other than one other person to help during the initial site survey, Chuck proposed that he would be the sole laborer at the meadow. He promised Jonathan and Elise he would use the latest in underground spectrographic imaging technology to minimize digging at the site, as he had for the connector road contract two years earlier. Upon completing the initial survey and assessment of the meadow, he suggested stringing only one excavation unit at a time rather than the entire site at once. And rather than stringing units with bright white cord as was customary, he proposed stringing each unit with earth-toned cord that would be invisible to passers-by.

Chuck staged the meadow to look like a run-of-the-mill construction zone. First, he created a visual barrier between the site and the village core by running a length of garish, orange, plastic-mesh construction fencing along the north edge of the site. Next, he had several abandoned pieces of heavy equipment brought to the meadow from the discard lot behind the South Rim Maintenance Garage and directed the arrangement of the inoperable pieces of equipment—two rusted backhoes, a small pavement roller, and an oversized Bobcat with a caved-in roof—just inside the orange fencing to create another visual barrier between the dig site and the village. To complete the scene, Chuck adopted the costume of a commonplace construction worker—ratty Carhartts, ripped T-shirt, greasy ball cap, and work boots with steel toes shining through holes worn in the leather.

The Marburys assigned Donald to help Chuck with the initial, above-ground field survey—they knew one another from Donald's oversight of Chuck's work on the connector road contract. Chuck and Donald worked their way from one end of the meadow to the other, Donald holding the surveying rod while Chuck shot elevations across the swath of blue grama grass and sagebrush with his transit from the site's primary datum point.

While they worked, Donald rattled on about what he thought of the latest Hollywood blockbusters, his belief in the existence of UFOs, the athletic exploits of his high-school-aged nieces back home in San Diego, and a slew of other topics. Chuck responded to each of Donald's monologues with little more than a grunt, after which Donald launched, unfazed, into a new subject.

Chuck paid only passing attention to Donald's stories as he shot and recorded elevations across the meadow. He took notice, however, when Donald repeatedly mentioned a female ranger named Rachel Severin who'd recently been assigned to the park.

"You're trying to play matchmaker, aren't you?" Chuck accused Donald.

"What? Me?" Donald responded, feigning surprise.

"What? Me?" Chuck mimicked.

Donald made a show of tapping his chin with his forefinger. "Now that you mention it, that's not such a bad idea."

"I didn't mention it."

"You just said you're interested in her."

Chuck blew a jet of air out his lips. "I said you're trying to set me up."

"I don't think so."

Chuck shook his head in defeat.

The next day Donald reported that the new ranger had agreed to swing by Donald's apartment for dinner with him that evening, and that Chuck's attendance was required.

"What about you and this Rachel?" Chuck asked as he repositioned the theodolite on its tripod before sending Donald off to the far side of the meadow with the surveying rod.

"She's not my type."

"What do you mean, not your type? You've been saying she's good-looking, athletic, intelligent—what's not to like about all that?"

"She's quiet."

"Quiet?"

"Yeah. Quiet."

"And?"

"And, well, somebody like me, she'd last about a week before she'd pound me into the turf just to shut me up. But you, you're quiet, too."

"Silence is, what, golden in this particular instance?"

"I didn't say silence. I said quiet. Big difference."

Donald was right. Dinner was a hit. Rachel's reserved, self-reliant nature mirrored Chuck's, which proved to be the one big plus of their on-again, off-again relationship over the years. But their kindred natures proved the one big minus of their relationship as well.

Each time it became logical for the two of them to up the ante in some significant way, to consider moving in together during Chuck's contracts at the park, or to explore the notion of splitting expenses on a place they both could use during their breaks from work, they shied away from the subject and drifted apart as a result. And while Chuck enjoyed the time he spent with Rachel during the weeks he worked the Backcountry Information Center site, the job itself proved to be the non-event he and the Marburys expected—until the very last day of digging.

Nineteen

9 p.m.

Chuck moved slowly through the parking lot around the Backcountry Information Center looking for the big black SUV. He circled the center twice but spotted neither the car nor anything else that appeared the least bit out of the ordinary. While monitoring the continuing stream of senseless group texts arriving on Janelle's phone, he angled toward the six buildings that comprised the Maswik Lodge complex west of the information center at the south end of the village.

Maswik was the only low-cost lodging option at the South Rim. Given the lodge's affordability as well as its location next to the information center, Chuck suspected Carmelita was being held in a room in one of its six motel-like buildings. But he didn't dare risk Carmelita's safety by knocking on random doors in advance of the exchange. He walked slowly through the grounds of the lodge complex. As with his loops around the information center, however, his walk turned up nothing of note, nor was the black SUV parked in any of the small parking lots fronting each Maswik building.

He settled in beneath a squat juniper at the edge of the forest, thirty feet south of the sprawling Backcountry Information Center parking lot. It was well before ten o'clock. Behind him, the pine forest stretched unbroken to the park's southern boundary twenty miles away. Ahead, beyond row after row of parked cars, the timber-frame information center with its south-facing wall of floor-to-ceiling windows sat dark and silent.

By now, Chuck was nearly recovered from his collapse on the trail. Though his head still ached from the severe bout of dehydration he'd suffered, he was fully alert. He lay on his stomach, propped on his elbows, just beyond the glow of the overhead lights lining the parking lot. The moonless night was comfortably cool after the heat of the day. His watch read 9:45. Fifteen minutes to go. He thumbed through the texts bouncing among the members of the tourist group, but found nothing useful.

He adjusted the strap on the compact set of night-vision goggles Rachel had retrieved for him from her patrol car at camp in anticipation of the nighttime exchange. The goggles weren't standard ranger issue. Rather, Rachel used them during her adventure races and kept them in her ranger duffel between competitions. He centered the goggles' binocular-like eye ports over the bridge of his nose. A ghostly, gray-green, infrared image of the darkened Backcountry Information Center settled into focus in the middle of the three-quarters full parking lot. The building was deserted, but even at this late hour the parking lot was alive with tourists making their way to and from their cars.

The selection of such a busy site for the exchange puzzled Chuck. How was he to make the swap for Carmelita with all these people around? The scene had been far different ten years ago when he'd won the contract to assess the expanse of grass and sage that was the proposed site for the information center.

The meadow never served as a regular gathering place for the Anasazi. But because of its location less than two hundred yards south of where Bright Angel Trail dropped off the South Rim into the canyon, it had served as a staging and encampment area for the hordes of prospectors in the late 1800s who ultimately learned the canyon was devoid of any large deposits of precious metals. In the wake of their departure, the prospectors left piles of trash along the South Rim that were sifted and resifted over the intervening decades by amateur treasure hunters who carted off anything of interest—brass bridle rings, unbroken bottles, discarded letters, and the like.

Chuck's initial survey of the site, completed with Donald's assistance, revealed the locations of two such debris piles in the meadow. After Donald returned to his regular ranger duties, Chuck excavated the first of the two piles. It contained but one item of marginal interest, a century-old, mildew-riddled canvas tent wrapped around a pair of wooden support poles.

The second debris pile, at the southwest edge of the meadow, turned out to be much smaller than the first. Someone had put a match to it at some point so that its remains consisted of ashes, chunks of blackened wood, and a few strips of charred burlap and canvas. Chuck moved outward from the center of the pile, digging and screening as he went, until he no longer encountered ashes or other signs of trash left behind by prospectors a hundred years ago. Just before he set about refilling the shallow hole he'd created, he noticed a splash of color, rose-petal red against the brown earth, at the very bottom of the hole. He froze, staring.

The spot of red, out of place at the bottom of the debris pile, had a natural tone to it that suggested the use of plant dye for coloration rather than modern chemicals. He set to work over the spot of color, loosening dirt with his fingertips, his breaths becoming more excited with each handful. He switched to a small paintbrush and within minutes uncovered a few coal-black turkey feathers strung together with yucca thread dyed solid red.

He set his camera on a tripod, aimed it into the hole, and programmed it to take pictures at one-minute intervals while he worked. He remained crouched in the depression, exposing the find using ever-smaller implements, as hours passed and afternoon gave way to dusk, then dark. He kept at it late into the night, using shielded spots for light, as he unearthed an extraordinary, thousand-year-old Anasazi burial shroud that somehow had ended up at the bottom of a hundred-year-old mining debris pile.

The majority of burial shrouds fashioned by the Anasazi were crude affairs made of turkey-wing feathers tied together with undyed yucca fiber. Only a handful of shrouds, collected across the Colorado Plateau early in the twentieth century before burial sites were declared almost entirely off limits to archaeologists, were finer than that. They featured threadwork of plant-dyed cord that served both to hold the feathers in place and demarcate simple geometric patterns. Yet the more Chuck uncovered of the shroud, the more he recognized its workmanship as a significant step above even those well-crafted shrouds.

He dug a trench around the shroud and continued the painstaking work of uncovering it feather by feather. When midnight came and went, he grew too exhausted to continue. Afraid to let the shroud out of his sight, he spent an uncomfortable few hours sprawled at the edge of the hole before starting in on the excavation again at dawn, using a tiny paintbrush to sweep minuscule bits of dirt and ash from the feathered sides of the shroud into the surrounding trench.

In addition to the red thread that had caught his eye, other thread colors appeared as he worked—three distinct shades of green, two yellows, and an additional burnt-orange tone of red. All were sewn together in interlocking geometric designs and a descending series of fanciful twists and intricate knots that appeared to replicate, in Chuck's mind, the plunging waterfalls and fern-bedecked grottoes of the sort hidden in the farthest reaches of the canyon.

As he picked and brushed, Chuck imagined what had transpired with the burial shroud. Maybe a prospector came across the shroud wrapped around the shoulders of an Anasazi corpse somewhere deep in the canyon. Unable to resist its finery, the prospector removed the funerary covering from the corpse and hauled it out of the canyon to the South Rim. Superstition caught up with the prospector—perhaps he turned his ankle or cut his hand and became frightened that bad juju cast by the shroud had caused the accident. Rather than reunite the shroud with its corpse deep in the canyon, he took the easy way out, burying it in the debris pile and setting the pile on fire.

A century later, Chuck worked to uncover what the prospector hadn't managed to incinerate, relying on a toothpick to remove the last of the dirt and ash bit by bit until well past noon on the second day. Chuck called in Donald when, late that afternoon, the artifact was ready to come out of the ground. Together they lifted the shroud and laid it gently on a clean, white, cotton sheet. They hoisted the sheet by its corners, creating a makeshift sling, and carried the artifact straight to the South Rim Museum, where they knocked unannounced on the door to the display-preparation room at the back of the building. Upon entering, they centered the sheet on the brightly lit preparation table in the middle of the high-ceilinged room and let the sheet corners fall away so the shroud lay alone on the table. Jonathan and Elise Marbury clutched each other, their eyes locked on the shroud. Then they gave Chuck and Donald hearty backslaps.

Weeks of study by the Marburys followed. Not until Chuck's dig was long completed and construction of the Backcountry Information Center well underway did the curators hold a press conference that amounted to a coronation ceremony for the shroud, with Chuck in attendance as an honored guest. At the press conference held outside the museum, with the shroud displayed in a glass case at their side, the Marburys took turns preening before a small phalanx of video cameras arrayed in a half circle before them. The press conference lasted more than an hour as Jonathan and Elise worked, page by page, through the thick media packet they'd produced, stepping on each other's sentences as they provided ever more detailed observations about the artifact.

Modern-day archaeological ethics decreed that, except in rare circumstances, all human remains uncovered during digs were to be covered back up and left undisturbed. It came as no surprise, then, that as news of the shroud's discovery spread in advance of the press conference, there were those who questioned Chuck's decision to remove the funerary item from its resting place—even though the mining-debris pile was not a burial site, and the shroud did not constitute actual human remains. Among the questioners were the members of a band of Navajo activists including Marvin Begay, then a Window Rock High School student already supporting the advanced Anasazi culture cause.

The activists showed up at the press conference to protest the shroud's disinterment and public display. They gathered in a cordoned-off area across the parking lot from where the Marburys made their announcement, pounding on a large wooden drum and wailing in the *Diné* tongue. The Marburys welcomed the protest. The activists' long muslin shirts, fringed leather pants, and beaded moccasins made for good television footage, and their mournful chants, used as filler between sound bites from Jonathan and Elise, gave the story of the shroud a dramatic and compelling edge.

"No such thing as bad publicity," Elise told Chuck. To this day, she and Jonathan referred to the shroud as the most noteworthy of their displays in the South Rim Museum, where Rosie and Carmelita had seen it only yesterday.

Beneath the juniper, Chuck pushed the night-vision goggles up on his forehead and glanced at his watch. It was almost time. He steadied his breathing and kept his eyes on the parking lot. The top of the hour came and went. 10:05. 10:10. His heart rate increased with each passing minute. Why was nothing happening? He was about to leave the shelter of the forest and show himself at the locked door of the Backcountry Information Center when Janelle's phone gave the elongated buzz of an incoming, single-party text. The message was from the 505 number now familiar to Chuck.

end of rr y. 15 min. alone, the text read.

"Dammit," Chuck muttered in dismay—and grudging admiration. The proposed rendezvous at the information center had been a ruse, while the new, end-of-the-railroad-wye location for the exchange was, from the kidnapper's point of view, superb.

The Grand Canyon Scenic Railroad hauled train buffs in vintage passenger cars to Grand Canyon Village from the town of Williams, sixty miles south of the canyon, each day throughout the summer months. After pulling into the village to drop its load of passengers, the train turned around on a quarter-mile-long, Y-shaped length of track that extended into a thick grove of spindly ponderosas just west of Maswik Lodge.

In response to wildfires that had ravaged northern Arizona in recent years, the forest south of the canyon had been thinned to leave nothing but widely spaced ponderosas and a smattering of piñons and junipers all the way to the park boundary—save for the dense stand of young ponderosas surrounding the railroad wye. The thick grove of young pines acted as a natural sound barrier between the village and the Grand Canyon Dog Kennel on the far side of the stand of trees. The kennel took in animals for campers, hikers, backpackers, and hotel guests. Its canine boarders, held in indoor/outdoor pens, barked incessantly, leading park officials to determine that the sound barrier provided by the thickly bunched trees between the kennel and village outweighed the fire danger the grove presented.

As a result, the end of the railroad wye provided a private setting mere steps from the Maswik room in which Chuck suspected Carmelita was being held—a perfect place to make the exchange. And by waiting until the last minute to reveal the true location of the exchange, the kidnapper left Chuck no time to survey the site in advance.

He sent off a quick *okay* text in reply and set out for the wye, angling south into the thinned forest, then west. In the viewfinder of Rachel's goggles, the trunks of the thinned forest's soaring ponderosas stood out as black bars against a green background. He approached the end of the railroad wye from the south, slowing as he entered the dense grove of young ponderosas standing between the kennel and village. To his left, the kenneled dogs offered desultory barks and yelps. The slight evening breeze directed his scent to the east, away from the kennel, masking his approach from the dogs' sensitive noses. Chuck crept past the outlines of the small trees, their narrow trunks spaced a few feet apart. He crawled forward to where, twenty yards ahead, the grove gave way to a hundred-foot-wide clearing with the terminus of the railroad wye at its center.

The tracks of the wye extended on a raised gravel bed from the village through a narrow cut in the trees to the middle of the clearing. There they ended at a stout, four-foot-high bumper constructed of steel I-beams. The clearing was lit only by the stars and the slightest hint of illumination filtering through the trees from the village.

For a minute, two minutes, three, there was no movement in the clearing. The kenneled dogs continued their halfhearted snuffles, offering nothing in the way of excited barks that might announce the arrival of the kidnapper with Carmelita in tow.

Five more minutes passed with interminable slowness.

Surely, if the kidnapper and Carmelita were here, the two would have made enough noise to alert the dogs. Had the kidnapper, like Chuck, come alone? Was he waiting in the trees for Chuck to show himself first?

Though Janelle's phone continued its double-vibration group texts, no long single buzzes announced themselves against Chuck's thigh. He held his ground for another minute until, like a change in wind direction, the kenneled dogs began to keen uncertainly. A couple of questioning woofs. A single explosive bark. Then the dogs erupted in a full chorus of crazed howls.

Twenty

11:30 p.m.

Chuck spotted movement, hazy green in the goggles' viewfinder, at the far side of the clearing. A human figure dislodged itself from the cover of the trees and strode across the grassy opening and up the graveled mound to the end of the railroad tracks. The howls of the dogs reached a fever pitch as the figure stopped and stood between the tracks a few feet from the heavy steel bumper that marked the wye's terminus.

Three gunshots sounded in quick succession. Each shot was accompanied by a bright muzzle flash from the edge of the trees to the right of Chuck. Unlike the muffled explosion of the pretzel bag that had sent Chuck scrambling for cover in the canyon earlier that day, each defined crack, unquestionably that of a small-caliber handgun, sliced distinctly across the clearing.

Chuck's chest tightened and his breath came in horrified gulps. He looked on in shock as the figure at the end of the wye crumpled to the ground before the sound of the shots faded away into the trees. He leaned forward, ready to rush to the aid of the shooting victim. But helping the victim would bring him directly into the shooter's line of fire.

The dogs' cries were wild and unrestrained in the aftermath of the gunfire. The acrid smell of spent gunpowder rode the evening breeze. The figure lay unmoving between the tracks on the far side of the steel bumper.

Chuck's body quaked, making the image in the goggles before him swim disconcertingly. He willed himself to stillness as his thoughts caromed inside his head.

What should he do?

Trapped by uncertainty, he did not move. A beat passed. Another. Then a second human figure detached itself from the trees, this one from the spot where the gunshots had sounded. The shooter crossed the clearing to the end of the wye, climbed the gravel embankment, and knelt beside the prostrate victim. In the blurry green glow of the goggles, Chuck discerned that the shooter wore a light-colored shirt and had what appeared to be a man's frame. The shooter held a pistol in his right hand. Would he put his gun to the head of the victim and finish the job? Should Chuck show himself, and risk being shot, in an attempt to scare off the shooter before he could deliver any *coup de grace*?

It was all Chuck could do, unarmed, to stay where he was. The shooter patted the downed figure, his left hand moving along the victim's torso. Then he stood and looked around the clearing. After turning a full circle, the shooter stepped away from the figure on the ground, descended the embankment to the clearing, and disappeared into the stand of trees in the direction of the village.

Seconds passed with no more movement in the clearing. The cries of the kenneled dogs subsided. The figure sprawled between the tracks groaned. The moan was deep and liquid. The dogs resumed their frantic howls.

Chuck worked his way to the edge of the trees, positioning the steel bumper between himself and the spot at the far side of the clearing where the shooter had disappeared. Chuck sprinted from the cover of the trees, across the grassy opening, and up the embankment. He knelt behind the bumper and peered between its horizontal beams.

The figure came into focus in Rachel's goggles. The man, his eyes closed, wore a ranger uniform. His badge shone bright green on his chest and his potbelly pressed at his shirt. Donald. The downed ranger was Donald Podalski.

Donald's legs twitched. He groaned again as the dogs howled from their pens. A stream of blood, black in the goggles' viewfinder against the eerie light green of Donald's face, ran from the corner of the ranger's mouth to his ear.

"Donald!" Chuck whispered. "It's Chuck."

Donald opened his eyes. He lifted a hand, reaching toward the bumper. Chuck rounded the steel beams and took Donald's upraised hand in both of his.

Donald's hand was cold and clammy. His breaths were labored. He turned his head to the side and gagged. A thick clot of blood fell from the side of his mouth to the gravel between the tracks.

Chuck tore off his daypack and settled it under Donald's head. He reached beneath Donald, feeling for wounds.

Donald looked up at Chuck. The ranger's body tensed and his eyes widened. Chuck shoved the infrared goggles up on his forehead. He no longer could make out the details of his friend's face, but he felt Donald relax in his probing hands.

"Chuck," Donald gasped.

"Don't try to talk."

"The girl," Donald said. Then, his words barely coherent, "Don. Have . . . to . . ."

Donald was referring to Carmelita. And himself. Somehow he had known Chuck was to make the exchange at the end of the railroad wye.

Donald reached up with one hand and took hold of the front of Chuck's shirt. He twisted the cloth in his fist with a firm grip.

"*Girl,*" Donald repeated forcefully. "Don. The music . . ." His voice faltered and his grasp loosened. He was slipping away, hearing things, some sort of song. His hand fell from Chuck's shirt and his body slumped to the railroad ties between the tracks.

Chuck tilted his head forward, cradling Donald's upper body in his arms. "We've got to get you—"

Three rapid shots rang out from the edge of the trees just as Chuck dipped his head to speak to Donald. The high-pitched whine of the small-caliber bullets filled Chuck's ears as the shots passed above the back of his neck, piercing the air where his head had been an instant earlier. One of the shots clanged off the steel bumper and ricocheted into the night.

Chuck threw himself sideways across the tracks. He reached over Donald's torso and yanked the ranger's heavy .45 from its holster. Sliding the night-vision goggles back down over his eyes, he released the pistol's safety, chambered a round, and squeezed off four quick shots into the trees in the general direction of the shooter. Donald's beefy gun kicked hard in Chuck's hand. The pistol roared and the flashes from its muzzle blinded him. He rolled away from Donald down the far side of the embankment to the grassy clearing as the shooter fired an errant shot in return.

Chuck stayed low and sprinted away from the end of the tracks, digging for the cover of the trees. He reached the grove and looked back around the trunk of a small ponderosa. Relying on his peripheral vision to scan the far side of the clearing for movement, he spotted at the edge of the goggles' viewfinder a bobbing green blur deep in the trees—the shooter, running away from the wye.

Chuck leveled Donald's gun and fired twice at the running figure, again blinding himself. He waited for his eyes to clear, then fired a third and fourth time with greater care, emptying the gun's eight-shot clip despite the fact that, with so many trees between Chuck and the retreating shooter, the shots stood virtually no chance of reaching their target.

Chuck blinked the muzzle flashes from his eyes and watched as the shooter disappeared into the depths of the grove. Chuck left the cover of the trees and hurried to the end of the railroad wye, the .45 hanging from his hand. He knelt at Donald's side, ready to grab the extra magazine from Donald's waist belt and give chase.

But that would mean leaving Donald behind. Chuck hesitated. The shooter was gone now. That was enough.

Chuck dialed 911 on Janelle's phone. He bent close over his friend after making the call and was relieved to find that Donald was still alive. Donald tried to speak, but his mouth moved only in silence.

The wail of approaching sirens reached the clearing seconds after Chuck completed the emergency call. He slipped his pack from beneath Donald's head, removed Rachel's goggles, and took Donald's spare magazine from its stiff leather pouch. He stuffed the goggles, magazine, and .45 into his daypack and flung the pack to the edge of the trees at the back of the clearing. He knelt again at Donald's side and held his friend in his arms, his hands growing wet and warm with Donald's blood, as the headlights of the oncoming park vehicles lit the clearing.

Chuck drew a sharp breath. Shots meant for him were taking Donald's life. And what of the shooter? Would he panic? Would Carmelita be his next victim?

Chuck fought to remain calm. He whispered reassurances in Donald's ear. The smell of creosote from the wooden ties beneath the tracks mingled in the night air with the musky odor of Donald's blood. The vehicles bounced down the tracks, an ambulance followed by a string of ranger patrol cars. Donald turned his head with great effort and looked up at Chuck, his body shivering in Chuck's arms. The headlights of the ambulance washed across Donald's ashen face. Donald's breath left him in a long, drawn-out sigh. His body slumped to the railroad ties.

Chuck checked Donald's neck for a pulse. Finding none, he bent over his friend's inert frame and began chest compressions. The ambulance slid to a stop twenty feet up the tracks, its headlights illuminating Donald with Chuck bent over him, compressing the ranger's chest. Two paramedics leapt from the vehicle as the sound of its siren died away. They hurried to Donald's side, gear boxes in hand, but even as Chuck made way for them he knew they were too late. Donald's face was tinted white now. His eyes were fixed and unseeing.

One of the paramedics placed a plastic mask over Donald's mouth and squeezed an attached air bag while the second took over for Chuck, pressing on Donald's chest. Chuck rose and stood on unsteady legs, looking down at the ranger's lifeless body.

Donald's death was Chuck's fault. Chuck had insisted on coming here alone. He'd told no one where he was headed, but his friend somehow had stumbled upon the site of the exchange.

Bile rose in Chuck's throat. His hands, wet with Donald's blood, hung at his sides. He stumbled down the gravel embankment and across the grass to the edge of the trees as the ranger sedans that had followed the ambulance from the village careened off the tracks and down the embankment into the clearing. The cars swung around one by one and came to a stop in the meadow with their headlights directed at the working paramedics.

Chuck bent double at the edge of the woods, retching. He wanted nothing more than to grab his pack and run. But he owed it to Donald to tell the rangers what he knew. He straightened and nudged his pack deeper into the forest with his toe, then followed after it. He glanced back to make sure he was out of sight among the trees before picking up the pack and heaving it as far into the woods as he could.

He reemerged into the open, wiping his mouth with one hand and clutching his stomach with the other. He entered the circle of light created by the parked patrol cars. Rachel was bending over the paramedics to check on Donald. She approached Chuck, her eyes wide. Chuck spoke softly. "We can't say anything about Carmelita. Not yet. Look what he did to Donald. He'll kill her, too."

"What happened?" Rachel asked, her voice shaking.

"He must've thought Donald was me."

"Donald," she said. She put a hand to her mouth. "You.

They were after you."

"I was trying to make the exchange. Donald stepped into the middle of it. He never had a chance."

Rangers gathered in front of their cars in the center of the clearing. Most wore street clothes, having responded from off duty. Among them was Hansen Conover, the ranger-in-training who had rescued Chuck in the canyon. Chuck stepped backward at the sight of Hansen and the rest of the rangers huddled together looking his way. But Rachel grabbed his arm.

"Someone just tried to kill you," she said. "You have to tell us everything you know. I'm with you on the girl, okay? But everything else."

"What 'everything else'? This is about getting Carmelita back. It's only about getting her back now."

Opposite Chuck and Rachel, Hansen bent his head to speak into the ear of a uniformed ranger.

Chuck thought of his pack, filled with incriminating evidence, less than a hundred feet away in the trees. What had made him think he could hide it, and the story of Carmelita's kidnapping as well?

Robert Begay's white Suburban bounced into the clearing and braked to a stop behind the ambulance. The chief ranger climbed out of his car.

"The phone calls," Rachel urged Chuck. "Where you went today. Tell Robert everything you know about what's going on. For Donald."

Robert left the Suburban with its door open and headlights shining and marched past the ambulance. He headed straight for Chuck, with barely a glance at Donald lying motionless between the two paramedics. Robert's steps were deliberate, his dark eyes menacing.

Chuck's heart hammered in his chest. How often was a national park ranger killed on duty? Essentially, never. Yet that's what had happened on Robert's watch. The National Park Service bosses in D.C. would want this incident off the front pages as quickly as possible. That meant naming an initial suspect, any suspect, to create closure in the public's mind.

And that suspect undoubtedly would be Chuck.

Robert could report that while, yes, one of his rangers had been shot and killed in Grand Canyon National Park, a suspect was in custody. The park would remain open and tourists would continue to visit. The park service would be subject to far less scrutiny than an open murder case would engender. No matter that the initial suspect wasn't the actual perpetrator of the crime; finding Donald's true killer could come later. Robert's first order of business would be to reassure the public on behalf of the park service, and that meant arresting Chuck right here, right now, at the scene of the shooting.

Chuck had Donald's blood all over him. Donald's gun, covered with Chuck's fingerprints, was stowed in Chuck's backpack a few feet away in the woods. A single sweep by Robert's rangers through the trees would divulge the pack with the gun inside, and the necklaces from Cope Butte as well. Chuck would be locked away for weeks, perhaps months, while he sought to prove his innocence. Janelle would be faced with trying to win Carmelita's release on her own. And Miguel would get what he wanted: Chuck away from Janelle. For her part, Janelle would see Chuck as a failure. She might well see him as a murderer, too.

Chuck took another step backward. Rachel clung to his arm. Robert picked up his pace. Chuck wrenched himself free of Rachel's grasp, darted across the clearing, and dove into the trees.

Friday

"Only the melancholy murmur of the wind ascended from the Grand Cañon of Arizona, that sepulchre of centuries. It seemed the requiem for a vanished world."

— John Stoddard
John L. Stoddard's Lectures, Vol. 10, 1898

Twenty-One

Midnight

Shouts rose in the clearing behind Chuck. The beams of the rangers' high-powered flashlights cut into the stand of trees, lighting the way ahead. Chuck scooped up his pack and sprinted deeper into the woods. The flashlight beams grew dimmer as the rangers, moving slowly through the grove to guard against ambush, fell behind.

Chuck exited the far side of the woods and slid to a stop on a thin strip of pavement at the rear of the dog kennel. Downward facing lights outlined the steel building's exterior. Between the strip of pavement and kennel, a dozen dogs in side-by-side pens lunged against a wire fence, their howls filling the night.

Chuck set off again at a run. He pulled Rachel's night-vision goggles from his pack, settled them over his eyes, and left the pavement where it turned toward the front of the building. Chuck disappeared into the forest that blanketed the broad plateau south of the village. He passed the wide trunks of towering ponderosas, holding to a southerly course. The cries of the dogs grew faint, then died away.

Breathing hard, Chuck slowed to a jog. He was a fugitive, alone and on the run. Every ranger and employee in the park would be on the lookout for him now, as would, by morning, every tourist at the South Rim.

He had to get out of the park and regroup. That meant continuing to the collection of chain motels, fast food restaurants, and parking lots that comprised the community of Tusayan immediately outside the park's South Entrance. He would work his way there on foot through the night, get his hands on a car, and ditch the area. Then he would call the 505 number. With the necklaces from Cope Butte in his possession, he would be in position to direct what would happen next. This time, the exchange would take place at a time and place of his choosing, not the kidnapper's, and in a manner that would ensure Carmelita's well being.

Miguel had to be ready for all this to end. He'd shot and killed Donald by mistake. Now the heat was on him in the village. No question he was loading Carmelita into his car this very minute, getting ready to leave the park. Logic said he would head for a large city, to blend in with the masses. Phoenix was nearest. Albuquerque a close second.

If Chuck kept moving through the night, he would reach Tusayan by daybreak, at which point he would check in with the kidnapper. Assuming Chuck managed to nab a car without wasting too much time, he could be in either Phoenix or Albuquerque by noon. His thoughts ran ahead of him. Where in either city could he safely pull off an exchange with Miguel?

He came to an abrupt halt.

Phoenix? Albuquerque? What was he thinking? No one was going to a big city. Not Chuck, and certainly not Miguel and Carmelita.

Grand Canyon Village would be in an uproar after Donald's shooting. No one would be able to make a move without raising suspicion. Moreover, both the south and east park exits would be secured by now, with every departing vehicle subject to search. Miguel wouldn't dare attempt to leave the park with Carmelita. The highway south of Tusayan, though outside the park boundary, was sure to be blockaded by now, rendering Chuck's plan impossible.

Chuck turned 180 degrees to face due north, his boots planted in the thick layer of pine needles covering the forest floor. The next chapter of this saga would not take place in Phoenix or Albuquerque. Miguel was trapped in the park, and Chuck was trapped here with him. Miguel had murdered Donald. He was holding Carmelita hostage. Chuck had to take the fight directly to him.

Chuck set off back through the trees toward the village. In his pocket, Janelle's phone continued its double-buzzes. He would check the latest in the stream of group texts soon enough, but he wanted to think things through on his own first.

A national park ranger had been murdered. The story would make headlines across the nation in a matter of hours. Donald's fellow rangers would not rest until they'd caught or gunned down a suspect, any suspect, in the killing—including Chuck, regardless of any defense Rachel might be mounting on his behalf. Having been posted on the Internet for much of the day, Carmelita's disappearance was destined to grow exponentially more public in the hours ahead as well. It wouldn't be long before someone linked Donald's murder with Carmelita's disappearance.

Tonight, it was easy enough to predict, most of Robert Begay's rangers would cruise the village and park roads while a core team developed a comprehensive strategy for moving forward at daylight. Robert's troops, along with an army of additional law-enforcement officers summoned from Flagstaff, Williams, the Navajo Nation, even Phoenix, would turn the park inside out, systematically searching every building and vehicle in the village and surrounding campgrounds and parking lots, and using bloodhounds to track Chuck's flight into the forest. The army of searchers would not stop until Chuck and Miguel and Carmelita were found.

Chuck had until daybreak, no longer, to track down Carmelita in advance of the rangers. He did not want to think of what Miguel might do to Carmelita if cornered by the authorities. Staying ahead of the rangers meant quickly arranging another exchange with Miguel, and this time making sure the handoff worked. By now, Miguel would have made his way from the railroad wye back to his hotel room in the village. He likely was lying low, possibly trying to reach Chuck.

As if on cue, Janelle's phone gave the single-buzz indication of an incoming phone call—but the call was from Clarence's number.

Before setting off for the Backcountry Information Center from camp, Chuck had insisted Janelle and Clarence not call him. Instead, he'd assured them, he would call them as soon as the exchange was complete and he and Carmelita were in the clear. But that had been before the shooting.

"Where are you? What's going on?" Clarence asked the instant Chuck answered.

"Let me talk to Jan," Chuck said.

"We need to know—"

"Jan," Chuck repeated. "I need to talk to her."

"Okay," Clarence grumbled.

"Chuck, is that you?" Janelle asked when she came on the line seconds later, her voice laced with fear.

Chuck's heart leapt into his throat at the sound of her voice. "Yes," he said.

"You're alive. You're okay." Her relief was palpable even as she tried to speak quietly. "Give me a minute. I'm walking away. It's a zoo here." A pause, then, a little louder, "They say there's been a shooting, that somebody's been killed. We heard the shots. They said it was an adult, not a child . . . but still . . . oh, Chuck."

"What about Carm? Anything?"

"You don't have her?" When Chuck didn't reply, she provided her own answer. "I knew it." Her voice gathered strength. "Everybody's checking in, but nobody's seen anything. They're all over the place. Rangers, too. They're everywhere."

"The rangers will be coming your way. It won't be long."

"They're already here, asking all sorts of questions. The shooting, I thought it was—" She stopped, then started again.

"I don't know what I should say to them. We have to tell them about Carm. It's time. But . . . you didn't call."

"I *couldn't* call."

"You were there?"

"It was Donald. He's dead, Jan."

"My God, Chuck. Donald? And you? You're all right?"

"I got away, but they think . . ."

"They think you did it," she finished for him. "They're being careful, what they're saying, the way they're asking, but I can tell. Where are you? We have to figure this out. We have to find Carm."

"Whoever's got her, I'm gonna kill him."

"I've been thinking about it. The voice. I'm sure of it now. It's not Miguel."

"You're right," Chuck agreed. He'd held that thought in the back of his mind since Janelle had first expressed doubt, back in camp, about the computerized voice.

The caller had known the correct pronunciation of Boucher, had been familiar with the network of inner-canyon trails, had pronounced BIC as a word, and had directed Chuck to the perfect ambush site at the edge of the village. All were things a small-time drug dealer from Albuquerque wasn't likely to know—though plenty of others would.

"We have to talk," Janelle said. "Now. Face to face. But you can't come here. They'll arrest you. They haven't said so, but I know they will. I can't think straight, Chuck. Carm. My baby." She began to cry.

"Okay, okay. It's gonna be all right," Chuck soothed. "I'll meet you south of the Backcountry Information Center," he continued, making a quick decision. "Back in the trees. It's quiet there, dark. But you'll have to get away from camp."

"They can't stop us, right?"

"Us?"

"Clarence and me. We're not under arrest or anything. *Mami* and *Papi* can look after Rosie."

"Fifteen minutes."

"Fifteen," Janelle repeated. "And Chuck?"

"Yes?"

"I love you."

Chuck swallowed, his knees weakening. "We'll get through this, Jan," he told her. "Carm's going to be okay. I swear to you, we'll find her."

He pocketed Janelle's phone and cut through the forest toward the information center, his thoughts turning to his mounting worries about Carmelita. It was closing in on twenty-four hours since she'd gone missing, a long time for a little girl. And, assuming she was being held by someone other than her father, someone who had ruthlessly gunned down Donald, there was no telling what might be happening to her now.

Twenty-Two

1 a.m.

As he headed toward the village, Chuck worked his way through the many possibilities for what lay ahead, growing increasingly perplexed.

The kidnapper knew the Grand Canyon well, and knew about Chuck's unreported find deep in the canyon, too. Who might that be? Any number of people. Even though Chuck had gone silent about his discovery around the time of the Bland of Brothers and Anasazi cannibalism controversies, most members of the Southwest archaeological community likely had heard something about it over the years. The question was, who might set enough store by what they'd heard to deem it worthy of kidnapping Carmelita?

He sifted through name after name until, taken aback by the outlandishness of his thought process, he stopped at one name in particular. What about Janelle? How well, he forced himself to consider, did he really know his newlywed wife?

The very idea was preposterous. But Chuck owed it to Carmelita to ask himself the question: could the beautiful young woman who'd just told Chuck she loved him possibly be taking him for a ride? Could she, in any remotely fathomable way, be responsible for Carmelita's disappearance and Donald's murder?

Janelle knew about Chuck's discovery, his "retirement fund" as he jokingly referred to it—though he'd never told anyone, not even Janelle, about the necklaces and disks. He'd wanted to keep them, the last pieces of the puzzle, to himself until he unveiled his discovery to the world. Other than that one omission, however, he had shared more details about his find with Janelle than with anyone else.

"It's worth a fortune," Chuck had told her. He'd explained

how explosive the discovery would be when he disclosed it publicly, and how working for Marvin Begay these last two years had convinced him the time had come to do so.

He'd told Clarence about his discovery, too, before Janelle had even entered the picture. Chuck shook his head in disbelief. Could Janelle and Clarence be in on this together? That could explain an awful lot. Chuck had told Clarence and Janelle plenty about the Grand Canyon, more than enough for the two of them to direct his movements, puppet-like, in the hours since Carmelita had gone missing. And as for the discovery on Cope Butte, though he hadn't told the two of them about the necklaces, he'd told them about the pots with their amazing exteriors, and hinted that there was much more to the find as well. Was it possible the two of them saw Chuck as nothing more than a meal ticket, a pathway to ill-gotten wealth?

Chuck thought of how easily Clarence had masked his knowledge of the discovery while describing Arturo Dinaveri's purported shrine to Janelle in front of Robert Begay at the campsite, and of how smoothly, in response, Janelle pretended Clarence's tale was the first she'd ever heard of any such rumored treasure.

It was Janelle who came up with the idea of visiting the Grand Canyon with Chuck and the girls. She and Clarence could have planned for Clarence's subsequent arrival at the canyon, after which Carmelita had gone missing. Clarence could have spiked Chuck's shot of tequila upon arriving at the campground. Janelle and Clarence could have taken Carmelita, planted the "NO COPS" note, and directed Chuck into the canyon and nearly to his death, with Janelle using her computer skills to disguise the caller's voice and set up Chuck's phone to supply its location.

Could Janelle and Clarence have been working with the man and woman from Albuquerque? The couple could have been charged with keeping an eye on Chuck when they had caught his attention with their juvenile antics on Maricopa Point. It would have been the woman, then, who called on Janelle's phone when Chuck arrived back at camp after surviving the retrieval of the necklaces from the alcove.

Janelle's involvement could explain why she'd suggested the quick City Hall wedding ceremony after Chuck proposed to her, and why she'd been so willing to leave Albuquerque, to take the girls away from their grandparents and the life they'd always known to move to Colorado.

If the gold-digger scenario had any grounding in reality, then Chuck had made for an easy mark, blinded by his love for Janelle, and blinded, too, by the trust he'd come to place in Clarence.

He remembered the night, more than a year ago, when he'd told Clarence about his find. They'd been overnighting along an isolated stretch of the transmission line right-of-way. It was after nightfall, a cold, late-spring evening, and they sat in front of a small campfire. Relaxed by the warmth of the flames, Chuck found himself regaling Clarence with the tale of his discovery and his plan to tell the world of its existence upon completing the transmission line contract.

"I owe it to Marvin, to the *Diné*," Chuck explained to Clarence. "All these allegations of the Anasazi as cannibals who ate each other for lunch and destroyed their culture in the process? One look at my find will put an end to every bit of that."

Chuck remembered his response when Clarence asked about the value of the discovery.

"Beyond priceless," Chuck said. "Don't think I haven't thought about it, because I have." He stared into the fire. "Never have to work another day in my life. But . . ."

"But what?" Clarence urged.

"But nothing, that's all," Chuck replied, prompting Clarence to shake his head and whistle.

Chuck had taken Clarence's whistle to be a gesture of admiration. But could Clarence simply have been stunned that Chuck wasn't planning to sell his find on the black market?

In a few minutes, Chuck was to meet Janelle and Clarence in the forest behind the BIC. The six necklaces in his pack would make the two of them rich, and they would enrich themselves immeasurably more when, upon circling outward from his phone in the canyon, they found the alcove and the remaining scores of necklaces.

Chuck walked blindly through the forest. Was Janelle keeping him off balance by declaring Miguel the prime suspect in Carmelita's disappearance, then saying the voice on the phone didn't sound like Miguel's? Her involvement in Carmelita's disappearance could explain why she'd announced the disappearance online, planning to use Carmelita's kidnapping to force Chuck to reveal the location of his discovery, then blame him for the kidnapping once he was dead. When Janelle turned up with Carmelita after alerting the entire online world to her daughter's disappearance, no one ever would suspect her of having engineered Carmelita's kidnapping in the first place.

But Donald had been shot and killed instead.

Chuck leaned his hand against the trunk of a ponderosa, his head hanging. No matter who had done the actual killing, it was he, Chuck, who was responsible for Donald's death. All his life Chuck had been a loner, and loners, by definition, were lonely. If Janelle and Clarence were playing him, then it was Clarence who, as a proven master at ingratiating himself with others, had alerted Janelle to Chuck's loneliness and attendant gullibility, after which the siblings had steered Chuck exactly where they wanted him to go.

Chuck raised his head. Even if Janelle and Clarence were innocent—as Chuck remained convinced no matter how far he spun things in his mind—he should not risk meeting up with them. Donald's killing had changed the game. It was best if Chuck stayed away from Janelle and Clarence, at least for now, and let things play out without him.

Everyone at the Grand Canyon was on the hunt. Sometime in the next few hours, rangers would discover the woman from Albuquerque holding Carmelita in one of the lodges on the South Rim. The woman, in turn, would finger the true culprit or culprits, and Chuck would be exonerated.

But what if someone else wound up being hurt or killed because Chuck stayed hidden?

Chuck owed it to Donald to do everything he could to shut things down before anyone else was harmed. It was time for him to do what he should have been doing all along: act rather than react.

He punched the 505 number into Janelle's phone. The computerized voice—it had to be the woman from Albuquerque—answered right away.

"I have what you want," Chuck said, "if you still want it."

"We do," came the disembodied reply.

"I'm willing to meet you again. But this time you have to show yourself first. And the girl."

There was a pause, then, "That will take some work, work, work. Sunup, sunup, sunup."

"What's that?"

"Sunup!" The strange repetitions resumed as the voice somehow went awry: "You're setting the terms, terms, terms; we'll let you know the place, place, place, place, place."

With that, the voice was gone.

The face of Janelle's phone glowed in the darkness. The caller had known to play for time—Chuck had until sunup, barely four hours from now, to make things right. He set his mouth in a straight line and punched a number he knew by heart into Janelle's phone.

Twenty-Three

2 a.m.

This was about Carmelita. At daybreak, she would be taken to a location that, as before, would not be disclosed to Chuck until the last minute. The plan would be to display Carmelita in order to lure him into the open and somehow take him out in the light of day.

But what if he could win Carmelita's release in the hours before daybreak?

"It's me," Chuck explained when Rachel picked up his call, "on Jan's phone."

Rachel's reply was tight-lipped. "If you've got something to say, Chuck, say it."

"Donald?" he asked.

"He's dead. You know that."

"They were still trying to bring him back when I . . ."

"When you ran away, like you have your entire life."

"I stopped running a few months ago."

"'She's really something.' Isn't that what you said?"

A vision of Janelle floated before Chuck. "There's a lot going on I don't understand," he said.

Rachel's voice was filled with equal parts anger and disgust. "Nothing new there."

"You know I didn't kill Donald."

"I know you were involved. I know you're off hiding somewhere while the rest of us are out here risking our lives looking for his killer. These are my people—your people, too—and you're putting them in harm's way."

"I didn't mean—"

"There's a murderer out there," Rachel pressed on. "You could be helping. All you had to do was stick around, talk to

Robert. We could have this all wrapped up by now."

"No," Chuck said quickly. Then, hard and determined, "No, Rachel. Robert would've fingered me as the killer. He'd have taken me in, shut down any search, and left the park exits open. They'd have gotten away. It's better like this, with the pressure still on."

"But you're the one we're looking for."

Chuck didn't dare let Rachel in on his over-the-top suppositions about who the real culprits might be. There was someone else he could turn her loose on, however.

"You remember the woman from Albuquerque, the one whose boyfriend fell from the cliff?"

Rachel's reply was guarded. "Yeah?"

"She's—" He stopped. How should he put it? "I don't think she ever left," he finished.

"You're saying Donald and that woman's boyfriend, their deaths are somehow related?"

"I think so."

"You *think* so?"

This was when he needed to let Rachel in on all the coincidences surrounding Janelle and Clarence. But he couldn't bring himself to do it, not when he didn't even believe them himself. "Just . . . she's still here."

"You have to come clean with me, Chuck."

"She's got Carm. She's holed up in the village somewhere. I'm sure of it."

"But she didn't kill Donald."

"No."

"And her boyfriend, who maybe could have done the killing, is dead."

"Yes."

Rachel exhaled vehemently. "Somehow this woman, who I have met and spoken with and personally know to be as dumb as a pile of bricks, you're saying you think she's the mastermind behind Donald's murder, her boyfriend's murder, and the girl's kidnapping? You're nuts, Chuck."

"She's not the mastermind."

"Then who is?"

"You just said I'm nuts."

"Try me."

He took a deep breath, then heard himself say, "My wife."

"*What?*"

"Janelle Ortega," he replied, forcing out the words. "My wife. I'm wondering if she might be part of it somehow."

Rachel guffawed. "You are nuts. You're stark raving mad."

Chuck let out the breath he'd been holding. He'd been right to confide in Rachel. Her response was reassuring beyond measure.

"Do you realize what you just told me?" Rachel continued. "That you think your wife might be a kidnapper and a murderer, this woman who is leading—*leading*—everyone in the village, and everyone online, too, I might add, in the search for her missing daughter."

"I know," Chuck said. "I didn't really—"

Rachel cut him off. "You were right when you told me you weren't the marrying kind. You never should have gotten hitched. It's driven you straight off the deep end."

It occurred to Chuck that he'd told Rachel about his find, too. That had been years ago and, true to her nature, she hadn't set much store by it. "You remember my discovery here at the canyon?" he reminded her.

"You're kidding me. *That's* what you think this is about? Let me get this straight. You told your wife about your hush-hush find, and you think she's trying to get her hands on it—" Rachel's tone went from dubious to incredulous "*—by kidnapping her own daughter?*"

"I'm sure I'm wrong. But Donald's dead. I'm just trying

to do something, anything, before the same thing happens to Carmelita."

"You *are* wrong, Chuck. I spent a lot of time with Jan today. She's innocent. I'd bet everything I have on it." There was a long pause, then Rachel asked warily, "What is it you want, anyway?"

"I need your help finding the woman from Albuquerque. You know her name. I don't."

"I'm supposed to be finding *you*—'no matter what it takes,' is how Robert put it."

"The woman is the key to everything. She's got Carm."

"You know that because . . .?"

"Trust me, Rachel."

"Trust you? The nutcase who suspects his wife of kidnapping her own daughter?"

"I don't think that, okay? I *didn't* think that. I was just working things through in my head, considering every angle. But the woman from Albuquerque, it's a process of elimination. She's a piece of this. She's gotta be."

Chuck could hear Rachel breathing over the phone. "Okay," she said. "For Donald." Then, her mind clearly made up, she said briskly, "Conrad's working tonight, lucky for you."

"Conrad?"

"Night auditor at El Tovar. You're not the only one who's moved on."

Chuck felt a slight tug deep inside himself. "You're thinking he could run her name for us? See if it shows up at one of the lodges?"

"I am. But I'm also thinking she can't be that stupid, can she?"

"I'm betting she grabbed a room with cash after she left the campground with Carmelita. He'd be able to check that, wouldn't he? How many people can there be paying cash to stay at the South Rim?"

"Okay. I'll head over, see what he can find out. I'll call as soon as I know anything." She broke the connection.

Chuck paced beneath the trees, fighting exhaustion. His ripped palm and raw chin throbbed, and his head pounded, an agonizing pain deep in his skull.

He pictured Janelle and Clarence moving through the woods south of the Backcountry Information Center, whispering his name and growing ever more anxious when he did not appear.

Rachel was right. They were innocent. And though he wanted with every ounce of his being to meet up with them, he knew he couldn't. Not yet. Still, it wasn't in him to simply wait in the forest for Rachel's call. He broke from the back-and-forth path he was tracing beneath the ponderosas and headed for the village. He angled west, keeping well clear of the information center, aiming to emerge from the trees at the rear of the Maswik Lodge complex.

Janelle's phone single-buzzed three times as he made his way through the forest. Each time, the phone displayed an incoming call from Clarence's number. Chuck let the calls go to voicemail. When he reached the edge of the trees behind Maswik, he punched in Janelle's voicemail ID, the numbers corresponding to the first four letters of Carmelita's name, and listened to all three messages. Each was from Janelle, and each was more frantic than the last. She asked where Chuck was, insisted he call her back, then, her voice breaking, begged him to call her the instant he was able.

The messages sounded legitimate—so legit, in fact, that it was all Chuck could do to keep from calling her that minute. But he wanted, needed, something to report to her first.

He put away the phone and stowed Rachel's night-vision goggles in his pack before making his way across the well-lit grounds of the Maswik complex. Two hundred yards east of here, Janelle and Clarence were working their way through the trees, looking to meet up with him. To the west, emergency lights flickered blue and red from the grove of trees surrounding the railroad wye.

Chuck left the front of the complex and approached Center Road, the village's main thoroughfare. The two lane road, running in front of Maswik Lodge and behind the string of hotels facing the canyon rim, was lined with parked vehicles. Though its driving lanes were bumper to bumper with passenger cars and RVs during daylight hours, Center Road was little traveled this time of night. He waited until the road was clear of traffic, then hurried across it and up a sloping rear driveway that led to the lower, service-level entrance of El Tovar Hotel. In his pocket, Janelle's phone continued its double-buzz announcements of incoming texts from the group of tourists. He wondered if any were reports of his having been sighted passing through the Maswik complex and crossing Center Road, but didn't take time to find out. His best response to any such sightings was to keep moving.

An empty ranger patrol car was parked at the rear of the hotel in the shadows of the service entrance loading dock. Chuck slipped past the car, climbed the stairs to the dock, and crossed the concrete landing to the service door with its small window of wired security glass. The gray metal door into the hotel's lower level was unlocked. He ducked inside and eased the door closed behind him.

A darkened hallway led into the bowels of the building. The deserted passageway smelled of bleach and detergent. He made his way down the corridor past a large unlit room lined with commercial-size washers and dryers. Beyond the laundry room, the hallway turned a corner. Chuck peeked around it. The corridor continued deeper into the building past a lighted open doorway. The murmur of voices came from the opening. Chuck crept down the hall and paused, listening, at the edge of the doorway.

" . . . agree with you," came the sound of a male voice Chuck did not recognize.

"Who else could it be?" came Rachel's voice in response.

Chuck stepped through the doorway into a windowless office. A balding, round-faced man wearing rimless glasses sat at a desk before a large monitor, his hand controlling a computer mouse. The man's forearms were thick and corded. His shoulders were broad and heavily muscled under his blue sport shirt. Rachel sat on a corner of the desk studying the monitor over the man's shoulder.

Chuck's sudden entrance startled Rachel and the man at the computer. They stared open-mouthed at him. Rachel's hand darted to the gun at her waist as the surprise in her eyes gave way to deep-seated sorrow; she'd known Donald since she'd started at the park a decade ago.

"Chuck, Conrad," Rachel said, dropping her hand and indicating each with a jut of her jaw. "Conrad, Chuck."

The auditor looked Chuck over before going back to studying the monitor in front of him.

"Looks like we found her," Rachel told Chuck.

"And?" He leaned forward, trying to catch a glimpse of the monitor. Janelle's phone continued its double-buzzes against his thigh, announcing group text after group text. Had he been spotted slipping inside El Tovar? Were members of the tourist group converging on the hotel's service entrance? Were rangers close behind?

"Francesca Calderon, that's her name. But, as you'd expect, there's nobody registered under it," Rachel said. "Plus, quite a few people are paying cash, fifty or so between all the South Rim hotels. That's the bad news. The good news is, they're pretty much all Europeans avoiding currency exchange fees."

"That's still fifty rooms," Chuck said.

Conrad explained, "I sorted and batched the cash-only

names and ran them as a subset. There are Heinrichs from Frankfort, de Fleurs from Paris—and one Francisco Contreras, supposedly from Santa Fe."

"You think?" Chuck asked the two of them.

"Registering under a guy's name?" Rachel said. "She might have tried that. But the Santa Fe thing? Who else could it be?"

"She's in Maswik," Conrad said. "Building One, Room 211."

"Bingo," Chuck said. Carmelita was little more than a hundred yards away.

"Just like you thought," Rachel told him.

"I'm already there." He pivoted to leave the auditor's office.

Rachel's hand returned to her gun. "You know I can't let you do that."

Chuck turned back into the doorway. "Go ahead, shoot. It's the only way you'll stop me." He left the room and hustled down the hall. A backward glance told him Rachel was jogging to catch up, with Conrad close behind her.

Chuck stopped at the end of the corridor to look out the window in the service entrance door, allowing Rachel and Conrad to catch up.

"I have to call this in, Chuck," said Rachel at his shoulder. "I have to."

"Go ahead. I'll still get there first."

Seeing no signs of movement in the shadowed loading-dock area, he opened the service door and stepped to the edge of the dock. Rachel muttered beneath her breath and followed. From the raised dock Chuck had a clear view up and down Center Road—and there, to the west, nearly a quarter mile away, was someone, no, two people, walking up the sidewalk alongside the road in the direction of the hotel. Rachel followed his gaze and held out a hand, bringing Conrad to a halt at the edge of the loading dock beside her.

The two pedestrians grew more distinct as they continued

up the sidewalk beneath the glow of the streetlights lining the road. One of the two was overweight. The other was much smaller and moved with a girlish gait.

Chuck's heart skipped a beat. It couldn't be, could it?

The two stopped at a white compact car parked at the near side of the road. The larger figure climbed behind the wheel while the smaller took the passenger seat.

Chuck leapt from the waist-high loading dock to the parking area below. Rachel hopped down with him.

"It has to be them," he told her breathlessly.

"You're sure?"

"A little girl like that? This late at night?"

"But she wasn't forced into the car."

"She knows to do as she's told. Hell, she may not even understand she's been kidnapped."

The car pulled a U-turn and headed east on Center Road, approaching the hotel.

"Come on, Rachel," Chuck said urgently as the compact passed below them, its interior hidden behind the sheen of the streetlights shining on its windows. "They're getting away."

He hurried to the passenger side of the patrol sedan and tried the door, but it was locked. Rachel moved to the driver's door, her eyes on the receding compact. Chuck laid his arms on top of the sedan, his wrists pressed together.

"Cuff me and throw me in back," he begged. "I'll be your prisoner."

Rachel ignored him and slid into the driver's seat. Chuck watched the taillights of the compact grow dim as the car headed east out of the village.

"Whatever you do, don't lose them," he commanded, stepping back from the patrol car as Rachel slammed her door. She gunned the car in reverse down the service drive and bounced backward into the road. She braked to a stop, turned hard, and accelerated in pursuit of the white compact, her emergency lights flashing.

Chuck studied Building One of Maswik Lodge on the far side of Center Road. "I could use your help," he told Conrad. Chuck led the way at a run down the sloping service drive and across the road to the front of the complex, the auditor's pounding steps following.

The sound of a siren rose from the east. Rachel had the compact in sight. More sirens sounded from the clearing at the end of the railroad wye to the west as rangers took up the chase. Chuck slowed as he approached Building One. A string of patrol cars, lights flashing and sirens screaming, sped by on Center Road. Conrad drew abreast of Chuck.

Like the other five Maswik buildings, Building One was two stories tall, forest green with a shake-shingle roof. The scuffed brown doors to its rooms opened onto a sidewalk on the first floor and an open-air balcony on the second. Chuck led the way across the strip of xeric landscaping surrounding the building to the foot of the nearest stairwell. He hurried up the stairs and along the second-floor balcony to Room 211. Wasting no time, he rapped on the door as Conrad caught up with him.

"*¿Quien es?*" came an inquiry from inside the room.

Chuck put his mouth to the edge of the closed door. "Clarence," he responded in a deep, Ortega-like voice.

The door to the room swung open and the woman from Albuquerque filled the doorway. Francesca Calderon's eyes widened. Before she could slam the door shut, Chuck put his shoulder to it and piled into the room.

Francesca fell backward to the nearest of the room's two double beds. She was barefooted and wore jeans and a black T-shirt. Chuck caught himself and straightened just inside the room. The sound of the receding sirens came through the doorway as the rangers raced eastward out of the village. Janelle's phone single-buzzed in Chuck's pocket, indicating an incoming call. He stepped aside and motioned Conrad to keep an eye on Francesca as he yanked out the phone.

"Janelle!" a woman's voice screeched into the phone the instant Chuck took the call. "They're chasing us! They're after us! What do we do? What do we do?"

It was Dolores. The sound of a lone siren came over the phone in the background.

Shocked, Chuck stood rooted in place, the phone pressed to his ear. The small pedestrian with the girlish gait had been Dolores making her way up the sidewalk in her tippy sandals, while the larger of the two had been Amelia. The generic white compact, Chuck realized, was Amelia's car. Janelle's friends had ignored his admonition that the members of the tourist group not drive to and from their assigned posts throughout the village, and now Rachel was pursuing them.

"Dolores, is that you?" Chuck said, speaking fast.

"Yes!" Dolores shrieked.

"Listen. It's me, Chuck. You've got to tell Amelia to slow down."

"They're after us! They're after us!"

"Slow down. Stop!" Chuck pleaded. "They won't do anything to you. They're rangers."

"Look out!" Dolores screamed.

In the motel room, Francesca sat up on the bed, ready to make a break for it. Before she could so much as stand, however, Conrad stepped to her side, spun her by the elbow, and planted her face down on the bed. He put a knee to the small of her back and twisted her forearm up between her shoulders.

"Jesus!" Francesca cried out, her voice muffled by the bed's flowered comforter. "You're breaking my arm."

"Snap it in two if you have to," Chuck told Conrad grimly.

The squeal of tires issued from the phone, followed by a second of silence. Then Dolores breathed, "Oh, my God. Oh, my God."

"Dolores," Chuck barked. "Are you all right?"

"That way!" Dolores screeched suddenly. "Amelia! Left, left, *left!*" Her voice was distant, as if she'd lowered her phone to her side.

"Dolores!" Chuck yelled. "Can you hear me?"

"Chuck?" Dolores asked, her voice full in his ear again.

"Where are you?"

"Some big building. A paved circle. We spun around, almost hit the car chasing us."

The paved circle had to be the shuttle bus turnaround in front of the South Rim Visitor Center at the east end of the village. And the car they'd almost hit was Rachel's.

Should Chuck try to reach Rachel and tell her to give up the pursuit? No. Making the call would take too much time. Nor was there any chance Rachel would answer her phone in the middle of the chase. His only hope was to stay on the line with Dolores and, through her, convince Amelia to pull over.

"Left. You said left. Which way are you headed?" he asked, trying to keep Dolores talking.

"Away somewhere. It's dark. No more lights."

Over the phone, Chuck heard the whine of the car's engine as it climbed through its gears, gaining speed.

"We gapped 'em," Dolores said, a hint of satisfaction in her voice. "Bought ourselves some time."

Chuck gulped. Precisely what Dolores and Amelia *didn't* have was time.

Before Rachel had caught up to them, Janelle's friends had been headed out of the village on Center Road, presumably on their way back to Mather Campground. When Rachel had come up behind them with her lights flashing and siren howling, Amelia must have gunned the compact past the turnoff to Mather and stuck with Center Road as it curved north to the visitor center. There she'd ended up at the shuttle bus turnaround in front of the center.

Amelia had spun a tight circle in the paved cul-de-sac and nearly struck Rachel's oncoming patrol car on her way out. The trailing patrol cars would have been approaching the visitor center along Center Road at about that time, prompting Dolores' cries for Amelia to turn "left, left, *left*" onto Desert View Drive from Center Road.

Desert View Drive followed the canyon rim east for thirty miles past a series of overlooks and trailheads to the park's East Entrance. Unlike dead end Rim Drive on the opposite side of the village, Desert View Drive was open to the public. For most of its length, Desert View Drive stayed well back from the canyon's edge. Half a mile from the visitor center, however, a shallow wash forced the road close to the edge of the canyon, then south at a hard ninety degrees to drop into the wash before climbing up and out the other side.

The low-walled drainage that forced the sharp turn in the road had been formed over millions of years by the intermittent waters of Pipe Creek, a seasonal stream that flowed north to the South Rim and plunged into the canyon and on down to the Colorado River whenever drenching thunderstorms swept across the Colorado Plateau. A thousand years ago, the Anasazi had dammed the wash at intervals to capture the infrequent rains of the high desert, creating a number of small reservoirs a mile or two upstream from where Pipe Creek poured off the canyon rim. The stored water had supported a handful of Anasazi families, whose abandoned, rock-walled homes still stood beneath the low overhanging cliffs that lined the wash. The Anasazi families were long gone from Pipe Creek, but tonight, this instant, Amelia was racing her compact through the darkness straight toward the ninety degree turn in the road where the wash fell away into the canyon.

"There's a curve!" Chuck yelled. "Dolores! It's just ahead of you. You've got to get Amelia to slow down!"

Dolores screamed in his ear. He clutched the phone as the screech of rending metal and the crackle of breaking glass choked out Dolores' shriek.

"Dolores! Amelia!" he shouted into the phone. But there was no response.

Twenty-Four

3 a.m.

Chuck crammed Janelle's phone into his pocket and slammed the motel-room door closed behind him.

First Donald. Now Amelia and Dolores.

He crossed the room to where Francesca was face down on the bed. He shoved Conrad aside and flipped Francesca over so she lay on her back looking up at him. Before he could say anything to her, Francesca kicked upward with both feet, trying to catch him in the groin. He jumped out of the way, then returned to her side and brought his boot down on one of her bare feet, pressing it into the room's beige carpeting.

Francesca sat up and scowled at Chuck. She cradled the arm Conrad had twisted behind her back. Her toenails were painted blood red to match her fingernails. Her hair was pulled back with a Harley-Davidson-orange bandana. The rouge on her jowly cheeks was uneven. Eyeliner trailed like tiny snakes from the corners of her eyes.

A single corner lamp lit the room. A pair of framed photographs of the Grand Canyon beneath a mantle of snow hung on the wall above the double beds. A bag of chips lay open on the side table between the two beds. A television droned on the bureau along the near wall. At the far end of the bureau, a liter bottle of soda rested on the edge of a detailed map of the inner canyon. The room smelled of stale food and unwashed clothes. No sign of Carmelita.

"Where's Carm? Where's the girl?" Chuck demanded, keeping his boot on top of Francesca's foot.

"I don't gotta tell you nothin'." She spat defiantly on the front of Chuck's shirt.

Chuck pressed harder on Francesca's foot. She'd been here at the canyon with her boyfriend at the start of all this. She was a party, somehow, to everything that had happened since.

Chuck lifted his boot and spun Francesca around so she again lay face down on the bed. Pressing her head into the mattress with a pinscher-like grip at the back of her neck, he removed his pack with his free hand and fished out the length of rope he'd taken from the alcove the afternoon before. He brought Francesca's hands together behind her back and wrapped the rope around her wrists. Moving fast, he trailed the rope to her ankles and tied them together as well. He pulled her knotted ankles toward her wrists and secured the rope, then swung his pack back over his shoulder and stepped away, allowing the trussed Francesca to slide slowly off the bed and land on the carpet with a resounding *whoomp*. She lay on her side, her belly spilled out before her, glaring sideways up at him.

"My daughter is missing," Chuck told her. "My *daughter*. And you know where she is."

"Your *daughter,*" Francesca imitated him. "For all of, what, a week?" She raised her head from the floor. "I don't know where she is."

"But you know where she's been. Which is right here in this room, with you."

Francesca looked away. "I don't know nothin'."

Chuck swung back a booted foot, feigning a blow to Francesca's midsection. Before he could find out if threatening a kick would elicit any information from her, Conrad took hold of his shoulders from behind and pulled him backward, then stepped around him and knelt beside Francesca. The auditor helped her to a slumped sitting position on the floor, her back to the bed and her roped legs off to one side.

"You'll only make matters worse for yourself if you keep lying," Conrad told her as he straightened and stepped back.

"Don't I get a lawyer or somethin'?" Francesca snarled, eyeing

Conrad from where she sat propped against the side of the bed.

"Your Miranda rights are waived during an active kidnapping," Conrad replied, his unruffled tone that of a television-show police detective. "You've heard of Megan's Law, haven't you? Your sentence will be doubled if it's found you didn't cooperate during the ongoing abduction of a child."

Francesca worked her thick brows. "I don't know what you're talking about."

"This is your one chance, Francesca." Conrad tapped the chest pocket of his sport shirt. "I'm recording every word of this interview. You know the sentencing guidelines for kidnapping? Ten years, minimum. Double that if you don't come clean right now."

Francesca's lips drew back. "I didn't do no kidnapping."

"That's good. Accessory to kidnapping is only probationary—" again Conrad tapped the chest pocket of his shirt, "*if* you're found to have been helpful from the start."

The auditor's shirt pocket appeared empty to Chuck. Even so, Francesca puffed her cheeks and said, "He came back and took her. Took my phone, too, the one we been using. Didn't say nothin' to me. He was in a big-ass hurry."

"Who was?" the auditor asked.

Francesca looked at Chuck, then back at Conrad. "He knows who," she said.

Chuck inclined his head, a short sharp movement. *Clarence.* Francesca had opened the door when Chuck had used his name.

"When did they leave?" Conrad asked, a note of urgency in his voice.

"Like half an hour ago."

"Where'd they go?"

"I told you. He didn't say."

Chuck broke in. "Did they go in the SUV? The one you had at the campground?"

Francesca's eyes flashed. "He made me drive it out of the park and leave it. Said it was too showy. Asshole."

"The girl, how is she?" Conrad asked.

"I kept her sleepy, like they wanted. She hardly knew what was going on."

Chuck glared at her. "Was she 'sleepy' when he took her? Did you drug her earlier tonight?"

Francesca glowered right back at him. "You're the reason my Ronnie's dead."

Chuck didn't hesitate. "It was you who pushed him. You were mad because he went down so easy to me. One lousy punch. But he was a jerk to you anyway, right? He beat you all the time, didn't he?"

Francesca's glower disappeared. Her breaths came fast and shallow.

"You were ready to be done with him, had been for a long time," Chuck continued. "You posed him for a picture out on the end of the point, got him up on the railing. It was so tempting, so easy. You gave him a little shove. Who would ever suspect?"

Francesca's eyes, darting from side to side, told Chuck all he needed to know.

"Francesca," Conrad said. He waited until she gave him her attention. "We have to know everything you know, and we have to know it now. Where do you think he took the girl?"

"He's crazy. He keeps getting crazier."

Chuck glanced at the map lying open on the bureau. "You were here when he directed me in the canyon?"

"We couldn't go out. None of us."

"He took the phone?"

"My phone," she complained.

"And the gun?"

"I could smell it. It'd just been fired. I knew to keep my mouth shut."

"But you let him take Carmelita." Chuck made no attempt to hide his disgust. "You let him take the girl."

"I told you. I didn't want to be next. He was, like, talking to himself. Don, he said. He kept talking about Don."

Donald. Chuck gritted his teeth. He'd heard enough. He backed to the door and pulled it open. "I'm out of here," he told Conrad. He pointed at Francesca. "Call 911. They'll take her off your hands."

He sprinted the length of the balcony to the back of the building, pounded down the rear stairs, and ran south through the Maswik complex and into the forest. He settled Rachel's infrared goggles over his eyes as he entered the trees. He slowed, weighed down by all that had happened—the car chase, the wreck, what he'd learned from Francesca Calderon.

Where should he go next? What should he do?

Francesca had opened the door to the motel room when Chuck announced "Clarence." Chuck drove his palm into his fist as he remembered what Francesca had said when Conrad had asked her about Carmelita. *"They,"* Francesca said. *"I kept her sleepy, like they wanted."*

And now "they" were set to use Carmelita as bait to direct Chuck to yet another out-of-the-way location at daybreak—in order to kill him.

He came to a stop deep enough in the forest to be surrounded by full darkness. It was time he checked in with the only "they" he'd come up with so far. He pushed the goggles up on his forehead and punched in Clarence's number on Janelle's phone.

"Where are you?" Clarence asked upon answering. "You didn't show," he sped on, his words tripping over one another. "And now all these sirens. Jesus, Chuck. Are you all right?"

"Do you still have Carm with you?" Chuck demanded.

"Carm? What are you talking about? Do you have her?"

"I was just at the room, Clarence."

"Room? What room?"

Clarence sounded baffled—and innocent.

"Let me talk to Jan," Chuck said, reconsidering.

"My God, Chuck. Where are you?" Janelle said as soon as she came on the line. She sounded truly worried, her voice high and tight.

Chuck bit his lip. Neither Clarence nor Janelle was putting up a front. The two of them weren't acting. They *sounded* genuinely concerned because they *were* genuinely concerned. They weren't kidnappers. They were the mother and uncle of a kidnapped little girl, afraid for her safety, and for Chuck's safety as well.

"We're back at camp," Janelle said when Chuck failed to speak. "We waited, but . . .where were you? The sirens. Do you think they've found Carm?"

"They're . . .they're . . ." Chuck ached to tell Janelle about Dolores and Amelia. But he couldn't. Not over the phone. And not now, not while he continued to wrestle with all the uncertainties ricocheting inside his head. "They still think it's me," he said. "They think I've got her."

"No." Janelle sobbed. "Chuck. No."

The phone beeped in Chuck's ear, signaling an incoming call. He glanced at the screen. The call was from the 505 number. This was it, his chance to prove Janelle and Clarence innocent beyond any doubt whatsoever. He put the phone back to his ear. "Is Clarence still there with you?"

"What?" Janelle sniffled. "Of course he is."

"Let me talk to him again. Quick. Please, Jan."

The phone beeped in his ear a second time; he only had a few more seconds.

"Chuck," Clarence said as he came on the line. "Christ, man, you're—"

Chuck stabbed Janelle's phone with his finger, taking the call.

"This is it," the computerized voice announced. A handful of unintelligible phrases followed. Then came a few words Chuck managed to make out: ". . . sunup . . . music festival site, site, site . . . alone . . . Don, Don, Don . . . have to, have to, have to." With that, the caller was gone.

Chuck lowered the phone.

The "he" Francesca had referred to in the motel room was not Clarence. The kidnapper, Donald's killer, was someone else.

Miguel. The name came to Chuck. Who else could it be? But Janelle had said the caller's voice wasn't Miguel's. Plus, there was Francesca's confounding reference to "they." And the fact that the kidnapper—or, now, kidnappers—knew so much about the canyon, and about Chuck's find, too.

Chuck mentally replayed the brief call from the computerized voice.

"Don," the caller had said, the same thing Donald had said as he lay dying in Chuck's arms. But why had Donald spoken his own name as he died? And why had the computerized voice just repeated it?

Suddenly the answer came to Chuck: Donald hadn't been saying his own name. He hadn't said "Don," he'd said "dawn," just as the caller had said seconds ago.

Chuck recalled Donald's last words: "The music . . ."

Donald hadn't been hearing things. He'd known what was going on before he'd been shot, and he'd died trying to tell Chuck what he knew.

The screen on Janelle's phone blinked off. In the pitch-black forest, Chuck rocked forward to the balls of his feet.

Dawn it would be, two hours from now, at the abandoned Grand Canyon Music Festival site two miles east of the village, on the very edge of the South Rim.

Twenty-Five

3 a.m.

Who would he face at the music festival site? Was Miguel the "he" Francesca Calderon had referred to? Did the "they" she'd referred to include someone who knew the park and canyon?

The easy way for Chuck to get the answers he sought was to ask Francesca. But he couldn't call her because she'd said "he" had taken her phone. Besides, Chuck was sure the opportunity to get the truth from her had passed; she'd be done answering questions at this point. And other than Francesca, there was no one he could turn to for the information he needed.

He pulled Rachel's goggles over his eyes and set off at a run through the forest in the direction of the music festival site. He stayed deep in the trees and cut a wide arc around Mather Campground, crossing park roads when no cars were in sight, then disappearing back into the forest. He pushed himself, his legs growing heavy, and thought through every suspect he could imagine as he ran.

Who might constitute Francesca's "they"?

His mind rewound two days to the visit to the South Rim Museum with Janelle and the girls.

The Marburys, Jonathan and Elise.

He stumbled, just catching himself.

Could they have kidnapped Carmelita? The Marburys were an eccentric couple, awkward conversationalists at the best of times, prone to nervous tics and stumbling over each other's words. But odd didn't necessarily mean evil. Did it?

In the museum, the park's two curators had been in quite a rush as they'd made their way through the grand entry hall, their heads bent together over the papers in Jonathan's hands. After nearly running Rosie down, Jonathan had joined Elise in closely eyeing Janelle and the girls. With a start, Chuck remembered Elise's last comment before she and Jonathan had headed deeper into the museum. "Work, work, work, work, work," she'd chirped.

Jonathan and Elise had been thrilled with Chuck's discovery of the burial shroud a decade ago. They'd been delighted by the olla basket from the connector-road dig two years before that, and by the double-ported urn from the latrine site dig two years ago. Chuck was their "magician," as Elise had confided to the girls.

Chuck never had told the Marburys about his find in the canyon, but they'd surely heard about it from others over the years. Had they somehow convinced themselves getting their hands on the discovery would provide a fitting capstone to their careers?

And there was more: in the museum, Jonathan had said he and Elise knew Chuck was visiting the canyon. How had they known he was here when he'd arrived at the park with Janelle and the girls only a few hours before?

The Marburys had entered the grand hall from the administrative wing. Perhaps they'd just left a meeting with Robert Begay, who at the time would have been freshly returned to the village from the scene of the fatal plunge of Francesca's boyfriend, Ronnie, off Maricopa Point. Had Robert told the Marburys he'd seen Chuck at the promontory?

Robert. The chief ranger had shown up without warning at the campsite after Carmelita had gone missing. And he'd been at Maricopa Point looking into Ronnie's death. Would the chief ranger of Grand Canyon National Park show up at the scene of each and every cliff fall at the canyon? The answer was yes, Chuck suspected, if the chief ranger was Robert Begay.

Robert was a known micromanager, as Chuck knew from personal experience. Two years ago, a few weeks after taking over the job as chief ranger, Robert had hiked all the way to Hermit Creek Backcountry Campground in the inner canyon to personally check on Chuck's contracted work at the proposed site for the campground's new latrine.

Though the odds of coming across anything of interest at the barren site were astronomically long, Chuck had done a thorough job. He'd surveyed, staked, and strung every inch of the open patch of ground where the latrine would be built. He'd worked each five-foot-by-five-foot quadrant in turn, digging to where the layer of soil atop the rocky shelf ended and solid rock began, as deep as eighteen inches in some places, as little as four inches in others.

At the end of each work day, Chuck had taken to exploring the ridges on each side of the creek. Though his contract did not require additional exploration beyond the confines of the latrine site itself, he was prompted to search the ridges on his own time because past archaeological surveys at Hermit Creek had turned up evidence of Anasazi presence in the form of potsherds, grinding stones, and hunting points along the creek bed, while more recent discoveries elsewhere across the Colorado Plateau indicated the Anasazi had made use of protected spaces beneath boulders and ledges as natural cupboards for storing urns and other clay items out of reach of rain. Three years prior to Chuck's work at the latrine site, in fact, a pair of youngsters visiting Durango, which was situated in a river valley once populated by the Anasazi, had come across a perfectly preserved Anasazi pot beneath a rock ledge two hundred yards up the mountainside from their motel room on the edge of town.

It was that find Chuck kept in mind as he zigzagged across the facing ridges above the latrine site during his evening hours, focusing on boulders and rock ledges large enough to provide shelter for stored Anasazi pottery until, just before dark one night, he crouched to look beneath a knee-high rock ledge and discovered the slender, double-ported Anasazi urn so similar to modern Navajo wedding vases. He photographed the urn *in situ* before packing it out of the canyon and turning it over to the Marburys at the South Rim Museum the next day.

A week later, Robert radioed Chuck, requesting permission to stop by the latrine site in a couple of days for a "brief show-and-tell," as he put it. Chuck spent the next forty-eight hours dreading the visit. New bosses invariably were out to prove themselves. What better way for the chief ranger to show his full-time employees at the canyon how tough he was than to make an example of a temporary contract worker by finding problem after problem with Chuck's work?

But Robert surprised him. The chief ranger arrived at the campground with just one other ranger, not the sizable entourage Chuck had expected. While the ranger visited with campers along the creek, Robert asked if Chuck would give him a tour of the dig site on its rocky shelf above the creek bed.

After a cursory look at the unremarkable site, Chuck led the way at Robert's request up the west-facing ridge to the spot where he'd found the double-ported urn a week earlier. He and Robert squatted side by side, studying the small cavity beneath the low rock ledge where an Anasazi Indian had tucked the urn a millennium ago.

"Did you think about keeping it?" Robert asked, straightening with Chuck and turning to look him in the eye.

"The pot?" Chuck replied in surprise.

Robert nodded.

"No. Never," Chuck said with a definitive shake of his head.

"It must have been tempting."

"What are you saying?" Chuck asked, treading carefully.

Robert shrugged. "You and I both know how much something like that is worth."

Chuck hadn't been sure how to respond. Yes, the idea of

stealing a artifact or two had occurred to him over the years. How could it not? Greed was an inescapable part of the human condition. Acting on such a thought, however, would have gone against everything he stood for as an archaeologist.

There was, of course, the fact that he'd kept the pots, necklaces, and disks in the alcove on Cope Butte secret all these years. But that was different. As he'd told Clarence, he never would profit from the Cope Butte find; he was just waiting for the right moment to tell the world about it.

As Chuck made his way through the forest toward the music festival site, a chill passed through him. He'd told Robert the truth: stealing wasn't for him. But was acting on such a temptation possible for the chief ranger of the park? It was Robert, after all, who had raised the subject with Chuck. Over the last two days, Robert had glared at Chuck on Maricopa Point, shown up unannounced at the campsite first thing the next morning, and come straight for Chuck at the railroad wye after Donald's shooting, with barely a glance at Donald lying on the tracks.

Robert's involvement in Carmelita's kidnapping certainly would explain the caller's knowledge of the canyon and its trails. It was conceivable that Donald had stumbled across what his boss was up to and had gone to the wye in an attempt to put a stop to it.

But why would Robert risk his long and successful park-service career to chase after a rumored Anasazi treasure? And why on earth would he pursue the treasure via the strange route of kidnapping a little girl? Was it possible he and the Marburys were involved in the kidnapping together? Was there something Chuck wasn't seeing? Something about Robert and the Marburys he didn't know?

Chuck grunted in frustration, his mind whirling, searching. Another name came to him: Hansen Conover.

The ranger-in-training had been positioned at Hermit's Rest

when Chuck had arrived there. Hansen had tracked Chuck's movements in and out of the canyon before coming to Chuck's aid when Chuck had collapsed on the Chalk Stairs. The young man had been on the scene of Donald's killing, too.

But why, if Hansen was involved in the kidnapping, had he called attention to himself by approaching Chuck at Hermit's Rest? Maybe the thrill of the risky game the young man was playing had made it impossible for him to resist accosting Chuck at the trailhead.

Had Hansen been among those at Maricopa Point working to retrieve the body of Ronnie, Francesca's boyfriend? Chuck couldn't recall the young man among those gathered on the promontory. But Robert Begay had been there. What if the chief ranger and Hansen were working together? What if the two of them, not the Marburys, were Francesca Calderon's "they"?

Bewildered, Chuck palmed sweat from his forehead and considered yet another name: Rachel.

He was sure the Rachel he'd known until the day of their last breakup two years ago was incapable of kidnapping a little girl and holding her for ransom. But two years was a long time. Had their final breakup sent Rachel over the edge? She'd transferred—albeit unsuccessfully—to Everglades National Park, indicating at least some level of dissatisfaction with her work, or her life, at the Grand Canyon. Could her discontent have anything to do with Chuck? Could she have kidnapped Carmelita to get back at him? He snorted at the thought. Was he really such a prize that breaking up with him could drive a woman crazy? Certainly not confident, self-assured Rachel.

Besides, if Rachel was involved, she never would have gotten hold of Conrad and disclosed Francesca's whereabouts to Chuck. Nor would she have hopped in her patrol car and given chase to Amelia and Dolores. No, Rachel wasn't a suspect. Which brought Chuck back to Miguel.

It was hard to imagine how Miguel could *not* be involved in Carmelita's kidnapping. The girls' father had kidnapped another little girl in the past, and he had at least three motives for kidnapping Carmelita: greed, getting back at Janelle, and going after Chuck. Janelle and Clarence agreed Miguel was smart. He'd successfully pulled off the abduction and return of his niece for ransom, and he'd dealt drugs all these years without getting caught.

What if Miguel had feared Janelle would recognize his voice through the phone-synthesizer app and so had coerced someone else, someone who knew the canyon well, into doing the talking for him? That certainly would account for Francesca's "they."

Chuck fixed his eyes on the black trunk of a massive ponderosa rising into the night sky. Of course Miguel was involved. After his failure to get his hands on the treasure at the railroad wye and his mistaken killing of Donald, Janelle's ex had to be ready to play the second proposed exchange straight, to hand over Carmelita to Chuck at the music festival site in return for Chuck's takings from the alcove before heading farther east, away from the village on Desert View Drive and out of the park. All of which meant it was critical for Chuck to get to the festival site and be ready to make the exchange when the sun came up.

But there was one thing he had to do first.

He'd avoided meeting Janelle and Clarence behind the Backcountry Information Center, after which he'd ended his phone call with them to take the incoming call from the computerized voice. He owed it to them to call back. Besides, they'd likely heard about the crash by now. Had Dolores and Amelia survived the accident?

Chuck stopped next to the large ponderosa, pushed the goggles up on his forehead, and dialed Clarence's number into Janelle's phone. One ring sounded. Two. Three. No answer. He began rehearsing the voicemail message he would leave when, on the fourth ring, Janelle's voice came on the line.

"What?" In a single word, Chuck heard it all: Janelle's frustrated, desperate love for her missing child, and the fact that, against all expectation, she was holding her well-deserved anger toward Chuck in check.

How, he asked himself, had he been so lucky as to find Janelle? And how could he even have conceived the idea of her involvement in Carmelita's kidnapping?

He would tell her the good news that the exchange was back on, that he would do whatever it took to return Carmelita safely to her. "Jan—" he began.

"Clarence wouldn't answer," she interrupted. "I had to grab the phone out of his hand. And you know why."

"No, Jan," Chuck said. "Please."

"Carm gets kidnapped, and what's the first thing you do? You send us off with your ranger friend while you disappear into the canyon. Then your friend gets killed, and I tell you I have to see you, I have to meet up with you so we can figure this thing out together, and you don't show up. Then, along about the time Clarence and I are going absolutely crazy with worry, you decide, oh, okay, I guess I'll check in—but then you hang up on us."

Chuck swallowed. "I—"

"Don't say a word, Chuck. Don't you dare say a word." Janelle began to cry, but through her tears, her words were clear and cutting. "The truth," she said. "Always the truth between us. Nothing but."

"Jan. Please."

"*Mami*, she had her concerns. But you won her over. *Papi*, too. And I was ready. I was so ready." She was crying hard now, speaking in bursts between gasping breaths. "The girls were ready, too. They needed you. I told myself you were the one. I willed myself to believe it."

"You are my one, Jan. Every time I've told you I love—"

"No," Janelle cut in sharply. "I don't want to hear that from you. I can't." Her voice shook. "The rangers, they . . . Clarence . . ." She fell silent.

"What, Jan? What?"

Clarence spoke in the background. "Here, Sis," he said. "Give me the phone." A second later Clarence's voice sounded in Chuck's ear. "Listen to me, Chuck."

"Clarence, I—"

"No. *You* listen to *me*. The rangers, they've been talking to us. They say you did it. We keep telling them no, no way, it isn't you, it can't be you. But you won't come back."

"Clarence—" Chuck tried again.

"You have to get back here," Clarence said, "to the campsite. You have to show yourself, prove to them it's not you. They're gunning for you, man. They're gonna kill you."

Chuck opened his mouth to speak, but no words came out.

"One more time, Chuck," Clarence said. "Come back here. Right now. We're waiting."

With that, the line went dead.

Twenty-Six

4 a.m.

Chuck turned a slow circle in the dark forest. He thought of how alone he'd felt when he'd run from Rachel and Robert at the railroad wye. That had been nothing. This—*this*—was what being alone felt like.

He was lucky Janelle and Clarence weren't buying the rangers' conclusion that he was involved in Carmelita's kidnapping. Not yet, anyway.

He lowered his head, staring at the forest floor. He had fallen for Janelle the instant he'd seen her in her parents' home. She'd said yes when, after a few whirlwind weeks, he had heard himself asking her to marry him. She'd left Albuquerque and moved with the girls to Durango unquestioningly, upending her life for him a scant three months after meeting him. A fresh start, she'd told him, that's what he offered her.

Look what her fresh start had turned into.

Chuck bent forward, his hands on his knees. The rangers were focused only on his apprehension. They weren't looking for Carmelita's real kidnappers. Which meant whatever happened next was up to him.

He straightened up beside the ponderosa. He understood why the park rangers saw him as their sole suspect. But he knew who he was and who he wasn't. He would win Carmelita's release and, in so doing, prove his innocence.

Only he knew the time and place of the second proposed exchange. He still had the necklaces stowed in the bottom of his pack. He would keep the rendezvous at dawn at the Grand Canyon Music Festival site. He would do whatever it took to secure Carmelita's freedom, including trading his own life for hers if necessary.

He checked the time. After four. Little more than an hour and a half until dawn. He would trade the necklaces for Carmelita when the sun came up, and he would do so on his own, as the caller had directed.

Chuck centered the goggles over his eyes and set off through the trees. The shallow wash formed by Pipe Creek was half a mile ahead, midway between the village and the festival site. The sounds of the car accident—Dolores' scream, the rending metal and breaking glass—reverberated in his head. He took another look at his watch, calculating. There was enough time.

He looped south and east through the forest, running until lack of oxygen overtook him, walking until he regained his breath, then running again. He refused to accept how tired he was, how much his head and body hurt. The forest floor, carpeted in ponderosa needles, was spongy beneath his boots. Tree trunks swam past his field of vision.

After a few minutes, he emerged from the forest at the rocky edge of the Pipe Creek drainage. The vanilla scent of the ponderosas on both sides of the drainage rode the early-morning breeze. The slightest hint of gray shone in the eastern sky, just above the serrated outline of trees on the far side of the low wash.

He found a break in the cliff along the top of the wash, made his way to the gravel bottom of the dry twisting creek bed, and headed downstream toward the canyon rim. Within a hundred yards, he came to a house-sized chock stone in the middle of the creek bed surrounded by several truck-sized boulders resting against one another. The accumulation of rocks blocked the way ahead, forcing him up a series of waist-high sandstone ledges to bypass the obstruction. As he rounded the topmost of the boulders, he came upon one of the long-abandoned Anasazi homes along Pipe Creek. The tiny structure was built beneath a low overhanging cliff. Its stone-and-mortar front wall remained in place under the rock face, fronted by a flat sandstone shelf. In the center of the wall was the black rectangular opening that had served as the one-room home's only entrance.

Though Chuck had never been contracted by the park service to catalog the Anasazi structures along the wash, he'd spent plenty of time in his off hours exploring them. Other than the surviving walls of the structures, there hadn't been much to see. Any items left behind by the Anasazi had been carted off more than a century ago by prospectors and other early visitors to the canyon.

Despite the lack of artifacts, however, the aura of the long-disappeared Anasazi clung to the crumbling walls of the abandoned homes. During his explorations, Chuck had come upon evidence, in the form of ancient meadows where trees had yet to fully reestablish themselves, indicating that the Anasazi families of Pipe Creek had hauled water from their reservoirs to irrigate crops on the flats above the wash, a task as labor-intensive as any Chuck could imagine. Perhaps it was no surprise, then, that the handful of families who had worked so hard to make Pipe Creek their home hadn't lasted long here. The small number of homes along the wash and the lack of any ceremonial kivas indicated that the band of Anasazi at Pipe Creek had inhabited the site for no more than a few decades. They'd likely been driven away by the same lengthy drought in the early1200s that Southwest archaeologists believed had pushed the Anasazi out of their cliff-wall communities all across the Colorado Plateau to settle far to the southeast in the broad Rio Grande valley with its year-round water.

Chuck had a sudden vision of two toddler-aged Anasazi children giggling as they played together on the shelf of sandstone in front of the doorway of the abandoned home. He gave his head a stiff shake, but the memory of the toddlers lingered as he made his way back to the drainage bottom and on downstream.

What must the day have been like when the Anasazi families of Pipe Creek had abandoned their world on the lip of the Grand Canyon? How heartbroken they must have been when the drought that parched the Colorado Plateau forced them to give up all they'd worked for—their homes and reservoirs, the fields they'd cleared and cultivated, everything they and their children had ever known. And how unlikely it must have been that any youngsters had survived the long and arduous trek from the high plateau to the lowlands of the Rio Grande.

As he jogged down the dry creek bed, Chuck felt the sorrow of the ancient families as if it was his own. This was what it meant to be a husband and father, to be a part of something more than just himself. His life now was inextricably intertwined with the lives of others, with Janelle and Carmelita and Rosie, and with Clarence and Enrique and Yolanda.

As he made his way down the wash, he came upon the remains of the dams the Anasazi had built, stone by stone, across the floor of the drainage. Centuries after their construction, the low rock barriers trapped broad expanses of silt that supported the growth of tall grasses and thick shrubs. Emergency lights flickered off the sides of the drainage as Chuck made his way through the high grass and bushes upstream of the third such dam he came upon. He topped out on the ancient water barrier and stopped, dreading what lay ahead even as he remained determined to bear witness to the accident on his way to the festival site.

He descended the face of the dam. The lights flashing on the walls of the drainage grew brighter and the sound of radio voices crackled in the night air. He rounded a final bend and stopped a hundred yards upstream from where, following big rains, the waters of Pipe Creek poured off the South Rim into the depths of the canyon. He had a full view of the accident scene before him, and from where he stood deep in the shadows, no one could see him if they looked his way.

Desert View Drive angled toward him into the shallow wash. The two-lane road, empty of cars, turned and crossed a small bridge over the dry creek bed fifty yards in front of him. The road climbed back up and out of the wash and disappeared in the direction of the music festival site to the east.

As Chuck had feared, the accident had occurred where the road turned hard away from the canyon rim to begin its descent into the wash—though his first glimpse of the wreck filled him with sudden hope. Amelia's car indeed had missed the curve and crashed through the guardrail. But the car had not plummeted off the South Rim into the canyon. It had sailed down the steep embankment from the road into the shallow Pipe Creek drainage. There it had come to rest, its nose buried in the rocky creek bed and its windshield broken out, a few feet from where the wash plunged off the cliff that marked the canyon rim.

A pair of spotlights beamed from poles extending from the rear corners of a fire-rescue truck backed to the guardrail fifty feet above the wrecked car. The bright lights prompted Chuck to remove Rachel's goggles. The front end of Amelia's compact was crushed where it had smashed into the scoured-sandstone bed of the creek, but the car itself was upright and largely intact. Beside the car, lit as if on stage, stood Dolores. She appeared uninjured. She wore a dark-colored jacket, her arms wrapped around her narrow waist to ward off the nighttime chill. She was deep in conversation with a park ranger.

Chuck spotted Amelia, her arm in a sling. She wore slacks in place of the white denim shorts she'd worn at camp. She stood at the foot of the embankment below the road, between her wrecked car and the spot where the compact had crashed through the guardrail. Despite the sling, Chuck could see that she, like Dolores, had suffered no serious injuries. He breathed a long sigh of relief.

A second ranger stood at Amelia's side, notebook in hand.

Amelia spoke into a phone, her head bobbing in cadence with her speech. Surely she was talking to Janelle. In Amelia's mind, Chuck nearly had succeeded in his attempt to kill her and Dolores by sending rangers in pursuit of them. Janelle's two best friends had been suspicious of Chuck before Carmelita's kidnapping. Now, like Robert Begay's ranger corps, they would be out for his blood.

A flatbed wrecker, its emergency lights flashing, was backed to the narrow hole in the guardrail where Amelia's car had plunged off the road. A mechanic in overalls edged his way down the slope from the wrecker, winch cable in hand. The cable unwound from a spool in the bed of the truck with a loud whine. Amelia looked on, immersed in her phone conversation, as the man backed past her toward her battered car.

But where was Rachel?

Several rangers, three in uniform and the rest in street clothes, looked down on the scene from along the guardrail. Two spoke into handheld radios. One appeared to be Hansen Conover. The rangers' patrol cars were parked haphazardly at the side of the road behind them. There was no sign of Robert Begay's Suburban.

Finally, Chuck spotted Rachel. She stood off by herself on the far side of the wrecked car, at the very edge of the precipice where the wash fell away into the canyon. Her back was to the accident scene, her shoulders bowed. She rocked back and forth in obvious distress. Rachel had disobeyed basic law-enforcement guidelines in continuing to give chase to Amelia and Dolores, innocent as they'd turned out to be, after they'd refused to pull over upon her first catching up to them on Center Road. Chuck had demanded that she do whatever it took to stop the escaping car. If fault for the accident lay with anyone, it lay with him.

Chuck had held it together through everything since Carmelita's disappearance—his ill-fated trip into the canyon, Donald's killing, the confrontation with Francesca—but this was too much. His legs gave out and he sank to the ground. Seated in the sand, he pulled Janelle's phone from his pocket and dialed Rachel's number. She flinched at the first ring and stood unmoving through the second. Not until the third ring did she slide her phone from her belt case and look at it. She brought it slowly to her ear. "Chuck," she said, her voice weary.

"Rachel."

"What was I thinking?"

"I'm the one who sent you after them." He spoke quietly to ensure his voice didn't carry to the accident scene. "I was wrong. About Janelle, too. I was wrong about everything." The void he felt inside himself was as gaping as the canyon.

Rachel straightened in response to Chuck's words of reassurance. "These women, they're already threatening to get lawyered up," she said indignantly, her tone that of the adventure-racing ranger Chuck knew so well.

His reply was impulsive: "Turn around." If he could have reached out and taken her in his arms that instant, he'd have done so. "Look up the creek."

She turned away from the canyon. "It's dark," she said. She was looking straight at him over the roof of the wrecked car. From this distance, in the glare of the spotlights, her face was a splash of white against the blackness of the canyon.

"I'm here," Chuck said, "with you. You're looking right at me."

Rachel did not reply. She set off in his direction, stepping around the smashed car and past Dolores and the ranger.

Chuck scrambled to his feet. "Rachel," he warned her.

The rangers along the guardrail watched with rapt attention as she walked away from the accident scene. No one made a move to intercept her.

Chuck took an involuntary step backward when Rachel reached the point where Desert View Drive turned at the bottom of the drainage and crossed the creek bed. She climbed up to the raised roadway, strode across the blacktop, and dropped back down to the wash on the other side. She left the glare of the spotlights behind and faded into the night, disappearing from the view of her fellow rangers.

A long second passed. The rangers peered up the wash into inky blackness. Then, one by one, they turned back to the scene of the accident, where the wrecker operator now lay on his back at the rear of Amelia's compact, attaching the winch cable to the car's undercarriage.

Rachel advanced through the enveloping darkness. She made her way up a low rise and wound through a clump of sagebrush until she drew abreast of Chuck.

"Over here," Chuck whispered, his nerves jangling. He cast a frightened glance at the rangers, who, thankfully, remained where they stood.

Rachel angled toward the sound of his voice, stopping only when she was so close to him he could feel the warmth of her breath on his face. She stood with her back to the brightly lit accident scene, silhouetted in front of him, her face an invisible mask.

He shrank from her when she raised her arm. But, as she'd done hundreds of times over the years they'd been together, she merely cupped the back of his neck in the palm of her hand. Her touch was just as he remembered it, both firm and pliant, as if in the simple act of reaching out to him she was both asserting herself and offering herself to him.

She drew his face to hers and kissed him.

Twenty-Seven

4:30 a.m.

Even as Chuck told himself to pull away, he gave himself up to the kiss, and to Rachel. He wrapped his arms around her and pulled her to him, the heat of her lips on his a miniature sun at his center.

Rachel's kiss was searching, questioning. Authoritative, too, as if she was laying down a marker with it, communicating something to him.

As quickly as she'd brought her mouth to his, Rachel drew back. But she kept her hand at the back of his neck, her face inches from him. "Chuck," she said softly. She looked down, then up at him again, the movement of her head barely discernible in the dark. She swept her fingers up his neck and caressed the side of his head. "Hmm," she murmured, a single falling note, a goodbye—to him, to all they'd shared as a couple.

He considered various answers, came up with nothing, and settled on the truth. "I'm scared."

She dropped her hand. "You should be," she replied.

Just like that, Chuck was back, rooted in the present, and rooted in the realization that Rachel was right, that it was okay for him to be frightened, that he *should* be frightened. On the heels of that realization came awareness—he loved Janelle and the girls, and if he couldn't spend his life with them, his life wouldn't be worth living.

And finally, he realized, dawn was coming far too quickly.

Unsure how much Rachel could see of his eyes in the light filtering from the accident scene, he looked away. He remembered how easily he'd found himself telling Rachel his ridiculous idea of Janelle's possible involvement in Carmelita's kidnapping. If he kept talking with Rachel now, it wouldn't be long before he'd find himself telling her about his plan to make the exchange at the festival site alone, even after Donald's killing.

"What is it?" Rachel asked, her eyes seeking his.

"Clock's ticking," he replied simply.

He looked past her at the accident scene and was startled to find that the ranger who'd been standing at Amelia's side was headed up the drainage in Rachel's wake, approaching the point where Desert View Drive cut across the wash. The ranger put a hand to his eyes below the brim of his hat, shielding the bright lights behind him and looking ahead.

Chuck pointed at the oncoming ranger. "They're worried about you."

She glanced over her shoulder, then back. "So what."

He took Rachel's hand, the one that had brought his lips to hers, and held it as he studied her silhouette. "I have to go."

Rachel leaned toward him and spoke into his ear. "Find her, Chuck," she said.

"I will," he told her. "For you. And for my wife."

"For the two of us." Rachel stepped back, and Chuck felt the warmth of her smile in the darkness.

He let go of Rachel's hand and headed back up the creek bed at a ground-eating lope, guided once again by the night-vision goggles. The cool breeze poured past him, an invisible fog that filled him with foreboding.

He continued a few hundred yards up the wash before climbing from the drainage and running eastward through the forest, Janelle's voice playing over and over again in his mind. "*I told myself you were the one*," she'd said. "*I willed myself to believe it*." Rather than appreciate his new family, Chuck had taken to running from them each and every morning. He'd made the leap all too easily to paranoia, to wondering if his wife could be involved in her own daughter's disappearance. He flushed with shame. What kind of person was he?

He was on a path leading straight to where his father had ended up—alone and forgotten.

He looked through the trees to the eastern sky, brightening with the coming day. He was not his father. Janelle and the girls were not a burden, not something to be discarded the way his father had discarded him. Janelle and the girls *were* Chuck's life. For their lives to continue together, he had to win Carmelita's freedom, had to focus on the here and now—including figuring out how, in light of the accident, Miguel would manage to get past Pipe Creek to reach the music festival site, particularly with Carmelita in tow. One possibility was Hansen Conover. If Hansen was working with Miguel, the junior ranger could get Carmelita's father past the wreck on Desert View Drive. Or perhaps Miguel was already waiting with Carmelita at the festival site. Or he'd hidden Carmelita somewhere else and would expect Chuck to hand over the necklaces in return for disclosing her whereabouts.

Chuck kept his eyes on the forest floor directly ahead of him and worked to keep his speed up, concentrating on getting to the festival site as quickly as possible to size things up before daylight arrived. He maintained his pace through the forest until, as best he could determine, he was roughly even with the site. He turned north, toward the canyon. The ponderosa forest gave way to scattered piñons and junipers as he neared the canyon rim. The scrubby trees, bent and twisted by the nearly constant winds that blew up and out of the canyon, rose no more than thirty feet above the broad swath of yucca and sage that marked the canyon's edge.

He reached Desert View Drive and found he'd judged well; he was a hundred yards beyond the turnoff from the road to the festival site. He crossed the empty roadway and crept from tree to tree toward the edge-of-the-canyon drop-off a quarter mile away.

The eastern sky glowed bluish gray. A handful of stars

shone overhead. Chuck left the goggles behind on the ground, unwilling to risk the slight sound of unzipping his pack to stow them inside.

He stifled his breathing and stuck to patches of sand and smooth expanses of rock until, fifty yards ahead, rising at the lip of the canyon, the roof structure over the festival performance stage emerged above the tops of the low trees. The dying night sky framed the metal roof, held aloft by thick, peeled-log posts.

Chuck made his way to the eight-foot, chain-link fence that enclosed the site on three sides, all the way to the canyon rim. Beneath the prowed roof, the open rear of the performance stage was separated from the canyon only by a waist-high metal railing. Several hundred blue fiberglass seats, bolted to concrete risers, half encircled the stage to create an intimate amphitheater providing views of performances and, through the unwalled back of the stage, the abyss of the canyon beyond. A pair of flat-roofed, single-story storage buildings sat close beside one another behind the seating area, separating the amphitheater from a large gravel parking lot.

The festival site was a perfect example of federal money sloshing around until it found a home. A decade ago, a loose consortium of musical groups out of Flagstaff had convinced local politicians and park service officials in D.C. that the national park, always struggling for funds, could earn some extra cash by hosting a local music festival each year to attract visitors to the canyon from among the park's local populace. The feel-good idea had gained ground quickly, prompting the musicians and park officials to team up and select the rim-hugging site east of the village for the proposed festival amphitheater.

Upon the public announcement of the site's selection, the tribal elder serving as president of the Navajo tribe declared the site sacred. Developing the site, he said, would amount to sacrilege. Chuck recalled that Jonathan and Elise Marbury had supported the tribal president, whose contention threatened the entire music fest proposal until someone in D.C. suggested offering the Navajo tribe's wholly owned construction company, Diné Constructors, a no-bid contract to build the amphitheater at the site. The tribal president's concerns about the site's sacredness faded away with the signing of the lucrative contract, and a hurriedly approved federal grant funded the facility's construction by the tribe.

The musicians who had pushed for the festival's creation played the new amphitheater for a few years, posting impressive videos of their cliff-side performances online, before losing interest in making the lengthy drive from Flagstaff to play before what turned out to be minuscule festival audiences. After the initial acts moved on, the festival's executive director struggled to find new acts to fill the bill because the federal grant that had paid for the amphitheater's construction stipulated that only local acts could play it. The festival continued for a couple more years as the tiny crowds dwindled further. The festival took a "one-year hiatus" that had stretched on for four, leaving the site abandoned and bleaching beneath the high-desert sun.

Chuck peered through the fence into the amphitheater. In the murky gray of pre-dawn, he spotted no movement on the stage or in the seating area. No light came from the windows set in the concrete block walls of the twin storage buildings at the rear of the amphitheater. The site's gravel parking lot was empty. The only sound was that of the strengthening morning breeze coursing through the branches of the piñons and junipers outside the perimeter fence.

Three outward-leaning strands of barbed wire atop the fence made clambering up and over the chain-link barrier impossible. The site's entrance gate, also eight feet high and topped by barbed wire, was closed by a length of looped and locked chain where the entry drive reached the gravel lot.

Chuck's goal was to be hidden and waiting somewhere inside the festival site before the kidnapper or kidnappers showed up. He followed the perimeter fence to the edge of the cliff at the east end of the festival site, hoping to swing around the far side of the fence and into the site where the fence met the lip of the canyon. Rather than come to an end at the top of the cliff, however, the perimeter fence made a 180-degree turn out and over the precipice, topped by three tilted strands of barbed wire, to end bolted into the rock face eight feet below the top of the cliff.

The cliff itself extended without a break from the east perimeter fence past the rear of the open performance stage to the west perimeter fence, which also was bolted out and over the edge of the cliff fifty yards away. The waist-high railing at the back of the stage followed the top of the cliff both directions until it connected up with the two ends of the perimeter fence. A sandy shelf, dotted with boulders and brush, extended from the base of the uppermost, hundred-foot cliff horizontally for thirty feet before a second cliff plunged deeper into the shadow-filled canyon.

Chuck could attempt to enter the site by climbing down one side of the inverted fence and up the other, using the cliff face for traction to overcome the tilted strands of barbed wire, but doing so would require him to negotiate the strands of wire while hanging a hundred feet off the ground. Before he could decide if he was capable of such a maneuver, he heard a car approaching along Desert View Drive from the direction of the village. The vehicle slowed, turned onto the gravel road leading to the festival site, and headed his way.

His decision made for him, he clambered down the links of the overhanging fence as fast as he dared. He dropped his feet below the base of the inverted fence and lowered himself until he dangled from its bottom, his hands positioned between barbs on the lowest strand of wire. He pivoted his body and reached blindly upward with his left hand to begin his climb up the inside of the fence, scrabbling with his feet on the cliff wall. His hand closed over a barb on one of the strands of wire, reopening the wound on his palm. Stifling a cry of pain, he repositioned his left hand and hauled himself upward, grabbing the chain-link fence above the strands of barbed wire with his right hand. He pulled himself hand over hand up the inside of the fence, his injured palm throbbing, until his feet regained their purchase on the bottom of the inverted section of fence.

He clung to the fence, struggling for breath, and edged his head above the top of the cliff in time to catch sight of the oncoming car as it raced up the entrance road toward the festival site. The vehicle, visible in the growing daylight behind the beams of its headlights, was Robert Begay's hulking white Suburban.

Twenty-Eight

5:30 a.m.

The headlights of Robert's car swept across the parking lot. Chuck ducked his head below the top of the cliff, holding on to the inverted fence, his heart pounding. He waited for the Suburban to come to a stop at the entrance to the site and for Robert to climb out and unlock the gate. Instead, the already speeding vehicle accelerated further. Gravel spewed and a solid crunch echoed across the festival site as the Suburban smashed through the chained entrance.

Chuck poked his head up in time to see the Suburban tear across the gravel lot with the gate, ripped free of its moorings, draped across the car's hood. The instant Robert's car disappeared behind the storage buildings at the rear of the amphitheater, Chuck scrambled up and over the top of the cliff. He ducked between the bars of the waist-high railing at the edge of the precipice and sprinted around the amphitheater, his daypack slapping his back. The Suburban skidded to a stop out of sight on the far side of the buildings, sending the gate clanging to the ground. Chuck flattened himself face first against the wall of the nearest of the two concrete block buildings and listened, trembling, as a pair of car doors opened, then slammed shut.

He tilted his head to peek through a window in the side of the building as snippets of conversation reached him over the sound of the car's still-idling engine. He leaned his head farther, aligning his view through the window with another window set in the rear wall of the storage building to allow a distorted view of the parking lot. Peering through the two windows, he saw a man standing in front of the Suburban, his back to Chuck.

Chuck caught most of the words as the man said with a Latino accent, "I won't do nothing of the sort, *cabron* . . . do as you're told . . . give her back . . . you and me both know . . ."

A second man, facing Chuck, spoke: "You, you, you . . . you're the one who . . ."

Chuck gasped. The man was Marvin, not Robert, Begay.

Stunned, Chuck gripped the lower frame of the window for support. He watched as the young tribal official raised a pistol and aimed it at the Latino man. Even in the half-light of dawn, Chuck saw that Marvin's eyes displayed callous indifference.

The Latino man spoke with more force: "You're out of your mind . . . never let you . . . can't even . . ."

"You don't get it," Marvin replied. His voice was flat, inflectionless. "There's no way you can understand, understand, understand."

The Latino man held out his hand and stepped toward Marvin. "You have no idea what you're doing." His voice was stern and controlled, yet vibrating with rage. "Give it to me, to me, right now. Do I have to—"

Marvin's hand twitched and a gunshot sounded, the same sharp, small-caliber crack as at the railroad wye. A puff of smoke rose from the barrel of Marvin's pistol. He fired a second shot, then a third.

The Latino man grunted. He stumbled backward and fell, out of Chuck's sight, to the gravel surface of the parking lot.

Chuck ducked away from the aligned windows before Marvin looked up from the downed man. Swinging his pack to the ground, Chuck clawed inside it until he came up with Donald's .45. A door to the Suburban creaked open, the car's engine died, and the door closed. A second door opened. Quaking with fear, Chuck looked back through the two windows in time to see Marvin wrench Carmelita from the back seat of the Suburban.

"Come on, you," Marvin commanded. Carmelita leaned against him, her eyes closed. Marvin shook her by the arm, causing her to open her eyes.

"You're hurting me!" she cried.

"Shut it," Marvin said. He hauled Carmelita by the elbow toward the amphitheater, his pistol in his free hand. The two disappeared from Chuck's view. Their footsteps crunched on gravel as they crossed the parking lot to the walkway that led between the storage buildings and into the amphitheater.

Chuck scrambled along the opposite side of the building and emerged at the back of the amphitheater seating area, Donald's gun in hand. He readied himself for the instant Marvin and Carmelita would come into view at the rear of the amphitheater. Then he remembered: he'd never reloaded Donald's gun after emptying it at the railroad wye.

Before Marvin and Carmelita exited the passageway, Chuck fled back around the building, his pack in one hand and the .45 in the other. Behind the building, he came upon the Latino man sprawled on his back in the gravel parking lot. Chuck did not recognize the man, whose arms and legs were askew, his head cocked to one side. The man was in his early thirties. He wore bright white sneakers, low-slung jeans, and a loose dress shirt opened to expose a pair of gold chains around his neck. Three crimson spots blossomed through the silky fabric of his shirt, forming a bloody triangle in the center of his chest.

Chuck hurried to the man's side. A glance at the passageway between the buildings told him the angle was such that he could not see all the way down the passage to the amphitheater, and was likewise shielded from Marvin's view. Chuck dropped his pack and Donald's gun, knelt over the downed man, and put his fingers to the man's neck, searching for a pulse but finding none.

The man's eyes were open and unblinking, adding to the look of surprise on his brown, clean-shaven face. Blood, dark red in the early-morning light, spread slowly through the gravel from beneath his body. Chuck dug his fingers deeper into the man's neck but still failed to pick up a pulse. The only sounds were the low moan of the morning wind and the ticking of the Suburban's engine as it cooled.

Chuck tugged the neck of the man's dress shirt to one side. There, running along the man's collarbone, was a string of Chinese letters in the fashion of bold brush strokes. Chuck pulled the neck of the shirt the other direction, uncovering a second string of matching Chinese letters tattooed on the man's collarbone. Chuck returned his fingers to Miguel's neck. Nothing. The girls' father was dead.

Chuck rose. Should he attempt to ease open one of the Suburban's doors and call for help on the radio? Would the arrival of the park's ranger corps at the festival site convince Marvin to give up? Or would the rangers' arrival make matters worse?

A terrified wail rose from the amphitheater. Chuck spun away from the Suburban at Carmelita's cry. He retrieved his pack and Donald's gun and sprinted back along the far side of the storage building, coming to a halt just shy of the amphitheater. He set the pack on the ground and reached inside it, shoving aside the towel-wrapped sack containing the necklaces and rooting around until he came up with Donald's extra magazine.

He stood with his back to the wall of the building, holding his breath, the gun in his right hand and the magazine, streaked with melted yogurt, in his left. The sound of two pairs of footsteps came from the direction of the performance stage, Marvin's steps sure and steady, Carmelita's half-dragging. The footsteps halted. Carmelita whimpered pitifully.

"I told you to shut it!" Marvin bellowed.

Chuck squeezed the magazine release button and sprung the empty magazine from the handle of Donald's gun, sending the magazine clattering to the concrete apron that surrounded the storage building. He wiped the fresh magazine on his shirt and slid it into the gun with a well-oiled click, then slung his pack back over his shoulder and stepped around the corner of the building to the head of a side aisle leading through the seating area to the festival stage.

Marvin stood in the center of the stage with Carmelita clutched at his side. He was broad and solid. Carmelita was tiny beside him. Marvin stood with his back to the amphitheater's seating area, looking out over the canyon through the open rear of the stage.

Chuck took a few tentative steps down the side aisle toward the foot of the stage, Donald's .45 outstretched before him. Marvin did not move. Afraid of what Marvin might do to Carmelita if surprised, Chuck spoke.

"Let her go, Marvin," he demanded.

Marvin pivoted to face Chuck, turning Carmelita with him. He gripped Carmelita's elbow at his side with one hand while pressing the barrel of his slender pistol to her head with his other. The brown skin of Marvin's wide face was tight across his cheekbones. His eyes gleamed. "Chuck," he said, a dark smile tugging at the corners of his mouth. "You came."

"I swear to God," Chuck said, aiming Donald's heavy gun at Marvin's face, "I'll blow your brains out."

"Now, now, Chuck. No need, need, need for anger. Besides," Marvin gave Carmelita a shake, drawing another muted cry from her, "you won't do any such, such, such thing." He kept the muzzle of his pistol pressed against her temple.

Marvin had worn pressed slacks and dress shirts to every one of his meetings with Chuck throughout the two years of the transmission line contract. This morning, however, Marvin wore moccasins, fringed leather leggings, and a long, light-colored, smock-like shirt gathered with a thick leather belt at his waist, just as he had as a youthful protester at the Marburys' burial-shroud press conference ten years ago. A headband of red cloth pressed his close-cropped black hair to the sides of his head. He licked his lips, making an odd smacking noise.

The odor of gunpowder from his just-fired gun mixed with the pungent desert smell of the morning breeze sweeping across the amphitheater.

"Chuck?" Carmelita asked. She wore her new hiking boots and favorite blue sweats. She slumped at Marvin's side, the top of her head rising just above the tribal official's waist. Her nearly shuttered eyelids, slack jaw, and trembling legs indicated she was drugged. Chuck hoped she had been unconscious when the Suburban had arrived at the festival site and therefore hadn't witnessed her father's murder.

"Shut up," Marvin snapped at her. He yanked her roughly by the arm.

"I'm here, Carm," Chuck told her, seeking to convey confidence he didn't feel, given the fact that Marvin had his gun pressed to Carmelita's head, a gun he'd used minutes ago to kill Miguel. "Everything's gonna be okay," Chuck continued. He took a step forward, Donald's .45 still leveled at Marvin in the growing morning light.

"Stay where you are," Marvin sputtered. He backed a step toward the rear of the stage, taking Carmelita with him.

"I've got what you want, remember?" With his free hand, Chuck took his pack from his shoulder and held it out before him. He took another step toward the stage as he did so. He was nearly to the bottom of the half-dozen stairs leading from the side aisle to the raised stage, close enough to see Marvin's face grow cloudy with confusion.

"I've already got what I want," Marvin said, glancing down at Carmelita. "What I need." He pulled her tight to his side.

"But I have the A. Dinaveri." Chuck gave the open pack a shake, trying to draw Marvin's attention to it. Instead of focusing on the pack, however, Marvin's eyes wandered away to fix on the brightening sky to the east.

"Dawn," he said. "Sunup. Have to, have to, have to."

"What are you talking about, Marvin? What is it you have to do?"

At the sound of his name, Marvin returned his attention to the front of the stage. He stared at Chuck as if seeing him for the first time. "What are you doing here?" he asked, eyes wide with surprise.

Marvin's grip on Carmelita loosened and she leaned away from him. Half a foot of space opened between the two of them, enough for Chuck to consider risking a shot. Even as the idea occurred to him, however, he rejected it. Despite his expertise with a hunting rifle, he'd proven himself a lousy marksman with Donald's heavy-triggered, hard-bucking .45 when he'd shot the pistol at the park firing range several years ago. At this distance, even with the benefit of the morning's increasing light, he was as likely to shoot Carmelita as he was Marvin.

Chuck lifted his pack higher, attempting to hold Marvin's attention. "The exchange, remember?" He took two more steps to the foot of the stairs leading to the stage, causing Marvin to jerk Carmelita back to his side.

Marvin's eyes wandered to the daypack, then away. His head lolled sideways, as if he couldn't quite control its movements. He turned to face the eastern sky, twisting Carmelita with him, his feet shuffling on the polished-concrete floor of the stage.

"Dinaveri," he muttered, straightening his head and looking off into the distance. "Din, din, din." Then, addressing the eastern sky, "Today. Sunup. Dawn, dawn, dawn."

Arturo Dinaveri's calendar, Chuck realized with a start. *That* was what Marvin was going on about.

According to Dinaveri, the shadow calendar discovered by the Italian archaeologist's team at Chaco Canyon called for the Anasazi to reemerge from beneath the Colorado River here at the Grand Canyon sometime this decade. Marvin's addled brain must somehow have settled on today for the reemergence, with dawn the most likely time for the Anasazi to come forth.

Dinaveri contended in his thesis that the reemergence would take place only if the A. Dinaveri necklace from the hidden Grand Canyon shrine was thrown into the canyon the instant the sun rose into the sky. Dinaveri claimed the necklace would serve as a suitable sacrifice to Chirsáuha, the Anasazi god of fertility, as long as it was accompanied, Chuck recalled in sudden terror, by one additional sacrifice.

When Dinaveri released his thesis in the late 1950s, archaeological teams from around the world had been busy announcing revolutionary discoveries at the sites of abandoned cities built by the Mayan Indians a thousand years ago in the jungles of southern Mexico. Capitalizing on those headlines, Dinaveri juiced the conclusion of his Anasazi thesis with the contention that, like the many human sacrifices documented in Mayan society, a human sacrifice would be required to bring forth the Anasazi from the underworld at the Grand Canyon—and not just any sacrifice, but that of a young female.

Twenty-Nine

Dawn

Shaking with dread, Chuck took the first step up the stairs to the stage. Carmelita was thirty feet away from him, teetering against Marvin, her elbow still trapped in Marvin's grip, her eyes closed. Chuck risked a second step up the stairs. How devoted was Marvin to Dinaveri's sacrifice theory? Would he kill Carmelita even if he got his hands on the A. Dinaveri necklace?

Marvin dragged Carmelita backward until the pair came to a stop facing the amphitheater, their backs against the cliff-top railing at the rear of the open stage. Like a light turning off, the tribal official's eyes went flat, just as they'd been when he'd shot Miguel. "Today, today, today," Marvin said, his words disjointed, his face slackening. "Sunup, sunup, today, today, today."

The first rays of the rising sun struck the cliffs at the top of the North Rim. Soon sunlight would flood the festival stage here at the South Rim as well, the instant Marvin's bewildered mind must be telling him he had to sacrifice Carmelita in order to summon the long-disappeared Anasazi back to the Earth's surface.

Chuck stared at the young Navajo official in horror. Marvin had come across as sane when they'd met in Tuba City three days ago. He had spoken coherently about the conference of tribal elders he was to have been attending in Page this very moment, and he'd discussed the upcoming deadline for the transmission line report lucidly. But Francesca had described Marvin as crazy and getting crazier when he'd taken Carmelita from the room in Maswik Lodge a few hours ago.

Was it possible for someone to go from sane to insane in less than three days? Or did Marvin somehow see his bizarre, return-of-the-Anasazi plan as entirely logical?

"Why'd you kill Miguel and Donald?" Chuck asked, hoping the bluntness of his question would pull Marvin back from wherever he'd gone.

Light returned to Marvin's eyes. "Your friend Donald blew it," Marvin said, sounding for all the world like the intelligent tribal official Chuck had come to know over the past two years. "All he had to do was keep you moving in the right direction."

"Donald was in on this?" Chuck asked in disbelief.

"He thought he was going to have all the money he needed."

"You told him you were meeting me at the wye?"

"I let him know what you were in for, yes. He got sentimental on me. Thought he was going to put a stop to this." Marvin waved his gun vaguely in the direction of the canyon before putting it back to Carmelita's head.

"You murdered him, Marvin. You tried to kill me, but you killed him instead."

Marvin's nostrils flared. "That's what Miguel said."

"You murdered him, too."

"He kept telling me I'd ruined everything. Thought he was going to jail. Wouldn't let it go. He wanted to take the girl from me."

"You killed Miguel *and* you killed Donald."

"I did what I had to do. For my people."

"You're wrong, Marvin," Chuck said. "The *Diné* way is the path of peace. The *Diné* way has nothing to do with murder."

Marvin recoiled. "This is not about murder," he hissed. "It's about rebirth." His eyes slipped from Chuck's face and began to dim.

"No," Chuck said quickly, fighting to keep Marvin tethered to reality—or whatever version of reality he now inhabited. "It's about kidnapping. You stole this little girl from her mother. You kidnapped her. You and whoever else."

Marvin's eyes brightened in recollection. "Clarence told me about the shrine one night in Gallup, the one you found in the canyon. He was drunk, hardly knew what he was talking about. He said he didn't know what was in it. But I knew. I've always known." Marvin's face lit up. "He kept talking. Talk, talk, talk, like always. He mentioned these people he knew in Albuquerque, Ronnie and Francesca. Lowlifes, he said. So I contacted them. Sure enough, they were willing to do what I needed done, and for a reasonable price." Marvin's eyes actually sparkled. "They were tracking you in Durango for me. Then you came here. It was perfect. Perfectly perfect."

"But you said Miguel took her."

"Sure. It was Ronnie's idea to bring Miguel in on the deal. The girl was happy to go along with her dad, do whatever he said." Marvin glanced down at Carmelita. He gave her a shake. Her eyes fluttered open. "Weren't you?"

"Miguel took her from the camper?" Chuck asked.

"She went to the bathroom," Marvin said, looking back at Chuck. "Miguel followed her. I snuck into the camper, left the note. You were snoring away." He nearly smiled.

"You're a murderer," Chuck said, wanting to wipe the smug look from Marvin's face. "A killer two times over."

Shame appeared in Marvin's eyes for an instant before he buried any hint of remorse away inside himself. His entire body shuddered and his eyes burned with zealous intensity. "This is about life, rebirth, reemergence," he said, choking on the last word.

His arms twitched and he took a stumbling step forward, nearly toppling to the stage floor. He regained his balance and pressed his pistol so hard against Carmelita's temple her head bent all the way to her shoulder. Carmelita's eyes were wide open, her body rigid. Marvin curled his finger around the trigger and stepped back with her to the railing, the canyon behind them.

Chuck thought of how simple it had been for Francesca to push Ronnie off Maricopa Point. It would be just as easy for

Marvin to send Carmelita to her death over the railing at the open rear of the stage when the first rays of morning sun struck the amphitheater.

The pink glow of dawn was disappearing from the cliffs along the North Rim, giving way to the bright light of day. Chuck glanced to the east. The tops of the piñons and junipers at the edge of the festival site were outlined by the first rays of the rising sun on this side of the canyon. Direct sunlight would reach the stage in no more than a few minutes.

Chuck climbed the last of the steps to the stage. "The shrine," he told Marvin, holding his pack out before him from the top of the stairs. "The offering. You must have this in your hand before the sun gets here. Chirsáuha demands it."

Marvin leaned away from Chuck, his upper body canted backward out and over the top bar of the railing, his pistol still pressed to Carmelita's head. "What, what, what?"

"The A. Dinaveri," Chuck urged. "If you're not holding it up to the east so the first ray of sun strikes it, the reemergence won't happen. Of course you know that. That's why you had me meet you here, remember? The offering from the shrine and the girl. You have to have both."

"The offering. The girl. Have to," Marvin repeated, breathing hard. He appeared lost and haunted, guilt-ridden, seemingly intent only on sacrificing Carmelita, and on killing no one else.

That, at least, was the instantaneous determination Chuck made as he turned Donald's gun so its muzzle faced the sky. He intended to show Marvin he meant no harm, but the movement startled the tribal official nonetheless. Marvin's body spasmed. He pulled Carmelita to him and leaned even farther back over the railing.

"Marvin," Chuck said. "You have to listen to me. I'm going to put my gun down and show you what I've got for you." Without waiting for acknowledgement, Chuck squatted and laid

Donald's gun on the stage floor.

Now was Marvin's chance. All he had to do was turn his pistol on Chuck and fire. With Chuck out of the way, Marvin could rummage through the pack for one of the necklaces, and have everything his crazed mind was telling him he needed to bring forth the Anasazi from beneath the river. Instead, however, Marvin kept his gun pressed to Carmelita's head as he leaned back over the railing and regarded Chuck with confused eyes.

Chuck set his pack on the stage floor beside Donald's .45. He showed his opened palms, still stained with Donald's blood, to Marvin. He reached inside the pack, loosened the neck of the sack containing the necklaces, and slipped one of them free from its plastic bag.

"You were right about my find," Chuck said, lifting the necklace. Marvin gasped as Chuck straightened, the piece of jewelry draped over the fingers of his hand. "*This* is what you want." He held out the necklace and stepped past his gun and pack. "*This* is what you have to have, for Chirsáuha. *Now*."

Marvin turned his face to the east. He looked down, taking in the precipice behind him. From there his eyes rose to the sunlit North Rim. He wagged his head from side to side.

Chuck took two more steps, still proffering the turquoise necklace. He was no more than fifteen feet from Marvin and Carmelita now. Marvin turned to Chuck and beheld the necklace before looking at Carmelita trembling in his grip.

"The girl," Marvin said. He looked again to the east.

Chuck jiggled the necklace, counting on the thousand-year-old braided yucca cord not to break. "There's a sun inscribed on the pendant," Chuck said with a quick glance at the large chunk of burnished turquoise. "It's just as Dinaveri wrote: 'The sun must face the sun when the first ray hits.' You know that, don't you? Everybody knows that."

Marvin nodded, though Arturo Dinaveri never wrote any such thing. As if for the first time, Marvin seemed to realize Chuck was unarmed. He pointed his gun at Chuck's torso.

Chuck raised his free hand in surrender. "Marvin," he said. "Enough."

Chuck lifted the necklace above his head. Marvin tracked its movement with his eyes but kept his gun centered on Chuck's chest.

"You've only got a few seconds," Chuck insisted, trying to ignore Marvin's finger tightening on the trigger of his gun. "If you—"

Marvin's eyes grew large. His moccasined feet skittered on the bare floor of the stage as he shoved himself back against the unyielding metal railing, his gaze fixed on something beyond Chuck's shoulder. Marvin reached around Carmelita's waist, lifted her off the stage, and pressed the barrel of his gun against her temple as he pivoted with her toward the cliff.

Chuck ducked low and charged, dropping the necklace as he hurtled himself across the stage.

Only at the last second did Marvin see Chuck barreling toward him, too late to get off a shot before Chuck, holding his crouch, rammed Marvin hard in the side with his lowered shoulder.

Chuck enveloped Carmelita in his arms as he crushed Marvin against the metal railing, his shoulder ramming Marvin's midsection. Marvin's feet left the floor of the stage and his upper body leaned past the top bar of the railing at an impossible angle. He cartwheeled up and over the railing and out into space.

Carmelita spun over the top bar of the railing alongside Marvin. Chuck corralled her tiny body to him as he plowed hard into the railing himself. For an instant, as he and Carmelita leaned over the railing's top bar, she threatened to spin from his grasp. Then his feet settled on the floor of the stage and he pulled her back over the railing to his chest, holding her close as Marvin plummeted, screaming, down the face of the cliff, his gun flying free from his grasp and his empty hands reaching for purchase in the cool morning air.

Chuck pressed Carmelita's face to his chest and watched over the top of her head as Marvin struck the boulder-strewn shelf at the base of the cliff. Marvin's scream ended abruptly as he crumpled headfirst among the rocks. His body spun a full turn and he came to rest on his back, one shattered arm flung outward, the other flopped across his chest. Marvin faced the sky amid the boulders, unmoving, his mouth open in mid-scream, his eyes closed. His gun clattered among the rocks, coming to rest in a patch of sand at his side.

Chuck knelt and hugged Carmelita to him. "Carm," he whispered in her ear, stroking the back of her head. "Carmelita. You're safe now, okay? You're safe."

Carmelita wrapped her arms around Chuck's neck and clung to him, sobbing. He stood, lifting her with him, and turned to find Robert Begay climbing the stairs to the stage. Robert's shoulders sagged beneath his wrinkled uniform. His face was lined with exhaustion. He came to a stop at the top of the steps.

"He asked me to meet him at my office," Robert said, his voice hollow. "He had the girl." He looked past Chuck and Carmelita to where Marvin had disappeared over the railing. "He wouldn't listen to me. He pulled a gun, took my keys."

Sirens sounded in the distance.

"I expected he would come here," Robert continued. "I made sure they were waved past Pipe Creek. I was afraid what might happen if they were stopped. I took another car, came in on foot. I thought I'd be able to talk some sense into him. I called dispatch as soon as I saw what happened back there—" he motioned toward the parking lot, "and Marvin up here with you." Robert lowered his gaze in weary defeat. "He was convinced this was where it would happen. But we have our own history, our own beliefs."

Chuck thought of his morning runs these past weeks. "Some of us are always convinced we have to have more," he said. "Whatever we have, we tell ourselves it isn't enough."

Robert walked past Chuck and Carmelita to the railing. He stared down at Marvin's body. Then he straightened, looked out across the canyon, and murmured a few lines of prayer in the guttural *Diné* tongue. He turned away from the canyon and took in the necklace lying on the floor of the stage. His eyes rose questioningly to Chuck.

"The A. Dinaveri," Chuck said. He pointed at his pack. "A whole bunch of them."

Robert's eyebrows lifted in further question. But when Chuck glanced past Carmelita at the sound of the sirens drawing closer, Robert tilted his head toward Marvin's body at the base of the cliff behind him. "Thank you," he said. "Hard as it is to say. You did the right thing."

"He killed Donald."

Robert looked away. "I thought you killed him, I really did. I'm sorry for that."

"He killed Miguel, too," Chuck said, holding Carmelita and aiming his chin at the rear of the amphitheater.

Robert clenched his square jaw. "Insanity, that'll have to be it."

"That's what it was."

"I know."

"You got here just in time."

Tears filled Robert's eyes. "He was a good boy. You know that, don't you? Smart. Such a hard worker. But we watched him change, my brother and I. He hid it for the most part, but we saw it. Last year, this year, it kept getting worse. There didn't seem to be anything we could do."

"He was always fine with me," Chuck said. "Fair. Good to

work with." He paused. "We get lost every now and then, Robert. All of us. Sometimes we can't find our way home."

At the word "home," Carmelita lifted her head from Chuck's shoulder. She looked at him with clearing eyes. "*Mamá*," she said.

Robert turned again to the canyon and gripped the top bar of the railing with both hands. His chin fell to his chest and his shoulders heaved. Beyond him, the North Rim shone in the morning light.

Chuck settled Carmelita on his hip and crossed the floor to the head of the stage. The first ray of sun to reach the amphitheater broke through the trees and shone full on Carmelita's face as they came to the top of the stairs. Chuck stopped and looked at Carmelita in the beam of sunlight. The tracks of her tears, nearly dry now, glittered on her cheeks. She studied him gravely in return.

"*M'hija*," Chuck said to her. He slipped a stray strand of hair, dark as Janelle's, behind her ear.

She dropped her head to his shoulder and nestled her forehead against his neck.

"Let's get you to your mother," Chuck said, heading down the stairs from the stage with his oldest daughter safely in his arms.

Acknowledgments

My thanks go to my earliest and toughest reader—my wife Sue—and to equally astute early readers Mary Engel, Anne Markward, John Peel, Kevin Graham, and Roslyn Bullas.

I cannot thank the dedicated folks at Torrey House Press enough for their belief in this book and its potential to share the Torrey House message of appreciation for the West with a new and wider audience, namely fun-loving mystery readers. Mark Bailey first selected this book for the Torrey House lineup, Kirsten Johanna Allen's keen insight improved the manuscript immensely, and Anne Terashima tightened my prose with a ruthlessly precise red pen. I am fortunate to now have all three championing my book out there in the bookselling world.

Which reminds me, my appreciation extends to booksellers everywhere, including my good friends at Maria's Bookshop in Durango, Colorado, whose belief in the power of story enables us writers to keep telling ours.

My respect goes to the rangers, staff, and employees of Grand Canyon National Park. I have loved and visited the Grand Canyon since I was a kid, and I look forward to exploring the canyon for the rest of my life thanks to those dedicating their professional lives to preserving and protecting the greatest hole on Earth.

Finally, my thanks go to the master, Tony Hillerman, in memoriam, for the advice he so willingly gave me years ago when, as a clueless young writer with my first book contract in hand, I picked up the phone and gave him a call.

About Scott Graham

Scott Graham was raised in the heart of the Southwest, where America's Native, Hispanic, and Anglo cultures co-exist—often uneasily—and where echoes of the ancient Anasazi Indians featured in *Canyon Sacrifice* resonate to this day. His home in Durango, Colorado, stands next to a thousand-year-old ruin once home to more than a dozen Anasazi families.

An avid outdoorsman and amateur archaeologist, Graham has explored the Grand Canyon all his life. He has backpacked deep into the canyon's farthest reaches, and twice has rowed his own eighteen-foot raft down the canyon's notorious Colorado River rapids. The author of several books about backcountry adventures, Graham won the National Outdoor Book Award for *Extreme Kids.* He enjoys hunting, rock climbing, skiing, backpacking, mountaineering, river rafting, and whitewater kayaking with his wife, an emergency physician, and their two sons.

About Torrey House Press

The economy is a wholly owned subsidiary of the environment, not the other way around.

—Senator Gaylord Nelson, founder of Earth Day

Love of the land inspires Torrey House Press and the books we publish. From literature and the environment and Western Lit to topical nonfiction about land-related issues and ideas, we strive to increase appreciation for the importance of natural landscape through the power of pen and story. Through our *2% to the West* program, Torrey House Press donates two percent of sales to not-for-profit environmental organizations and funds a scholarship for up-and-coming writers at colleges throughout the West.

Printed in the USA
CPSIA information can be obtained
at www.ICGtesting.com
JSHW022323140824
68134JS00019B/1268